KINGSCASTLE

KINGSCASTLE

SOPHIA HOLLOWAY

Allison & Busby Limited
11 Wardour Mews
London W1F 8AN
allisonandbusby.com

First published in Great Britain by Allison & Busby in 2021.

A CIP catalogue record for this book is available from
the British Library.

First Edition

ISBN 978-0-7490-2783-4

Typeset in 11/16 pt Sabon LT Pro by
Allison & Busby Ltd.

FSC
www.fsc.org
MIX
Paper from
responsible sources
FSC® C020471

The paper used for this Allison & Busby publication
has been produced from trees that have been legally sourced
from well-managed and credibly certified forests.

Printed and bound by

CPI Group (UK) Ltd, Croydon, CR0 4YY

For K. M. L. B.

CHAPTER ONE

MR TIDESWELL WAS ILL AT EASE. He found the bustle of a naval home port too much for one used to a quiet market town, and the sight of a small group of sailors, unsteady on their feet and lurching along Portsmouth High Street at two in the afternoon, filled him with horror as well as a degree of fear. He looked at the directions he had been given at the posting house, and made his way towards St Thomas's church. The High Street passed by it on the south side, and a row of decently proportioned houses formed an L shape on the west and north sides. He was impressed, having been prepared for some low, ill-kept boarding house, and when he rapped the polished brass knocker of the house bearing the correct number, a respectable-looking man came to the door and enquired his business.

'I am come to see Captain Hawksmoor. My name is Tideswell, and I am his family lawyer.'

'If you would be pleased to come into the hall, sir, I will find out if the captain is in. I believe he returned about noon.'

The man stood back, and Mr Tideswell entered the house. The doorkeeper, who appeared to be more of a housekeeper, went up to the first floor, and Mr Tideswell heard a brief, muffled conversation. The man returned and declared that Captain Hawksmoor would be pleased to see him, and would he please follow him up.

At the top of the stairs Mr Tideswell was shown into a neatly furnished room, at the end of which a gentleman in naval uniform sat at a desk. He rose, and it could be seen that he was a few inches above average height, his face a little tanned from exposure to sun and wind, and a trifle thin.

'Captain William Hawksmoor?' Mr Tideswell queried the rank, for the officer had but one epaulette. Surely captains wore two?

'Yes indeed.' The gentleman saw where the lawyer's gaze had fallen. 'Ah, you wonder at my shoulder? I received my promotion to post rank in '14 and so have not yet the three years' seniority that gives me the second epaulette. I really am Captain Hawksmoor, I assure you. Now, I am informed you are my family lawyer, yet I have never seen or heard of you before.'

He gestured Mr Tideswell to a chair, and took his seat again.

'I have the honour to be the family lawyer to the Marquis of Athelney,' volunteered Mr Tideswell.

'But I am merely a scion of the cadet branch, Mr Tidesell.'

'Tideswell, sir,' corrected the little lawyer, with a cough.

'Mr Tideswell. I am the younger son of a youngest son and . . .'

'You are the surviving son of Lord Edward Hawksmoor, by his wife Celia, daughter of Sir Nathaniel Barton of Oswestry in Shropshire.' Mr Tideswell rattled off the captain's parentage as if the Hawksmoor family tree was imprinted upon his memory.

'I am. My elder brother Thomas fell at Vittoria.' Captain Hawksmoor frowned. This seemed ponderously formal.

'I have to inform you that your uncle, Alexander Hawksmoor, fourth Marquis of Athelney, died these four weeks past and—'

'I am sorry to hear it. Do not tell me he has left me some bequest in his will. I would not have thought he even remembered my existence.'

'Not a bequest as such. You, sir, or rather, my lord, were the heir presumptive, and now, once the documentation is provided, fifth Marquis of Athelney.'

If Mr Tideswell expected an exclamation of surprised delight, he was to be disappointed. Captain Hawksmoor did indeed raise his brows, but then shook his head, smiling a little lopsidedly.

'You have become muddled, Mr Tideswell, and have had a wasted journey. The heir presumptive to the title is my cousin, the son of the middle brother, Lord Willoughby Hawksmoor. He is also called William, which is why, no doubt, some clerk made the mistake. Though if you are the family solicitor, I would have thought that you would know it well enough.' He looked slightly suspicious.

'Mr William Hawksmoor regrettably met his death one week before his lordship, in an accident.'

'From what I ever heard of my cousin William, are you sure some cuckolded husband did not shoot him in a duel?'

'Er, no, my lord.' Mr Tideswell blushed. 'He died as the result of an accident with his curricle, in the course of some wager.'

'That was another possibility, of course. You will not expect me to rend my clothes at the news, I take it. It would be both insincere and expensive, for a junior post captain on half pay receives but ten shillings and sixpence per day, and it is a long time till Quarter Day.'

'It would be appropriate for you to show some sign of mourning when you return to Kingscastle, my lord, but no, I do not expect grief.'

'Return to . . . If it is certain . . . Oh Lord, yes, I suppose I must do so.' Captain Hawksmoor, for he could not as yet imagine himself as anything else, sighed. 'Mind you, with the peace there are so many of us on half pay and so few ships, the chances of a command again are slim. Perhaps I should adjust to commanding estates instead.'

He spoke almost to himself.

'That might not be as easy as you would think, my lord.'

'I have commanded a fifth-rate, Mr Tideswell, one of His Majesty's warships. I do not see a problem.' The response was terse, and Captain Hawksmoor's grey eyes narrowed.

'There are certain provisions of his late lordship's will, however, my lord. If I might show you?'

Mr Tideswell withdrew a sheet of vellum from the bag that he had been clutching, as if from habit, to his bosom, and laid it upon the desk. Captain Hawksmoor read the contents with a growing frown.

'But this is ridiculous, outrageous . . . the estate to be held in Trust in perpetuity unless my nephew, William Hawksmoor, marries and produces a legitimate male heir within two years of my decease?'

'His lordship was thinking, not of you, my lord, but of Mr William Hawksmoor. He believed that marriage might settle him.'

'So if I am to have any control over the estate I have to marry. That is absurd enough, but the other part is simply madness. Even if I were to marry, there is no guarantee that my wife would bear a child within what was left of the two years, let alone that it would be of the male sex. Such things are in God's hands, not a man's.'

'I admit, my lord, that the stipulation is problematic. I made the strongest of representations to his lordship that those phrases be removed, but it was shortly after

Mr Hawksmoor's affairs became rather more scandalous than normal, and his lordship was in no mood to see reason. I have consulted with other members of my profession, and it would seem likely that the clause could be contested and declared invalid, since, as you say, such things are outside human control. The requirement to wed, however, will stand.'

Captain Hawksmoor ran a hand through his dark hair, which rebelled against tidiness, however much he combed it. 'This is an awful lot to take in.'

'Understandably so, my lord. Perhaps it would be best if I returned tomorrow morning, when you have had some time to become adjusted, so to speak. I would hope you would see your way to accompanying me to Kingscastle, perhaps via the capital, since you will be requiring civilian attire of a quality befitting your position. We could also deal with any matters pertaining to your taking your seat in the Upper House, should you so wish.'

'Yes, though how would I pay for all . . .'

'The Trust would provide monies for such needs as you might have, my lord. And you must remember that in your case, the Trust will not be concerned that any money that is released will be misused. Mr Hawksmoor left debts, and his manner of living was . . . excessive. Your probity is not in doubt.'

'Thank you. I am not sure if I should be relieved or flattered,' murmured Captain Hawksmoor, wryly.

* * *

It was some time after Mr Tideswell's departure that Captain Hawksmoor stood up and went to gaze into the street below. Here was Portsmouth, a place where he felt as much at home as anywhere upon land. He had gone to sea, under the patronage of his mother's cousin, at fifteen, which meant half his lifespan had been within the Royal Navy. He had been at sea for most of that time, and had only heard of the deaths of first his father and, last year, his mother, some months after the event. He had been ashore when his elder brother had been killed at Vittoria, but there were no obsequies to attend for a man buried anonymously upon a Spanish battlefield. If he was honest, the service had become his family, and he would miss it badly, now that Hawksmoor family duties were thrust upon him.

He did not see his unexpected elevation to the peerage as different from duty. He could not avoid it, so he would simply do the best he could. He feared idleness, and with so many men ashore, what chance had he of a command? Perhaps turning from the sea, from the ships that would not be there for him, would be a good thing; yet the 'family' of the navy had been his for so long that being parted from it was a difficult thing to assimilate. A naval officer was what he 'was' to his core; he was as comfortable with it as he was in his faded sea-going uniform. He was not even sure what a landed aristocrat actually 'did' in life. As a child he had not questioned what those without 'employment' did from day to day. Was a marquis expected to sit in aloof state while minions did everything? If that was the case, well, he would simply be one marquis who did not conform to the norm.

He was lifted from this melancholic mood by the sight of a uniformed gentleman stepping out smartly along the street. The officer looked up, smiled broadly, and touched his hat. Captain Hawksmoor waved him up. A minute or so later, a cheerful voice and familiar tread were heard upon the stair.

'Come on in, Mr Bitton.'

The door opened, and a fair-haired man, some five or six years the captain's junior, came into the room.

'Good afternoon, sir. I just heard Bradford got the *Phoebus*, lucky dog. I wonder if he might put in a word for me.'

'He might. Take a seat, for I have news that may surprise you nearly as much as it surprised me.'

Captain Hawksmoor told Lieutenant Bitton, who had been his first lieutenant aboard his last command, of his change of circumstances. The cheerful lieutenant was suitably amazed.

'I did not know you had such aristocratic connections, sir, my lord . . . er . . .'

'I don't feel like a lord.' The captain sounded gloomy again.

'That will come, my lord, given a few weeks.'

'Perhaps.' He sighed. 'I have no desire for this elevation.'

'Think of it as a promotion, as if . . .' Lieutenant

Bitton tried to think of an analogy. 'You had been given a first-rate ship of the line.'

'It will probably be as unwieldy.' Captain Hawksmoor did not appear visibly cheered.

The younger man was silent for a moment, and then smiled as a new thought occurred to him.

'I'd give a month's pay to see Royston's face when he hears. Always puffing himself up because his father's a baronet. What's a mere baronet in comparison to a marquis!'

Captain Hawksmoor managed a wry smile, but sighed. 'There is another part to the surprise as well, though.'

'There is?'

'Yes. I have to get married.'

Lieutenant Bitton laughed, until he realised that his superior was deadly serious. Then he simply blinked, for there was nothing he could think of to say.

It could not be said that Captain Hawksmoor viewed Mr Tideswell's return with eager anticipation upon the following morning. The little lawyer was considerably put out, having expected that, once the reality of his surprising news had sunk in, the new marquis would be in good spirits. It was, however, a stony-faced officer, with a valise already packed, whom he met in the lodging house. Captain Hawksmoor enquired what time the mail coach departed for London.

'Mail coach, my lord?'

Captain Hawksmoor still winced at the appellation. 'Indeed, Mr Tideswell, the mail coach.'

'But, my lord, I have engaged a post chaise.'

'You have done what?' Captain Hawksmoor's response would have given men of sterner heart than Mr Tideswell cause to tremble.

'I . . . You ought not . . . I mean,' gabbled the little man, clutching his hat very tightly, much to its detriment, 'the Trustees would not expect you to arrive in London upon the common stage. It would not be fitting.'

'You will be telling me next I must put up at the grandest hotel in London.'

'I have made enquiries, my lord, anticipating the need to visit the metropolis, and I believe the Bath or Grillon's would be entirely suitable.'

'They would? I have heard of neither, but then I am unfamiliar with any hotel in London other than Fladong's on Oxford Street, which is where I have every intention of taking a room. It is much used by officers who have cause to visit the Admiralty, and I have stayed there on three occasions before.'

'Would it be suffici . . .' Mr Tideswell was wise enough to abandon his question, seeing the set of Captain Hawksmoor's mouth. 'Yes, my lord, as you wish. Have you a preferred tailor?'

'Tailor? I have had no need for any garb but that of my uniform these fifteen years past. My ignorance is a problem. I am in uncharted waters, Mr Tideswell.'

'This I also envisaged, my lord. Lord Somborne, who

16

is one of the Trustees, was good enough to provide me with advice upon several subjects, and has suggested that you present yourself at his London abode. He generously said that he would be happy to introduce you as required at various establishments.'

'Somborne. You mean my Uncle Somborne, Aunt Elizabeth's husband?'

'Yes, my lord. You were aware that Lady Somborne died some three years ago?'

'I was informed.'

They had now reached the posting house, where Mr Tideswell paid his shot and directed Captain Hawksmoor to a waiting vehicle.

'Has your lordship directed your other luggage to the hotel you have chosen in London?'

'No,' replied Captain Hawksmoor, removing his hat and climbing into the chaise, 'I have but a trunk of books, a few personal possessions and my sea rig, and I have arranged for them to travel by carrier to Kingscastle, via Wells.'

Mr Tideswell eyed the single valise with a mixture of respect and faint horror.

The journey was accomplished in good time, Mr Tideswell enjoying the luxury of travelling post, and Captain Hawksmoor shutting his eyes, folding his arms and feigning sleep. This proved impossible to continue once the chaise crossed the Thames. The pace was necessarily slow. Mr Tideswell had only visited London to call upon Lord Somborne, who, even out of the

Season, came to attend lectures at the Royal Society. Bath and Bristol were busy enough for Mr Tideswell, and he found London rather overwhelming; so too did Captain Hawksmoor, though he disguised the fact well. The chaise deposited them at 144 Oxford Street, in front of Fladong's Hotel. The little lawyer tried to take Captain Hawksmoor's valise, but was politely told that would not be necessary. He accompanied his client into the vestibule of the hotel, where the captain was greeted with the deference due to his naval rank.

'Certainly, Captain—'

'Lord Athelney,' interjected Mr Tideswell, rather to Captain Hawksmoor's embarrassment. He would far rather keep his 'true' title as long as possible.

'My apologies, my lord. Your valise will be taken to your rooms immediately. Would you care to—'

'Hawksmoor, as I live and breathe!'

Captain Hawksmoor turned, and his hand was clasped warmly by a ruddy-faced gentleman, greying at the temples.

'Curdworth! I thought you in the Mediterranean still.'

'No, no, paid off last month at Chatham. Are you up to see their Lordships?'

'No, I . . . it is a mad tale. Dine with me.'

Mr Tideswell murmured that he would attend his lordship on the morrow at ten, and withdrew to take a cab to a more modest lodging off the Strand, which had been recommended by his senior partner.

* * *

The comfort of being among his own sort did not remain for long. Captain Hawksmoor was taken by Mr Tideswell to Lord Somborne's house, where he had the distinct impression that his naval career was something 'the family' would prefer to forget, quietly but swiftly. This did not put him in the most pliant frame of mind.

'My dear boy, delighted, delighted. One ought to say in tragic circumstances, but young William was . . . lacking in many . . . qualities. It is true to say the trustees of the estate are relieved, yes, relieved; there is no other term for it. Of course you will need assistance, in your changing circumstances.'

'Yes – writing, using the correct knife and fork . . .'

Lord Somborne's eyes opened wide in horror, as did his mouth.

Captain Hawksmoor could not keep a straight face. 'I assure you, sir, I am quite civilised. My weaknesses lie in an ignorance of where to provide myself with the attire and accessories of a gentleman both for town and country, and in the running of my estates, which is something I shall simply have to learn step by step.'

'It should not prove too demanding. One's stewards deal with the vast majority of the detail, and occasionally bring the accounts or a problem that requires attention. However, you ought to be free much of the time.'

'To do what, sir?'

Lord Somborne looked startled. 'Whatever you damned well please, my boy. Myself, I have a great interest in science, conduct experiments back home, you know, and my friend Coleorton catalogues butterflies. Hasn't got to be science, of course. You might become a patron of the turf, but I warn you that is damnably expensive. Some choose philanthropy, but for every deserving case I fear there are a dozen simply setting out to fleece the goodhearted.'

Captain Hawksmoor kept his own counsel. If he was head of vast estates in name, he would at least wish to be as an admiral upon his flagship, in charge not of the ship in its day-to-day affairs, but dictating where it, and the rest of the fleet, should be heading.

'Anyway,' continued the elderly earl, 'I can certainly take you about town, show you what is what, direct you to sniders, and so on. Have you a preference for Stulz? The military fellows tend to like his cut. Personally, I would go to Weston.'

'I have no preference, and would be happy to be guided by you, sir.'

'Good, good. Then I suggest we toddle down to Hoby and sort out some footwear, then on to Lock's for your hats, of course.'

'This hat is from Lock's. They have my measurements.'

'Excellent. Then we will visit Weston. The bills can be sent to me in the first instance until such time as the Trustees have advanced funds to your account. You won't want to be forever running to us just because you want to purchase a nightcap.'

'Indeed not,' averred Captain Hawksmoor. 'Which leads me to ask about the requirement, the frankly ridiculous requirement, to marry and produce an heir male in two years or I shall never have control of my own destiny.'

'Ahem, well, yes, that was going rather far, I will admit. Has not Tideswell said that the heir part is likely to be overturned, since it is patently a matter of chance? But marriage, well, it cannot be that difficult to find a girl. Come up for the Season, watch 'em trotted out, the young ladies, and take your pick. Good title, reasonable-looking chap, the mamas will be beating a path to your door. You'll have to push them from your doorstep just to get indoors.'

'The prospect does not fill me with glee, sir.'

'Well, never mind. There's Bath if you prefer less of a squeeze, but my dear wife always said it had gone downhill from when she was young.' Lord Somborne sighed, but then shook himself, in a gesture which reminded Captain Hawksmoor of a horse shaking off flies. 'No point in dwelling on what is past, eh. Let us be off to St James's, which reminds me, I shall put you up for White's, of course.'

With which generous offer Lord Somborne rang the bell and called for his coat, hat, cane and gloves.

The transformation of William Hawksmoor, Captain in His Majesty's Navy, into William Hawksmoor, Marquis of Athelney, was not simply a matter of his outward appearance. However, when he saw himself in the mirror, some days later, clad in buckskins and blue superfine, he sighed. The tailor smoothed an infinitesimal crease from the sleeve, and assumed the sigh was of satisfaction. He might think what he wished. Though the blue of the coat and the pallor of the buckskins were not so far removed from his uniform, he was very aware of crossing the Rubicon. From choice he would have continued in the security of his uniform, since he still held his commission, but knew that he had to become accustomed to the new 'rig' and accept that he had made the step from naval to civilian life. Not only was the cut and cloth alien to him, but so was the bewildering variety and number of items it was considered that he required. Shirt makers, waistcoat makers, hosiers – his person was under scrutiny and being measured by them all. Lord Somborne did not appear in the least discomposed by the cost of the new wardrobe, indeed almost complained when his protégé put down his neatly shod foot at the thought of a second pair of dancing shoes.

'My lord, I cannot see that I will get much use from a single pair. I am not going to spend my life prancing about at balls. I cannot even dance, beyond a few clumsy steps of a gavotte.'

'Good God, my boy. We will employ a caper merchant this very day. Being able to cut a figure upon the dance floor is terribly important with the ladies.'

William Hawksmoor thought, privately, that if ladies counted dancing ability over character and intellect, then it did not say much for the fairer sex, but submitted to 'learning to prance'.

It was on the eve of his departure from London

that a gentleman in scarlet regimentals, and with an angry countenance fast assuming a similar hue, entered Fladong's Hotel and demanded to see the Marquis of Athelney. The receptionist eyed him with concern, but directed the military gentleman to a private parlour, and sent up the major's card. A few minutes later, a rather perplexed Marquis of Athelney entered the room. The army officer was standing before the fireplace, looking belligerent. His eyebrows rose slightly; Athelney was not quite what he had expected, but then he was not in the sort of establishment he had expected either. He was looking at a tallish man, who held himself well, but whose face, whilst any man would say he was a 'well-looking fellow', was a little weathered and thin-cheeked.

'So,' barked the major, his eyes narrowing, 'I do not expect you anticipated meeting me.'

'Well, no,' replied Lord Athelney, very reasonably, 'I cannot say I did, since your name means absolutely nothing to me, Major . . .' He looked down at the card in his hand. 'Ratlinghope.'

'Means nothing to you?' spluttered the major, becoming even more apoplectic. 'How dare you stand there, as cool as a cucumber and say . . . after . . . You do not even deserve the courtesy of being called out. I should simply thrash you within an inch of your life here, you cur.' He advanced menacingly, his large hands forming very serviceable fists.

'I hope you will do neither, sir,' remarked the marquis, placatingly.

23

'Ha! Lily-livered! Should have guessed as much.'

'Well, you really ought not to trust to guesses; they are so often wrong.' Athelney remained unruffled.

If this was meant to lighten the atmosphere, it failed miserably. Major Ratlinghope made a sound akin to a mastiff about to launch itself at an intruder, and Athelney held up a hand.

'No, before you attempt to tear my throat out, and that is clearly what you would like to do, be so good as to explain what possible reason you might have to wish me ill. I say again, your name means nothing to me.'

'And does my wife mean nothing to you, scoundrel?'

'Nothing at all.'

'You heartless, shameless, ba—'

It dawned on Lord Athelney that the irate gentleman might be under a significant, if not dangerous, misapprehension. 'Ah, wait. I assume you are hot for the blood of William Hawksmoor.'

'I am, sir. Do you deny the name?'

'Not at all, for I am indeed William Hawksmoor.'

'Then . . .'

'I should rather say "a" William Hawksmoor, not the William Hawksmoor you undoubtedly seek.'

'If you think to bamboozle me, sir, you have the wrong man. I demand satisfaction.'

'You will not get it from me, I am afraid. Please, take a seat, and let me ring for,' he glanced at the clock upon the mantelshelf, 'a glass of burgundy, even though the sun is most certainly not over the yard arm.'

Major Ratlinghope wavered. His host seemed most unlike a rake and seducer, and a shadow of doubt entered his mind. He sat, and realised that he had done so as if obeying a command, however politely phrased. Lord Athelney rang the bell, and ordered the hotel's best burgundy. He felt his guest might at least seek solace in a palatable glass of wine.

'The William Hawksmoor whom I fear has done you wrong was my cousin. You see,' he explained gently, 'we were both, most unfortunately, christened William Hawksmoor. The name is, I assure you, all we have in common. He was the son of the Marquis of Athelney's younger brother, and his heir. I am the son of the youngest brother and hold the rank of a post captain in His Majesty's Navy.'

'You said "was" your cousin.'

'I did. My cousin, rather to the relief of the trustees of the estate, it seems, and probably to a number of gentlemen such as yourself, sir, met with a fatal driving accident but the week before my uncle died, thereby leaving me the heir to a title and responsibilities I never envisaged and did not seek.' Lord Athelney paused. 'Forgive me, but why have you sought out my ne'er-do-well namesake so late? I would have thought . . .'

'I am but this week returned from the Army of Occupation in France, my lord,' declared Major Ratlinghope, in a more civil and equable tone. 'My wife has been residing with my sister and her husband. I received a letter . . . from a third party, which . . .' He frowned.

'And so you came home to find out if report was true. I see. From what I have heard, my cousin was a man without morals, but of a damnably seductive manner when he chose, and quite heartless. A "vulnerable" beauty, and I take it your lady wife is attractive, would be the sort of challenge he could not resist. I would have thought you would have kept her close by in France, now there is peace. I hear it can be quite social.'

'Ironically, I thought her more at risk there. My wife is very beautiful, but seeks attention.' He sighed. 'I should indeed have kept her under my eye.'

'I have no experience of the gentle sex, but if she seeks attention, perhaps the best thing you could do is to pay her that attention.'

There was a knock, and a servant came in with the wine. Major Ratlinghope, with all hope of revenge gone, looked quite dejected.

'In retrospect that is what I should have done.' He accepted the proffered glass and took a rejuvenating sip of the dark liquid. 'Damn it, it is what I shall do. She is young, and rather spoilt, but . . . I am dashed fond of her, really.'

'Then I wish you well, Major, and can only apologise as a Hawksmoor.' Lord Athelney entertained his uninvited guest through several glasses of burgundy, and it was a considerably mellowed major who finally shook him by the hand, and departed.

The encounter gave him food for thought, and

neither of the two that occurred to him were happy ones. It seemed quite possible, if not probable, that he would find himself 'haunted' by his cousin's bad behaviour, and entering the married state was not a recipe for happiness.

CHAPTER TWO

IT WAS A FORTNIGHT LATER WHEN the Marquis of Athelney, still uncomfortable in his newly made civilian dress, was driven to the home of his ancestors. Kingscastle had indeed been a royal castle in the dim and distant past, but had passed to the Hawksmoor family when they were but barons. The gatehouse was thirteenth century, and the site, on higher ground in a loop of the river, marked it as a defensive position. The 'castle' itself had been rebuilt in Tudor times as a grand residence, and then much of it again after the destruction of the Civil War. It was a slightly rambling building, with a more homely air than in its past, and Lord Athelney remembered it dimly from visits as a child, when his grandfather had been alive. He certainly had not set foot in it for the best part of twenty years.

The staff stood outside, despite the chill October wind, and were introduced by Sturry, the butler. There had been much discussion below stairs about the new marquis, some even fearing that he would be wanting to flog anyone who disobeyed him. Sturry and the upper servants wondered if he would have the bearing that befitted his lineage, but all were agreed that far better it was 'the naval William' than 'Master William', who had terrorised the maidservants and invited wild friends until his uncle had banished him from the castle in his lifetime.

His lordship was not deceived. He was under more scrutiny than his servants, but then that was always the case when taking up a command. One was watched, assessed, perhaps tested, though he could not see the equivalent of his 'ship's company' at the castle causing him any problems. The butler had been in family service, man and boy, for forty years, and the housekeeper he vaguely remembered also. She turned quite pink when he mentioned it, though he omitted the 'vaguely' part. He knew from experience how useful recalling an old face with whom one had served before could be. He was not going to run Kingscastle like a ship, but the managing of men was the same ashore or afloat.

He was shown around, with a mixture of pride and requests for improvements and repairs. The cook was desperate to have a cooking range installed instead of the huge spit and mediaeval fireplace, which had been excellent for roasting whole wild boar but played havoc with modern recipes. Lord Athelney thought that might be paid for by the Trustees, none of whom, he was sure, had archaic cooking methods in their own residences. The Great Bedchamber, which had been prepared for a visit by Queen Elizabeth I, but thankfully never used by Her Majesty, who would almost certainly have bankrupted the family as she had others who had 'enjoyed' her presence, had been used by his uncle. Sturry announced, reverently, that it had been his late lordship's desire to pass from this world in it, and he had been granted his wish. Looking at the bed, his successor thought it looked so soft it might have engulfed and suffocated him to death. Years in hammock or cot had given him a preference for something firmer.

Sturry looked almost surprised when the new marquis declared a preference for the green bedchamber, which faced eastward, where the ground dropped away to the narrow swathe of flat land before the river, where the Dower House now stood. It was a square, ashlar-faced building only about seventy years old, and gave a sense of scale to the landscape beyond. Lord Athelney was not a man to lie abed for most of the forenoon, and liked the idea of rising before the sun's rays left his chamber. The bed was also smaller and a lot firmer, but Sturry assumed that his lordship had no desire to sleep in the bed in which his relative had so recently died.

Having viewed the bricks and mortar, Lord Athelney requested sustenance, and arranged to speak with the steward thereafter.

The steward, Mitchum, was a worried-looking individual who looked as old as the aged estate books, and peered at his employer myopically, with milky eyes.

'It has been more difficult of late, my lord, my eyes being not what they once were.' Mitchum wheezed as he spoke, and Lord Athelney thought he looked as if retirement could not come a moment too soon. Provision would surely be made for him.

The ledger thumped open, and Athelney stared in horror. The page before him bore no relation to any ship's book he had ever seen. The columns wandered, and the handwriting, which had once clearly had form, was a jumble that he could not even begin to read. He turned back several pages, back towards normality, for five years ago all was well laid out and legible.

'I think you will find all in order, my lord,' declared the steward, more in hope than confidence.

Lord Athelney did not know what to say. The man was honest enough, and had served the family many years, but this was an unholy mess. He wondered if the state of the fabric of the estate was as dilapidated as the books. His uncle had been frail some time from what Sturry had said, and perhaps unable to keep firm control of matters. An estate run by two elderly gentlemen whose experience had been overlaid by senility did not bode well. Would the Trustees see that more might be required to get Kingscastle shipshape? Hopefully, the other estates down in Devon and Dorset were under better management.

'Has the estate been profitable, Mitchum?'

'Oh yes.' Mitchum then qualified this statement: 'But I fear, my lord, of late less so. There is a problem with drainage, and his late lordship did permit Mr William to take a hand in arranging work upon that, some years ago.' He paused. 'That was at the beginning of Mr William's racketyness. The money was paid, but no work was done. His lordship was very angry but was persuaded it was the fault of whomsoever Mr William had engaged. I think, in truth, Mr William paid off his Oxford debts with it.'

Lord Athelney groaned. Mismanagement through infirmity of age was one thing, but syphoning off money with intent was another.

'It was only later that his lordship realised the extent of Mr William's excesses. That was after Mr William invited several other wild young gentlemen to Kingscastle, and,' Mitchum coughed, 'young females.'

'Good God, my cousin did not try to hold an orgy here, did he?'

'I am thankful to say I was not present, my lord, nor have I any experience of such lewdness, but from what Mr Sturry reported, that would seem likely. I believe Mr William thought that if it were confined to the west wing, his lordship would not become aware of it. However, it was impossible not to notice scantily clad females screeching round the courtyard in the small hours.'

'You would have to be,' Lord Athelney nearly said 'as blind as a mole' and thought better of it, 'very fast asleep, not to notice that, indeed.'

'And then the "gentlemen" tried to make very free with the maidservants, who are good, respectable girls.'

His lordship's expression grew grim. 'I see.'

'Thereafter his lordship cut all connection with Mr William, despite her ladyship, Lady Willoughby Hawksmoor, my lord, pestering him something terrible.'

Lord Athelney rubbed his chin, and made a decision. 'How old are you, Mitchum?'

'By my reckoning, my lord, I shall be three and seventy come Candlemas.' He sounded proud of having attained such age, as well he might.

'You must have served the Hawksmoors over half a century.'

'Aye, my lord, would be a little over that. All through Enclosure and everything.'

'I am afraid your eyesight has become a problem. These last few entries,' he really meant the last six pages, 'are difficult to make either head or tail of, for figures and words. Would you give your years of experience to a younger man, and take your ease, as is your due? You would be provided for, as a loyal pensioner of the family.'

Mitchum sighed. 'I cannot but say it would be a relief, my lord, but there is none hereabouts as I would recommend. I was never blessed with sons, or I would have trained one in my stead years back.'

'I may have the answer to that,' replied Lord Athelney, 'but first I must write a letter.'

* * *

Courtesy demanded that Lord Athelney pay a social call upon his aunt at the Dower House as soon as possible, and as well as writing a letter, he sent a message down the hill that he would call upon the morrow, when he would not be travel-stained. He had very dim memories of both the late Lord Willoughby Hawksmoor and his lady, though he knew that his mama disliked her. It was not a visit to be made after a long morning in a carriage, which, ironically, made the sea-going marquis feel distinctly queasy, and Lady Willoughby would undoubtedly expect him to contact her in advance.

He retired early, after a dinner, which, for all the cook bemoaned her archaic workplace, was very good, and far more than would have graced his simple table in his Portsmouth rooms. He rang, reluctantly, for his valet. It had been borne upon him that the employment of a gentleman's gentleman was required of a man of his rank, though he knew himself perfectly capable of fending for himself, until he saw the array of different ensembles it was thought necessary that he possess. Having lived in uniform, with no more than a decent supply of shirts, clean linen and a dress uniform, from adolescence, he found himself, as he had remarked, in uncharted waters. Evening wear was not difficult, barring the distinction between a private dinner and a formal ball or party, and the severe black was not so unlike a uniform, but the variety of coats and breeches and pantaloons for different daytime situations left his head reeling.

Mr Tideswell, having arranged that Lord Somborne

would direct the new marquis with regard to apparel, took it upon himself to make enquiries as to where his lordship would find a suitable valet. In the end, the erstwhile Captain Hawksmoor, feeling as ill at ease with his title as his new clothes, interviewed five candidates for the position. The first was patronising, the second too fastidious. The third seemed fearful, and the fourth kept referring to 'we' as in 'we will have to make ourselves at home in civilised society, my lord', as though his prospective employer had spent his life among Barbary apes.

Lord Athelney was getting desperate by the time he interviewed the fifth valet, and heaved a sigh of relief.

Cottam had valeted a former military gentleman for some years, and had become accustomed to the more pragmatic view of dress. His objective, and he used the word knowing that it would sit well with the gentleman sat before him, was to turn his master out neat and tidy at all times, to ensure that his garments were kept in good order and condition, and to offer sartorial advice only when it was requested. He had been taken on with immediate effect.

It took Cottam some minutes to reach his master, for which he apologised. 'The house, or rather castle, my lord, has many passages that appear the same to one unused to them, and I confess that I got lost.'

Lord Athelney laughed. 'I am not surprised, Cottam. I almost wished I had a map. It will take us both a few days to find our way about. Now, tomorrow I must pay a call upon my aunt, who is in deep mourning. Please lay out something suitably sober.'

'Of course, my lord.' He assisted his lordship from his top boots. 'Will you be driving or riding to the Dower House?'

'It is only down the hill, in perfect view. I shall walk.'

The valet refrained from commenting that it would mean arriving with muddied boots, and prayed that it might be so inclement as to make his master change his mind.

Cottam was a man whose prayers were answered. The following day dawned with a strong westerly gale and lashing rain. Lord Athelney had spent innumerable days out in such conditions, but recognised that arriving at the Dower House dripping wet would not create a good impression. He therefore had the horses put to, and was driven the short distance down the hill, though it went against the grain.

Lady Willoughby Hawksmoor wore black well. It gave her ramrod-straight posture added definition, and enhanced what was, for a woman of over fifty, a good figure. She managed to combine the vulnerability of the bereaved with the natural steel of her mien, and was feared by most of those with whom she came into contact, be they relatives, acquaintances, or servants. Her son had rarely visited of late years, finding his mama's animadversions upon his way of life not dissimilar to being thrashed at school: unpleasant to contemplate, painful to endure and lingering in effect. Her married daughter visited dutifully upon occasion, knowing that she would be told how she was raising her children incorrectly, wore her hair wrong and dressed like a dowd. Her younger daughter, having been so overawed by her strictures during her first London season that she behaved like a mouse fearing to leave the security of the edge of a room, had returned home to the Dower House unattached and in deep disfavour, Lady Willoughby seeing Charlotte's failure as intentional and designed to embarrass her.

Her son's sudden demise had caused her genuine distress, although his exploits had become so wild that such a calamity could not be entirely unforeseen. After the initial shock, she saw that it was yet another failure on his part, for had he but lived a short time longer, she might at least have been 'the mother of the Marquis of Athelney', which added to her consequence. That a different William Hawksmoor should succeed to the title irked the more so because of the name, and she greeted her nephew with thinly disguised dislike.

Lord Athelney bowed over her hand, and raised eyes that were not intimidated by her frosty greeting. 'My condolences, ma'am.'

'Really? Since you profited from the disaster that has befallen us, I can hardly believe them to be sincere.' Her ladyship used 'profited' in a very derogatory tone, as though he had won a wager for the title.

He wondered if the 'us' pertained to the other ladies

present, or was like a royal 'we'.

'I appreciate your grief as a parent, ma'am, and I can assure you that I do not consider myself to have "profited" by my change in circumstances.'

'Do not be ridiculous. You have inherited a marquisate, and before that you were nothing.'

'I was Captain William Hawksmoor of His Majesty's Navy, ma'am,' he responded tartly, flicked on the raw.

She sniffed, unabashed, and disregarded his reply. 'You did not come to Kingscastle with any urgency. Was that indolence or indigence? I assume officers receive some meagre form of remuneration, since they work.' She said the word as if it were dishonourable.

'I needed to go to London with Tideswell, the lawyer, and also provide myself with suitable attire for civilian life. Striding about the countryside in uniform would occasion remark.' He was not going to discuss his finances with her.

'Striding about the country at all would do so. Surely you were taught to ride a horse, before you ran away to sea, Athelney?'

'I can ride, ma'am, of course, and I did not run away to sea, nothing so romantic.'

'I do not approve of "romantic". It is foolishness.'

The youngest lady present gave what might have been a sigh. Lord Athelney glanced at her. She was pretty in a delicate way, with very fair hair and blue eyes. She looked as if permanently intimidated. The older daughter, he assumed, took more after her father, whom he dimly remembered as having dark brown hair like himself. She was petite also, but not frail-looking. She had the same straight back as his aunt, and her eyes were watchful.

Lady Willoughby saw him glance at Charlotte. 'Thankfully, you are here at long last, which will expedite matters.'

'Matters, ma'am?'

'Yes. The requirements of the late Lord Athelney's will are specific. I am in many ways glad that my poor boy was spared them,' she dabbed a handkerchief once only at the corner of her eye, 'but see that all is not lost. Since you have been so long absent from the family, you may not recall my younger daughter, Charlotte,' she indicated the fair-haired damsel, 'who will be your bride.'

Miss Hawksmoor let out a shocked squeak, and her eyes opened wide. Lord Athelney stared at his aunt in blank stupefaction. There followed an uneasy silence.

'I would be happy to see her wed in a quiet, private ceremony, but would suggest that you wait at least another month, lest it be perceived as hasty.'

'The hastiness, ma'am, is in your assumption that I will make my cousin an offer,' declared Lord Athelney, recovering the power of speech.

'Of course you will. It is eminently sensible. Where else will you find a wife of breeding outside the London season? And your case is urgent.'

'I do not know how you come to be in possession of this information, ma'am, but . . .'

'I demanded to see the will, of course. One cannot

trust menials. The provisions for myself and Charlotte were adequate, but no more.'

Even in his anger, Lord Athelney was confused by his aunt's lack of acknowledgement of the elder daughter. If she was going to thrust one upon him, why had she selected the younger?

'And your elder daughter?' He looked at the brunette.

Lady Willoughby followed his gaze, and looked quite shocked. 'My elder daughter is provided for, very well, by her husband. That,' she pointed at the young woman, 'is no daughter of mine. It is Eleanor.' She gave no more than the name.

'Forgive me, my lord,' Eleanor stepped forward and made her curtsey. 'We have not been introduced. My name is Eleanor Burgess, a connection of Lady Willoughby's, and her companion. I am employed, my lord, and,' she gave a tight smile, 'thus am also a person in receipt of remuneration.'

She looked him in the eye. Her voice was controlled, cool, but he thought that however subservient her outward demeanour, she disliked being treated as an object, and had inner spirit. He bowed, far lower than was required to 'a person in receipt of remuneration'.

'It is you who should forgive me, Miss Burgess.'

'I do not see that anyone need be forgiving except me. Who else has been insulted?' Lady Willoughby disliked the fact that Eleanor Burgess had distracted his lordship from the matter in hand. 'As I said, your case is urgent, Athelney. A wife is a wife. You will find Charlotte biddable, unobtrusive,' she gave her daughter a glance that held disdain, 'and perfectly suited to the role she will assume.'

Lord Athelney could think of few less appealing descriptions of a future spouse. Had he ever contemplated the married state, it would not have been with a girl like Charlotte Hawksmoor.

'You are under a gross misapprehension, Lady Willoughby. If I make any lady an offer, it will be my choice. I will not have a wife thrust upon me.' He looked visibly annoyed.

Lady Willoughby realised that she had been too forceful. Lord Athelney was not the sort of man with whom she had much contact.

'I apologise if I seem too pragmatic, Athelney. I understand that you may wish to get to know Charlotte better before coming to your decision.'

Lord Athelney was unsure what to do. His experience with the female of the species was exceedingly limited, and he did not think that reiterating his position more forcefully would succeed in getting through to this extraordinary woman. He therefore did what any good sailor would do when faced with having to head directly into the wind; he tacked.

'I do not think either Miss Hawksmoor or myself would wish to undertake any commitment without a vastly greater understanding of a potential spouse.' He phrased it as politely and vaguely as possible.

Miss Hawksmoor murmured something unintelligible,

and gave him a look of nervous gratitude.

'Then I expect to see you at dinner tomorrow evening. There is no point in dilly-dallying.'

Lady Willoughby was clearly not crushed. Lord Athelney wondered if he might invent some prior engagement, but realised that his aunt would quite reasonably ask what other acquaintance he might already possess in the district.

'Thank you, ma'am, I am sure.'

'We keep country hours and will sit down promptly at six. Do not be late.'

This injunction was obviously also a dismissal, and Lord Athelney withdrew, in as good an order as he could muster.

CHAPTER THREE

LORD ATHELNEY RETURNED THE SHORT DISTANCE to the castle in contemplative mood. His aunt was not entirely wrong in what she had said. The number of young ladies with whom he might become acquainted was, in the country, very limited, and he had no great desire to go to London for the Season, and a round of 'tight squeezes', evenings at Almack's, and simpering damsels. He wondered if he might manage upon his prize money and such advances as the Trust might make to him. Since the Trustees would not, as both Tideswell and Lord Somborne had assured him most frequently, fear that he would spend money recklessly, it might be assumed that all he need ever do was make representations to them whenever he required funds. He resented, however, that it would rob him of independent action and would mean him going cap in hand at every juncture. No, if a suitable young lady appeared upon the horizon, he would at least consider the option of marriage. Miss Hawksmoor he would not count as suitable. He felt sorry for her, but had even less intention of marrying out of pity than out of need. A pretty face was of no interest to him, if there was no substance to the personality behind it. He wondered if his cousin had even been permitted to develop a personality, so much was she in the shadow of her mama.

He was brought from contemplation of the unsuitability of Miss Hawksmoor to the present, seeing a groom walking the single horse from a jobbing carriage up and down in the courtyard. He stepped from his carriage, thanking the coachman, and was greeted by a very worried-looking Sturry, who had obviously been awaiting his return in some perturbation.

'My lord, I regret . . . I was not sure . . .' The old butler looked very flustered, and wrung his hands.

'What is it, Sturry?'

'A female, my lord, and one whom she declares to be her niece.'

Lord Athelney was conscious of a sense of déjà vu. Well, it was very unlikely that these two 'ladies' were about to threaten him with violence, which was a definite advantage over Major Ratlinghope. He smiled reassuringly.

'Really? You seem undecided about the validity of the relationship. Would I be right in thinking this woman is seeking William Hawksmoor, the new Marquis of Athelney, with an eye to profit?'

'Indeed, my lord.' Sturry, however shocked, was glad his lordship was so quick of understanding. 'I did not want them hammering upon the door and creating unseemly disturbance, and thought that perhaps once they see . . .'

'Oh yes, Sturry, I understand perfectly. Where will I find this "aunt and niece"?'

'In the small, panelled parlour, my lord, out of the way, so to speak.'

'Very good. You will announce me, but then you would in any case have to lead me to it, since I have no idea where the small, panelled parlour is situated.'

'If you would be pleased to follow me, my lord.' Sturry, relieved, sounded almost avuncular, and led the way down a corridor with several side turnings. At the door of the requisite chamber, they halted. Female voices sounded within.

'Getting the story right, no doubt.' Lord Athelney grinned, and then schooled his features into the semblance of aristocratic aloofness.

Sturry's lips twitched, but it was a very stone-faced butler who opened the door and declared loudly, 'The ladies are here, my lord.'

The two 'ladies' turned. One was middle-aged, though her dress would have suited a far younger woman, and her cheeks bore spots of colour that came from a rouge pot, which made her look like an ill-favoured doll; his lordship identified her correctly as very tough mutton dressed as lamb. The younger was striking, in a voluptuous way. Her guinea-gold hair was elaborately coiffed beneath a small, fussy hat, and her gown was overembellished, rather as she was overendowed. Lord Athelney could see instantly what had attracted his cousin, for they were scarcely hidden from view. Not a man of taste or discernment, Mr William Hawksmoor, he decided.

'Lord Athelney,' announced Sturry, and withdrew, slowly enough to hear the first shots of the engagement.

The older woman's eyes narrowed.

'No you ain't,' she averred, in a voice given an edge by years of being shrill, and indicating her far from genteel London origins.

'Oh, I am, ma'am, I assure you. But you have the better of me, for I have not the slightest notion who you might be, though "what" is more obvious.' He smiled, but his voice was cool, and his grey eyes glittered.

Both women looked confused. This was not what they had expected at all.

The senior made a recovery. 'No need for you to get offensive, sir . . . my . . .'

'"My lord" will do.' The chill in his voice had become more pronounced.

Sturry shut the crack in the door, and smiled to himself. His lordship would not need any assistance beyond his availability to show the women out at the end of the interview.

'We are here,' declared the woman, 'to see Lord Athelney, and there is an end to it. Until you bring him to us to explain hisself, we shall remain.'

As if to confirm this statement, she sat down, heavily, upon a rather aged chair, which creaked at the unaccustomed usage, her kid-gloved fingers clamping, claw-like, over her reticule.

'But I am Lord Athelney, as I have already told you, and if you are going to try and tell me that your . . . niece . . . or so I was informed, had any "dealings" with my uncle, I shall be astounded, for he was nigh on seventy, and in frail health for some years.'

The younger woman withdrew a rolled cutting from the *London Gazette* from her cleavage, in a highly theatrical gesture.

'Lord, no, not the old 'un. I has me pride.' She sounded affronted.

'Ah, I erroneously assumed you only had your price. Such a difference one letter makes, does it not,' murmured his lordship.

The golden-haired doxy digested this remark, threw him a look of dislike, and continued. 'It says here as the new Lord Athelney, formerly Mr William Hawksmoor, is taking up residence at the family seat, which is here. We have come all this way from the metro-pollis to see him.' She enunciated precisely, clearly proud of her refined terminology.

'Ah, you really ought not trust what you read in newspapers. Or rather you should have read and trusted the edition in which it said that Mr William Hawksmoor had suffered a fatal accident.'

'What do you mean?' The painted harridan was still suspicious, but showing signs of worry.

'I mean, ma'am, that you have had a wasted journey.' Lord Athelney was beginning to enjoy himself. 'It is perfectly clear. The gentleman you intended to see is no more.'

'But it states "William Hawksmoor", in black and white.'

'Yes, but unfortunately for you, it should have said "Captain William Hawksmoor, Royal Navy". My cousin William, who really does seem to have led a most colourful existence, died the week before my uncle, the, er, "old" Lord Athelney. I say again, I am Lord Athelney.'

The two women exchanged glances. Lord Athelney watched them as his information sank in. It did not take a man conversant with the ways of women of their trade to see their thought processes, which immediately set to work to see how they could still make money from the situation.

'Well, if that is who you are . . . my lord,' the title was given grudgingly, 'you will not wish to see the family name sullied by the revelations my poor deluded Antoinette could reveal.' The older woman eyed him speculatively.

'Antoinette?' Lord Athelney raised his brows. 'How . . . aspirational.' He paused. 'She does not look one who could be easily deluded. Up to every trick, I should say.'

'Antoinette' opened her mouth, and, with a smile as false as the red of her lips, was about, out of habit, to enumerate her 'tricks' when her 'aunt' interjected quickly.

'You would not look so, nor talk so clever, if it were made known how your wicked cousin seduced, yes, seduced, my innocent niece, my lord.'

'No, ma'am, indeed not. That is, if you are in possession of a niece, which I think a matter of conjecture, let alone one who could be described as innocent, which strikes me as highly unlikely.'

'How dare you suggest—'

'Oh, I am not suggesting, I am stating. And if this young woman is any blood relation of yours, her days of innocence must be long since departed, especially dressed like that. I have seen "ladies" of your profession half the world over, and I promise you, the look is much the same.'

'It doesn't make it any the likelier that you would want the Hawksmoor name dragged through the mud.' The harridan was persistent.

'Certainly not. I would not drag it so, myself, but, you see, while he lived, Wicked William dragged it perfectly well on his own. In fact, his death is in many ways a great relief. If you were to waste your breath declaiming him as a ravisher and seducer, nobody would listen, for it is news to none, and from your very painted lips the suggestion would be perfectly ridiculous. Now, since you will wish to reach Bath by dark, I suggest you leave at once.'

He reached for the bell, but the 'aunt' had one last card to play. 'Would his poor, grieving mama feel the same way, my lord?'

For a wicked moment, Lord Athelney imagined a confrontation between the two women, and it took all his self-control not to let his lips twitch. He had little doubt who would emerge victorious, though the similarities between the two did not elude him. Lady Willoughby was determinedly foisting her daughter upon him with as little interest in her wishes as any 'abbess' pushing one of her girls at a client, and how many other matchmaking mamas would not effectively sell their daughters to the man with the highest rank or fattest purse? It would, however, be unfair to Lady Willoughby to have to face such a class of female in her drawing room, loudly denouncing her son, however well aware she was of his peccadilloes, and however blind an eye had been turned to his many faults. It would be pointless to ask the women to be charitable, and so he gave them the truth, only slightly embellished.

'His mama was well aware of his failings, and of the low company he kept. If she grieved it was while he lived, that he should have conducted himself as he did. She is a very upright woman, very strict, and now confines herself to praying for his, one has to admit, rather blackened soul. I do not know for certain how she would deal with the likes of you, but you can be sure you would never forget it. A redoubtable lady, is my aunt. Have you been ejected from a residence, forcibly? I am sure you must have, over the years. My aunt's house has quite a flight of steps to the front door. I am not sure you might not suffer considerable injury. Your safest course is most definitely to return whence you came, and straight away.'

Before any response could be made, Lord Athelney tugged at the bell rope, and Sturry appeared just as if he had been right outside the door, which of course he had.

'You rang, my lord?'

'These ladies are leaving, Sturry. Will you be so good as to look about the room to ascertain whether everything is in place. I am unfamiliar with its contents. And then show them out.' He looked the women up and down, as they bristled at the imputation that they would stoop to common thievery. 'Good day to you both, and might I suggest that you let it be known among the sisterhood that my cousin is no more and that no advantage can be gained by telling of his exploits. They are all well known.'

With which Lord Athelney gave the slightest of bows and left, making his way back to the great hall, from which he could find his way to the library. It was there he gave way to mirth.

He had regained his equilibrium by the time he rang the bell some minutes later. Sturry arrived looking as if he had found a guinea in his sock. His face, usually a suitably inscrutable mask, was wreathed in smiles.

'My lord, that was masterly. I apologise for not sending them to the rightabout immediately but you see,

51

I have no experience with such females.'

Lord Athelney let out a crack of laughter. 'Thank you, Sturry. That assumes that I do.'

'No, no, my lord, indeed not.' The butler coloured, and hastened to reassure him.

'It is all right, Sturry. Actually, it was much better that I dealt with them. Hopefully the news of my cousin's demise will now circulate widely in that level of society he chose to frequent. Unfortunately, it seems that the newspapers have "Mr William Hawksmoor", which has led to misunderstanding. I fear it may yet lead to other unsavoury characters turning up at the door, threatening to dun me, or inflict violence upon my person.'

'I do hope not, my lord.' Sturry looked most concerned.

'So do I, Sturry. I am not a violent man.'

'You aren't, my lord?' Sturry sounded both relieved and yet slightly disappointed.

'No. Oh, you see naval officers as spending their lives with a cutlass between their teeth and a pistol in their hand? That is a very romantic and unrealistic view. There are short hours of battle and many months of fighting the elements.'

'I understand, my lord.'

He did not, and Lord Athelney knew that to be the case, but his lordship smiled nevertheless.

'We will hope that violence will not be required. I had to face a very angry husband in London. Fortunately he discovered his mistake before he tried to take out his ire upon my person. I had not anticipated that bearing

52

the title could prove so dangerous. I would rather not be forced into taking an advertisement in the *Gazette* reminding all and sundry that I am not my late and unlamented cousin.'

'I am sure that will not be required, my lord.' Sturry sighed. 'His old lordship was frequently distressed by Master William's exploits, and shook his head over them, those that came to his ears. We tried to keep as much as possible from him, but some things . . .' Sturry frowned, and paused. 'Some things could not be hidden.' He gave another sigh. 'In his youth, of course, his lordship had cut up larks of his own, as many young gentlemen did, but he never besmirched the family name. Of course, there was the advantage of "abroad" then. They could get the worst of their youthful high jinks out of their systems where it did not matter, and the Frenchies were always an immoral lot, even before they started cutting off the heads of all and sundry.'

Lord Athelney contained his surprise. 'I take it you have never been abroad, Sturry.'

'Oh no,' announced the old retainer proudly. 'Never been further than London, and that was when I was young in service, and a footman. There had been nasty contagion in the metropolis, and her ladyship thought it safer to take some of the Kingscastle servants than employ new ones up there. Nasty, noisy place it was, my lord. Never saw why folk wanted to go there.'

'It is indeed very noisy, I agree.'

'Never approved of abroad, and London might as

nearly well be. Bath, now that is a pleasant city.'

Sturry's natural predilection for his home shire was, felt Lord Athelney, rather touching.

'I think I shall take a glass of sherry before luncheon, Sturry. It has been a most interesting forenoon. Oh, and I shall be dining at the Dower House tomorrow evening, so could you warn Mrs Ablett. I would hate her to prepare something for it to go to waste.'

'Of course, my lord.' Sturry bowed and withdrew.

His lordship stood, hands behind his back, feet apart, as he had often done upon his own quarterdeck, except now this was upon the oak boards of his library floor, and instead of the whip of the wind and the vastness of ocean, there was the crackle of a good fire, and the view from the library window down to the loop of the river and the edge of the Somerset levels a little beyond. The interlude with the London 'ladies' had been enlivening, but he returned to contemplating the prospect of having to find a lady with whom he could comfortably, happily, spend the rest of his days. This morning had not shown off the gender to advantage in any way. It was most depressing.

Sturry returned with the sherry. His expression was one of worry.

'My lord, I was wondering. If by any mischance, individuals with violent intent should present themselves at the front door, should you wish me to call for assistance and bar the door? I am not, I admit, so strong that I think I could manage on my own.'

Lord Athelney imagined Sturry grabbing one of the ancient halberds off the wall.

'I think that eventuality unlikely, Sturry. If such persons have not appeared by now, I expect most have become aware of Mr Hawksmoor's demise. The gentleman who accosted me in London had been with the army in France. Those to whom he owed money would be the most likely to know of his movements, and that they ended suddenly. I do not think we are likely to be attacked.' He smiled at the butler. 'And if I am lucky, I will shortly receive news of reinforcements before we should have any need to repel boarders.'

CHAPTER FOUR

THE FOLLOWING EVENING, SUITABLY DRESSED AND with his hair as tidy as his own efforts and those of Cottam could make it, Lord Athelney presented himself at the Dower House for dinner. He did not expect it to be an evening of pleasure. He was the only gentleman present and stuck between his aunt and cousin. Miss Burgess sat opposite, and had obviously been instructed to keep silent unless directly addressed. Charlotte, on the other hand, sounded as if she had been given a list of topics upon which she must discourse, but her mother could not resist correcting her at every turn, and gradually taking over. Lord Athelney felt as if he were closely blockaded.

'Have you been in many battles, Cousin William?' enquired Charlotte, with a look at her mama that gave him the impression that she would be asked to repeat any list before going to her bed.

'A fair few engagements, yes. I first saw action at Copenhagen in 1801 as a midshipman aboard the *Monarch*. Her captain, Captain Moss, was a connection of my mother's family, and it was through him that I got to sea.'

'You must have been very young, my lord,' commented Miss Burgess, and earned a look of reproof from Lady Willoughby.

'I was fifteen, a good age to go to sea. There have been some but twelve years or younger, and that to my mind is far too young for a midshipman, who must learn command.'

'But in the navy promotion is not based upon breeding, merely merit,' Lady Willoughby interjected. 'At least in the army a gentleman may purchase advancement. Heaven knows what sorts of person one might have to acknowledge in so egalitarian a service.'

'Indeed, ma'am, one might have had to "acknowledge" Lord Nelson, whose father was a country parson,' his lordship riposted.

'But he was different.'

'Yes, ma'am, he was, in that he was a most brilliant leader of men, but I have been honoured to serve with, and under, men whose origins were as lowly, if not more so. What advances a junior officer is hard work, and good fortune.'

'Good luck?'

'Good luck in being in the right place at the right time, and not being in the line of a musket ball or splinter.'

'A splinter.' Lady Willoughby snorted derisively.

'I do not think, ma'am, that his lordship is referring to the sort of splinter one might find in one's finger,' murmured Miss Burgess, daring to smile across the table at him.

'The splinters I mean can be several feet long and cut a man in half or eviscerate him.' Lord Athelney did not care if his words shocked.

'And is it not so, that the most dangerous thing is for an enemy ship to cross behind one's own vessel, for the shot may run the length of it and cause great loss of life and limb, my lord?' Miss Burgess was clearly not shocked at all.

'That is true, ma'am.'

'I hardly think that a discussion of naval warfare is suitable for my dining room,' declared Lady Willoughby, in a repressive tone.

'It sounds positively appalling,' whispered Charlotte, who had gone quite pale.

'The tactic or the effect?' Miss Burgess enquired innocently, and regretted her recklessness.

Lady Willoughby glared at her. There would be a summons to The Presence for a lengthy lecture upon 'her place' before she could retire.

Lord Athelney, who felt very much that Miss Burgess had sacrificed herself in an attempt to come to his support, smiled across the table at her, despite the strategic placing of an epergne, which had clearly been placed to make any speech between the two of them dependent upon leaning somewhat to one side.

Charlotte ploughed on, showing little interest in the answers she received, or perhaps, he reflected, she was simply so used to not expressing an opinion that she had ceased to hold any. When the covers were removed, his aunt rose majestically from the table, and informed him that he might linger for no more than ten minutes with his port 'since you do so in solitary state', and that thereafter he might play spillikins with Charlotte.

Staring at the ornate timepiece upon the mantelshelf, he was convinced it was in league with his hostess and running fast to spite him. He took his glass of port, and was tempted to brood over it. The evening had done nothing more than confirm that never in a hundred years would he offer for his cousin, that his aunt was a petty despot, and that Miss Burgess had a spark to her. Gazing into the bottom of the glass, he sighed, and steeled himself for the unbounded excitement of parlour games.

When Lord Athelney, with what Miss Burgess thought patent relief, made his farewells for the evening, she immediately set about tidying up the spillikins and setting the tea things upon the tray. Any hope that this display of menial service would enable her to slip quietly away to bed was short-lived. Lady Willoughby permitted her daughter to kiss her cheek and sent her to her room. She then resumed her seat, and folded her hands in her lap, very precisely.

'At what point did you decide to ignore my instructions, and monopolise conversation, Eleanor?'

'Monopolise, ma'am? I spoke but twice, and barely more than a few words.'

'Three times, madam, and impertinently also. I do not pay you to flaunt yourself before your betters. You will remember that in future.' She paused, and then said, 'I do not wish you to engage in conversation with my nephew.'

Eleanor blinked in surprise. 'It would be exceedingly rude to cut him dead, ma'am.'

'You may respond, as politeness dictates, but no more. I am not a fool, Eleanor. Charlotte has not made a good impression, silly child. Athelney is not going hunting for a wife. You can tell he is inexperienced with women. The only two women of marriageable age he is likely to see more than once in a full moon are you and Charlotte, and however ineligible you are, laughably so, he has not had the upbringing to realise its implications. To a simple sailor, what harm could there be in marrying a parson's daughter, especially since he is so proud of Admiral Lord Nelson's equally humble ancestry. He has no more idea of what is due to his position as Marquis of Athelney than I have about warfare, which is thankfully nothing whatsoever.'

Eleanor opened her mouth to speak, to deny that she was any threat to Charlotte's chances, but Lady Willoughby held up a hand to stop her.

'You have been warned, Eleanor, and if you value your position in this household, you will act upon the warning. Goodnight. You are dismissed for the evening.'

Her ladyship inclined her head in gracious dismissal. Eleanor had little alternative but to curtsey and withdraw, however much it rankled. She maintained her composure until she was in the privacy of her own chamber, where she vented her frustration in brushing out her hair so aggressively that her eyes watered.

Only when she was actually lying in bed did she think about the man whom she had now been commanded to avoid, and who thus became instantly more interesting. It was true that Charlotte had done nothing to advance her cause with her cousin, but Eleanor could not see that she was in any way responsible for Charlotte's 'failure'. She had said so little, and if he had smiled at her, well, he was grateful, no more. He had smiled, though, and it was a nice smile, a smile of understanding, of appreciation. The poor man had been so beleaguered, she could not but have shown him compassion. Forgetting that he must converse with women when living ashore, and with no notion that captains occasionally took their wives upon passage, nor that a few women lived upon the lower decks, she imagined him unused to even the proximity of the fair sex. To be seated at dinner with none but females, and with no topic upon which they might discourse upon equal terms, must have been a torment. Perhaps, if Charlotte had been sweetly captivating, he might have relaxed, but poor Charlotte was even more stressed than he was.

Eleanor smiled, remembering his blank surprise when his cousin had asked him if he slept in a hammock in the castle. She thought it had been Charlotte's own question, and based upon the picture, painted by her mama, of Lord Athelney being some salty sea dog. Well, he looked perfectly at home in evening dress; in fact, it showed him to advantage, and his table manners were unexceptional. Whether these things had pleased Lady Willoughby, or had merely reduced the number of faults she would find with him, was unclear. However many faults she found, Charlotte would be pushed at him, regardless, because of his title. Both he and Charlotte had looked astounded when informed that the poor girl was to become the Marchioness of Athelney. Eleanor could not see the match coming to fruition on the evidence of this evening, but, if marriage was the only way Lord Athelney could take control of his own estates, his own destiny, would he set compatibility aside? Lady Willoughby must think he would do anything, since she now thought he would 'even' look at her paid companion. It was laughable, although Eleanor did not laugh.

Eleanor Burgess was five and twenty, and, in her own eyes, beyond marriage by virtue of both age and employment. She had entered Lady Willoughby Hawksmoor's employ the previous year, after much soul-searching. Her mama had kept in occasional contact with her more elevated relations, and this included Lady Willoughby Hawksmoor. That lady, having had, most unfortunately, to part with her secretary, thought that a paid companion during her daughter's come-out would take from her those uninteresting tasks such as dealing with responses to invitations, sending them out, and reminding her of the things she wished to do. She had written back to her relative, offering to 'take one of your many daughters off your hands', as a gesture of generosity that was based upon the fact that it would look better than placing an advertisement, and would almost certainly be cheaper.

The Honourable Mrs Thomas Burgess showed the letter to her husband, and then her daughters, of whom there were six. Emily and Georgina were too young, at fourteen and seventeen. Mary, who was undoubtedly the beauty of the family, had formed an attachment, and looked set to contract an advantageous alliance before her twentieth birthday, with the heir to a baronetcy whom she had met at the Chester Assembly Rooms. Jane suffered from a loss of hearing in one ear, but the new curate, a young man of bookish temperament and gentle manners, was showing a degree of interest in her that encouraged her mama to think that she too might find the security and happiness of marriage. That left the two eldest, Eleanor and Margaret. Margaret had declared her intention never to marry, but to be a comfort and support to her parents in their declining years. Since neither the reverend gentleman nor his wife felt the slightest signs of decline, this was felt to be precipitate by her parents, but Margaret had what her papa considered an unhealthy streak of the martyr in her character, and remained resolute that she would immolate herself upon the altar of filial devotion. This left Eleanor, eighteen months her junior, as available, and certainly the most suitable.

Eleanor was bright, had a neat hand, and was a very competent young woman. It was her mother's belief that she was perhaps too competent and practical. The gentlemen generally seemed to prefer girls whom they saw as needing protection, and Eleanor had always exuded an air of calm self-sufficiency that they found off-putting. She was of trim and tidy appearance, not tall, for none of the Burgess girls could claim to be much over the average, with rich brown hair that glinted with coppery highlights in sunshine and a slightly lop-sided smile. This added to her air of amusement at the folly of the world, and its male inhabitants in particular. Mrs Burgess had offered the hint often enough that young men did not like to be laughed at, to which Eleanor's reply was that they should therefore not behave so stupidly. Her mama feared that her attitude reflected the bruising of her youthful heart by the squire's younger son, and entertained unchristian thoughts about that gentleman, now happily far distant, and serving in India.

No pressure was brought to bear upon Eleanor's decision, but she herself saw the sense of taking up the offer. A parson's stipend was not large, and did not extend to luxuries with already seven adults in the house, and the wages of cook, a maid and the gardener. Even with the likelihood of this diminishing by two, there was the launching of Emily and Georgina to consider, be it only upon the edges of more fashionable Cheshire society. Besides which, she was underemployed at home. A wrench it would be to leave the rectory, but it was a sensible move, and Eleanor was a sensible woman. Considering every aspect, she had, with only the most private tears, left home. She had not, of course, met Lady Willoughby Hawksmoor.

Once she had done so, Eleanor found it hard not to despise the woman. Lady Willoughby's knowledge was limited, and she was proud of those limitations. Anything that she did not know was not suitable to be known by one of her station, or smacked of being the mark of a bluestocking. She was utterly selfish, and had a waspish temperament. Eleanor could easily see where her son had got his reckless disregard for anything except his own pleasure, and could only assume that, in character, Charlotte took after her long-deceased papa. So often had she wanted to shake Charlotte, and tell her to be herself, for she was a very pretty and sweet-tempered girl, and not as witless as her mama made her feel. In Eleanor's opinion, the only reason that Charlotte had emerged from her first season unbetrothed was that she had been too concerned always at what her mother was thinking, and that interested young men had been scared off by the bullying presence of that lady.

Only once before had Eleanor thought of resigning her position, and whilst she did so tonight, her reasons were very different. The other had been when Mr William

Hawksmoor, on one of his rare visits to his surviving parent, had decided that the position of companion to his mother gave him the right to make Eleanor the companion of his bed. She had found him in her bedchamber, half-cut and half-dressed, reeking of spirit, and intent on forcing himself upon her. Taken by surprise, she had not been able to prevent him grabbing her and pressing most unwelcome kisses upon her, but thankfully she had been able to free one arm and grab the bedside candle in its twisted oak candlestick and thrust it in his face. Lurching back from a singed cheek and letting her go had enabled her to pick up the poker, and to prod him far from gently in the ribs towards the door. She had then wedged a chair under the door handle, and accepted that unless she awoke very early, the maid would not be able to get in with the pitcher of water for her ablutions in the morning. She had considered resigning very definitely that night. Returning to the rectory would be a sign of defeat, however, and so, as now, she gritted her teeth, took a deep breath, and carried on.

Lord Athelney laid aside the muslin of his cravat, stretched his neck, and sighed. Unpleasant aunts were a fact of life, and indeed many a lively evening in the gunroom had been spent by the young gentlemen aboard ship telling more and more exaggerated tales of them, much as one would about sea serpents, but to have one less than half a mile away, one's nearest neighbour and capable of almost daily contact, was grim. The evening had been one he would wish to forget at the earliest opportunity, and he hoped he would be able to create a long list of excuses through which to work when invited to dine without the presence of other guests. Of course, he had not anticipated that tonight he would not have other company. He had, foolishly, hoped that even at short notice, his aunt would have invited the vicar, or some local landowner, to make his acquaintance.

Over the next few weeks he must expect to receive visits and invitations from about the county. He was not an antisocial man, and foresaw that at least a few of these would be pleasurable. If he was really fortunate, he might meet a pleasant and unattached young woman. Cousin Charlotte had even more firmly proved herself the sort of woman he would never be able to face across a breakfast table. She would undoubtedly talk all the time, and yet say nothing. If he had a preference, and now he considered the matter, he did, it was for a woman more in the style of Miss Burgess, the paid companion, who had an air of restful competence about her. Such a woman would allow a man to break his fast in peace, and only raise matters of importance for the day.

He gave himself a mental shake at how vivid the image was in his mind. It was even definitely in the breakfast parlour below, and there was sunshine streaming in through the leaded panes of the casement window and casting diamond patterns upon the sleeve of her gown, a green gown, and she was eating toast. Ridiculous. The trials of the evening must be addling his brain, and he would need a clear head in the morning because he was going to ride round the nearest of his tenancies, and Sittford, the village across the stone bridge that crossed the loop of river on the south side. It was effectively 'his' village, and he wanted to see it and be seen by its inhabitants as soon as possible.

He wondered, sleepily, how old Mitchum managed upon horseback, and smiled at the thought that the pace the elderly steward would choose would suit himself. He had ridden in youth, and occasionally since, but he would be lying if he did not admit it would take a month or so before he felt entirely at ease on horseback again. He was suddenly struck by a thought; he had no idea what horseflesh stood in his stable beyond the pair of carriage horses that had taken him to and fro between the castle and the Dower House. His uncle had been too old and infirm to have ridden. Perhaps there were no longer riding horses there at all. He should have asked about it, but now, it was far, far too late.

He fell asleep and dreamed of an enormous silver epergne that kept him from something unknown that he really wanted.

CHAPTER FIVE

Lord Athelney awoke to pale sunshine casting aside the pinks and greys of an autumnal dawn. He did not like the heavy brocade curtains to be drawn, either those across the window or about his bed, though it made the room colder in the mornings. He was used to fresh air, above decks at least, and a far horizon. He enjoyed both, but when he opened his eyes his head swam slightly. He frowned. He had most certainly not drunk too much the previous evening, but Lady Willoughby's port was poor quality, so perhaps that accounted for a slight muzziness of his brain. Cottam entered shortly after he tugged at the bell, rather too bright and breezy for his lordship's head.

'Remind me, Cottam, to never finish even one glass of port at the Dower House,' murmured Lord Athelney, rubbing the back of his head and making his hair stand up even more than usual.

'I shall endeavour to do so, my lord. I take it her ladyship does not keep a good cellar.'

'Correct, Cottam. I have imbibed some interesting beverages in the course of my service, but few could give me a clouded head after only two glasses.'

'Might I suggest you speak to her butler about it, my lord, quietly. It is often the case that unless intimations are given, better vintages are kept back, and even used below stairs. Not,' he added, hastily, 'that your lordship need fear that here. Mr Sturry is a very reliable gentleman, and besides, the Dower House is inhabited by ladies, who do not drink port, so they would never know.'

Lady Willoughby's butler looked very reliable too, but, considered Lord Athelney, if she was as unpleasant to her staff as to her relations, it might be a covert form of redressing the balance, a safe revenge upon her.

'I shall do that, Cottam. Now, I am going about with my steward today, so I require riding dress, and a good warm coat. That is if I possess an animal to ride.'

'The garments I will lay out immediately, my lord. The equine, I regret, is beyond my abilities to procure.'

Lord Athelney laughed, and then groaned.

Mitchum appeared as the marquis finished an abstemious breakfast, which left Cook worrying that she was failing in her duties. The old man was kneading a rather battered round hat, and regarded him with a rheumy eye.

'Good morning, Mitchum. We have a fine day for being out and about.' Lord Athelney tried to sound alert and keen, however little he felt like it.

'Yes, my lord.' He did not look particularly delighted, and Lord Athelney wondered if his old bones really disliked riding.

'I am sorry if it means a hard day in the saddle, Mitchum. Be consoled with the fact that I have not ridden for an extended period for many years, and will pay for it tomorrow.'

'I am sorry, my lord.'

'No, no, Mitchum, it is I who am sorry, but I do need you to guide me about and introduce me, at least initially.' He got up from the table. 'However, I must first ascertain if I have a mount, for I will be damned if I shall run behind you all day.' He smiled.

'To the best of my knowledge there is still his old lordship's favourite hunter, my lord. He is exercised occasionally.'

'Then let us take a look at him.'

The horse had once been a fine animal, but looked a little arthritic. The head groom swore that Sulphur was still up to being ridden.

'Sulphur, you say?' Lord Athelney looked suspicious.

'Why yes, m' lord. A'cos his lordship said he went like somethin' out o' hell, back in his prime.'

'Ah.' This was not the time to admit that he wished the horse had been named something more sedentary.

'He won't be up to no tricks now, leastways not many,

just so long as you 'members he don't like things up near his face sudden like, m' lord.'

'Thank you, I shall endeavour to bear that in mind.'

Mitchum was mounted on a pony already well into its winter coat, and they presented an odd couple, the old man upon the shaggy pony and the marquis on a bay hunter of over seventeen hands. Lord Athelney, being a reasonably tall gentleman, did not look out of place upon Sulphur, but felt a long way from the ground. Fortunately, Sulphur did not exhibit the desire for speed that he had possessed in youth, and seemed content to amble beside the sturdy pony, even if that poor beast was almost at the trot. They descended the hill, following the south track that hugged the wall of the castle and led down to the Sittford bridge. It was a sturdy stone construction, quite flat and with two piers in the flow of the river. Beyond lay both the village and the church, built in the community at the Restoration, before which the parishioners had to trail up the hill to where the little mediaeval church stood conveniently for the lords of Kingscastle. It was a linear village based upon one street with a few short side turnings, one of which led to church and parsonage. Mitchum pointed out those few houses of greater size than a cottage and gave names to the inhabitants. A few were encountered and introduced, which took up time, but Lord Athelney considered helpful, since his memory for names and faces was good, and for stone buildings quite poor. As they left the village he turned in the saddle, frowning.

'There is something concerns your lordship?' the old steward asked, his voice wavering a little.

'Yes, Mitchum. I know nothing of land management, but I do understand the ways of water. They are quite simple. Primarily, when there is too much to be contained, water overflows. To my eye, all round the south and east side of the castle promontory the land appears either the same elevation as the course of the river, or lower.'

'That is true, my lord, but it means good growing land even in gardens, and the river has not burst its banks these eighteen years. Bad it is when it happens, but, God willing, it happens so rare as folks can manage, and look about you, my lord. Where else hereabouts has height like Kingscastle? That is the end of the higher ground, and all the rest is low-lying. You head further to the south and west, my lord, and you get true wetlands that flood each winter with the rains. We lives where we was born to live, and dies where we was born to die.'

The old man seemed content with his philosophy, but it worried the marquis. They proceeded to several of the larger farms and met the tenants. There were requests from one or two, requests eliciting a nod of approval from old Mitchum, or a snort and dismissal as being an attempt to get what they had no right to expect. Lord Athelney ruefully acknowledged that he could not tell the difference.

'Ah, that, my lord, is where experience comes in. You needs to know what they has a right to expect of you, and also what manner of men they are. Nathaniel

Potter is as honest as a midsummer day is long, and he will not ask for anything he don't truly believe is right and proper, though he might be mistaken. On the other hand, the Tachbrooks would grasp all they would think they could get from you, and never think it enough.'

'What of the land that was meant to be drained?'

'That lies a bit beyond, my lord, but we have just enough hours of light for me to show you if we trot on a bit.'

It was well past three in the afternoon, and the warmth had long gone from the day, when the two riders crossed back onto the castle hill, this time via the wooden crossing at Sittford Mill. The miller, who announced himself as Jacob Flowers, was a prolific man, for Lord Athelney counted upward of eight children about the mill buildings, and Mrs Flowers looked shortly to be delivered of another.

'Ah yes.' Mitchum chuckled. 'Not only does he grind grain, our Jacob, but sows many seeds, my lord.'

He was still inclined to mirth as they crossed the bridge, with the horses' hooves clattering on the wooden planks. They turned to the left, following the loop of the river back towards the stone bridge. As they approached, a cloaked female figure crossed ahead of them, and turned a bonneted head to see who it might be. It was at that moment that a flock of chattering sparrows were disturbed from a bramble patch immediately to their right, and flew out in alarm. Whatever their alarm was as nothing to Sulphur's. He jibbed and reared, and his hind legs slithered in the wet turf. A good rider would have kept his seat, but Lord Athelney was not a good rider. Thrown forward onto the animal's neck, he then began an inexorable slide down the horse's back, slipping over the hindquarters and being deposited upon the ground, where an angry hoof lashed out and missed his nose by a hair's breadth. He swore, in language that was far more lower deck than quarterdeck, but thankfully not so loudly that Mitchum's old ears caught more than the intent of it.

The woman was hurrying towards them, holding her skirts up as best she might, and getting muddied stockings for her trouble. Mitchum, for whom dismounting was a slow process, had grabbed the hunter's reins by the bit and looked down at his master, his mouth open.

'My lord, my lord, are you all right?' Miss Burgess cried in concern.

'Damn it, madam, I merely slipped from the beast's rump, and have bruised my pride and muddied my raiment,' growled his lordship, wishing she were a hundred miles away, and that none but his steward might see his ignominious dismount.

'There is no need to swear, sir,' responded Miss Burgess tartly, as an illogical flood of relief swept through her. She stopped a few feet short of him, lying in the mud, and glaring up at her.

'I am sorry, ma'am, sorry, but . . .' He attempted to get to his feet and slipped again. She held out a gloved hand, and he took it. Her clasp was firm and she pulled quite strongly. His second attempt saw him stand before her, more than just spattered in mud; he was plastered in it. He held out one arm like a scarecrow, and pulled a face. Without in the least wishing to do so, Miss Burgess laughed.

'I fear, my lord, that if your bruises, the physical ones, that is, are as extensive as the mud, you will be very sore upon the morrow.'

'You laugh, ma'am, but think what Lady Willoughby would say about my dignity.'

'In your current state, my lord, I am not sure that you possess any.' A dimple peeped, and then she blushed, for his eyes laughed, though his voice was a groan.

'Alas, I shall never make a recovery then. I must implore your silence, ma'am, for the sake of the family honour.'

'Oh, in that case, my lord, my lips are sealed.'

He looked down at her, his flash of annoyance gone, looking at her smiling mouth, and suddenly both realised that he was still holding her hand. They started, and he let the hand drop as if it were a hot coal.

'Thank you, Miss Burgess, and my profound apologies for my intemperate language.' He spoke quietly, privately, as though they were quite alone.

'It is forgotten, my lord.' It was, but the laughter in his eyes was not.

Miss Burgess reached the Dower House as the gloaming slowly conceded defeat and slunk away, leaving darkness to take total command of the skies. She was greeted with some concern by Barwell, whose eyes widened at her muddied hem.

'Yes, Barwell, the day was fine, but the ground was . . . difficult. Has her ladyship been asking after me?'

'No, miss, you are, dare I say it, in luck. Her ladyship took on one of her sick headaches after you left, er, after luncheon, that is, and has been laid upon her bed all afternoon. Miss Charlotte attended her for a while but I apprehend that her services were dispensed with some time since.'

'Ah, I understand perfectly, Barwell. Thank you. I think I shall make good my chance and remove all evidence of good West Country mud from my person before I am taken to task for not avoiding it, though how one could do so without floating in the air, I cannot imagine.' She smiled conspiratorially at the butler, who nodded his approval.

'I shall send up Maria, with a bowl of hot water for your feet, miss.'

'Thank you.'

'And perhaps there might be some tea, as a restorative.' He had an avuncular side.

'Oh yes, Barwell, that would be nice.'

Tea was normally only made upon Lady Willoughby's instruction, but since Eleanor had not ordered it, nor Barwell specifically offered it, both consciences were clear.

She went to her room, and lit the fire, which in her

chamber was only permitted after dark settled, Lady Willoughby's reasoning being that Eleanor would be in attendance upon herself in the day, and needed no fire. She removed her shoes, stripped the wet and muddy stockings from her cold legs, and, with a sigh, changed both gown and petticoats. A knock at the door announced the arrival of Maria, tongue protruding slightly between her teeth in concentration as she balanced a pitcher of hot water, carefully, in a large basin. She set the latter upon the floor in front of the fire, and poured in the water.

'Oh dearie, miss, your poor clothes. You give me them undergarments, miss, and I will see them put to soak, for whites will not get white again easily if you let the mud stain, not the peaty mud we have here. And then I shall come back with your tea, miss. You put your poor feet in that bowl, now.'

The maid departed, and Eleanor did as she had been told. The water was hot, but not so hot as to make the skin tingle for more than a moment. She relaxed, and as she did so, she smiled, and was still smiling when Maria brought the tea.

She had disobeyed Lady Willoughby, there was no doubt about it, talking to Lord Athelney, but she felt liberated by the disobedience. It would, she told herself, have been unthinkable to have ignored the incident. It might have been that his lordship had suffered some injury, other, and her smile lengthened, than to his muddied dignity. She wondered at herself, for the man

78

did make her smile, but not in the way most men did. Normally she stood back from them, mocked their inflated egos, their assumption of superiority. She rarely smiled because she had shared a moment with one, and this was the second time. She told herself that she had laughed at his lordship because he had looked foolish and his pride had been deflated, but she knew that what had made her laugh was the admission in his eyes that he knew he looked ridiculous, and as for his snapping at her, well, he had just landed in cold, wet mud, and must have felt acutely uncomfortable as well as embarrassed. She wondered how he had been received at the castle. A single bowl of hot water would certainly not suffice to remove the mud. They must have the coppers heating water for a bath, and . . . She stopped thinking about Lord Athelney, and concentrated very firmly on the tea.

Lord Athelney was by this time standing before a good fire, and with a blanket wrapped about his waist. Cottam had sighed and shaken his head over the muddied clothes but remarked philosophically that 'better mud than blood', and had removed the garments for cleaning. The hip bath had been brought up and placed before the fire, and a succession of staff, with any large receptacles that would take water, were bringing them as fast as they could, as if delay would see their master in a state of collapse.

In fact, he was made of far sterner stuff, and had been a lot wetter, and a lot colder, for a lot longer, much more often than he could possibly recall. The mud, he admitted to himself, was an unpleasant addition, especially as it started to cake dry in the warmth, but no worse than salt irritating drying skin. When the bath was as full as it might sensibly hold, allowing for the displacement of his body, he thanked and dismissed the servants, dropped the blanket to the floor, and climbed with a luxuriating sigh into the hot water. His height might mean his knees stuck out of the water like twin islands, but the feeling was good, very good. His thighs and buttocks had started to seize up, simply through the unaccustomed length of time in the saddle, and the heat would be good for them too. Tomorrow he would ache, but there. Miss Burgess was quite right. Miss Burgess. She had the look of a young woman who was often right. She was probably the managing type, but even as he told himself this, he saw her laughing, and knew it for a lie. 'Capable', that was a better word for her. Those married captains under whom he had served were generally espoused to capable women, for it took such a one to cope with the long absences, the not knowing whether one was wife, or indeed widow. These men had seemed contented, but, a voice argued, was that because they were at sea, and the capable wife was at a safe distance, dealing with running the home, perhaps the estate?

No, that had not been so, and the contentment lay deeper, beneath the worries that absence brought. He had never thought of marriage as a sea-going officer, but had he done so he imagined he would have contemplated it with a capable woman. No doubt that had affected his attitude towards Charlotte. He smiled to himself, for a less capable woman he could not imagine. Perhaps the degree of capability might not have to be as high if one were on hand almost all the time, but if he married, his wife would need to be able to run the castle home, and he would want a woman who could stand beside him, not cower behind his back.

He closed his eyes, and sighed, half asleep. Miss Burgess. Miss Burgess would not cower. The water grew cold.

CHAPTER SIX

LORD ATHELNEY DID NOT GO RIDING the next day but walked, albeit with a stiffness in his normally striding gait, to church. That he should arrive on foot caused something of a stir among the parishioners, a few of whom sided, unconsciously, with Lady Willoughby, who thought it common. However, with the vast majority his lordship's reliance upon his own two feet showed him a gentleman who wanted to get close to his land, and more attention was paid to him than to the new incumbent, for whom this was only his third sermon. Miss Burgess managed a whispered interchange with him as Lady Willoughby gave the parson, a keen and rather optimistic-looking young man, her opinion of the sermon. She regaled him with what she had overheard among the locals about him being close to the land, but added that the land seemed to have been rather more successful at getting close to him. She gave him a sympathetic look, and wished him the best of luck walking back up the hill.

'Yes, it dawned upon me during the last hymn that the return journey will play havoc with those muscles I discovered upon horseback, or off it, yesterday, ma'am. Think of me, I beg.'

She did.

The marquis had hoped to get a reply to his letter early in the week, but instead got a visitor. Sturry knocked upon the study door with the information that a naval gentleman was in the hall, a gentleman by the name of Bitton. Lord Athelney scraped back his chair and beamed at his butler.

'Bring him in, Sturry, bring him in.'

A few moments later, the happy countenance of Harry Bitton was before him, and the young man was shaking him by the hand.

'When I got your letter, sir, my lord rather, I did not have to think hard or long about your offer. The only doubt I have is if their Lordships of the Admiralty send me to sea, though the chance would be a fine thing. It is mighty thoughtful of you to invite me to live here and sort out your books and such, for a lieutenant's half pay dwindles, and I have not your prize money to fall back upon. It is why I would hope to get another appointment, and the chance of promotion, but there.'

'You may not thank me when you see the mess I am in, and it is I who am grateful. You were ever a good one with the ledgers. I was concerned that you might think the job of steward, particularly if it ends up being acting temporary steward, beneath you, though I assure you it is a job that might become more than it has been. I hold over two thousand acres in this county, and estates in Devon and Dorset also, though they have stewards of their own, and I fear that the age and infirmity of the incumbent means it has gone to wrack and ruin these last few years.'

'Two thousand acres. By Jove, that is a fair slice of the map. But, my lord, though I can tackle figures, I know nothing of land work.'

'Nor do I, Mr Bitton, nor do I, but though old Mitchum may be mostly blind and his head three parts senile, the quarter that remains has more knowledge of the land in it than we could assimilate in a year. If we take the sense of what he has to teach us, we might keep the estate from running aground yet. Not that I know it to be that bad, but until we know what in Hades is going on with the accounts, who is to say, especially if you add in the possible dabbling of my wicked namesake, whose reputation is far from savoury. In fact, not to put too fine a point on it, he was a dashed loose screw. If he got a hand in the finances we could find ourselves paddling up the River Tick in no time.'

'I should have brought a boat's crew with me then, my lord.'

84

'Not a bad idea. Now if you are to stay, you'll need quarters, which leaves me in a quandary. I rattle around this labyrinth like a pebble in a jar, and would be very glad of the company, but in the longer term there might be problems with a paid employee living as a guest.'

'What about your gatehouse?'

'Unless you want to live in the true mediaeval style, with thick stone walls and a smell of long disuse, I doubt it is a real option. I was shown one of the lower chambers, and it seemed to be a lumber room. We will ask Sturry's advice. Oblige me by pulling the bell, Mr Bitton.'

'Aye aye, my lord.'

They were both still laughing when Sturry entered.

His lordship laid the problem before the butler, but rather to his surprise, Sturry disagreed with him.

'I can see as how you would think the gatehouse nothing but a glorified ruin, my lord, and 'tis true it has been much neglected these thirty years, but I recall it being inhabited when I first entered service as a lad. The upper chamber, the constable's chamber, had been panelled, and looked quite grand, and it had a big fireplace. I think the steward then used it for his work. Old Mr Mitchum, uncle of the current steward, he moved to the house at Pilcombe because his second wife disliked it. The cooking facilities were rather basic, I believe, and the steward ate in the kitchen with the staff when single.'

'We might take a good look after all. You have the key, Sturry?'

'Yes, my lord. Might I suggest that the gentleman's

uniform might become rather, er, soiled, if we investigate, my lord.'

'Good point, Sturry. Have you anything less reputable, Mr Bitton?'

'Er, I have a few "sea-going shirts", my lord, where the cuffs are wearing, and a wet weather coat.'

'Ah. Sturry, is there anything you might find that Mr Bitton might wear in a temporary capacity?'

'I am not sure, my lord. Mr Bitton appears to be a similar size to the second footman, so I might be able to procure some legwear. If you would be so kind as to wait here, sir, I will see what can be done. My lord, should I send Mr Cottam to you?'

'Yes, for he would not be best pleased at removing dust and cobwebs from this coat.'

Some twenty minutes later, and with Sturry enveloped in a very moth-eaten topcoat, the trio crossed the courtyard, armed with two lanterns, and Sturry unlocked the door, which creaked open in a strangely satisfying manner. The room they entered was the one Lord Athelney had seen before, and was used for lumber. To one side a narrow entrance gave onto a stone stairway that ran up to the floor level with the chamber above the gate. The door into the chamber needed the combined shove from two naval shoulders and then they half fell into the room. The window to the courtyard had been made much larger than originally built, but the glazing was so begrimed that they needed Sturry, bearing both lanterns, to see much in the Stygian gloom. The lights showed a spacious chamber some thirty feet long and about twenty feet wide, with a large open fireplace on the east side. It was inches deep in cobwebs and dust, which made them choke as they disturbed it, but the room was panelled in oak and furnished with a large refectory-style table and several heavy seventeenth-century high-backed chairs, with seats that had once been upholstered.

'I don't know about sleeping, my lord, but this really would be a grand place to work from. Plenty of room for a chart, I mean a map, and all the ledgers.' Mr Bitton had vision.

'There is a living chamber on the other side to where we entered, and another above, with two bedchambers above this room, my lord. The access to them is from the other side,' Sturry managed, between sneezes.

They forced open the other door, which had a spiral staircase leading up from the corner nearest the front gate, set in a chamber the same length as the main one, but only two thirds the width. The floor had a hole in it on the far side near a small fireplace with a stone hood.

'Needs some work in this room,' remarked the lieutenant cheerfully, treading cautiously to the spiral stair, which went down as well as up. They ascended and entered an equivalent room, though the door into the chambers over the gate was more central. The upper chamber over the constable's was divided into two by a narrow, panelled, central passage, which ended with a small closet chamber at the other side. The bedchambers were empty, and the windows rather small, but they too were panelled. Used to living within the dim wooden walls of a ship, Mr Bitton was completely at home.

'My lord, this is . . . a palace. It needs a dashed good clean and some repairs but . . .' He looked like a child with a first pony. 'The only problem would be food and somewhere to cook it.'

Lord Athelney rubbed his nose, and then sneezed. 'Quite a lot of repairs to my mind, but it is spacious enough. Why did we not enter on the west side of the gate, directly to the room with the spiral staircase leading up from it, Sturry?'

'The key was lost, years back, my lord. And since it was not used . . .'

'If you conducted business from the constable's chamber, and visitors entered by what is now the lumber room, the door to the west side could be a private entrance. It might be possible to turn the ground floor into a kitchen with a passage to the stair.'

'But who would cook?'

'We could employ a woman to cook and keep things ship-shape. But that is, I agree, longer term. If we set about things straight away I could see you living here by Christmas, and as for eating, well, I would be very glad of the company at my table, very glad of it. Besides, until you take over from Mitchum, you are my guest, not my steward.'

'My lord?' Sturry frowned.

'Yes, Sturry.'

'What of Mr Mitchum and the house at Pilcombe,

if he is no longer working?'

'What do you mean?'

'He and Mrs Mitchum have no family to go to, my lord.'

'I know he has no sons, but . . . oh, you mean you think I would throw him out?'

'My lord, no, not exactly, but . . .'

'Mitchum has given his life to this estate. The least we can do is give him tenure for life, and to Mrs Mitchum should he predecease her. That and a pension are his due as I see it.'

Sturry, thinking retirement might not be that many years ahead for himself also, was heartened both for his friend and on his own behalf.

As they emerged, blinking, into the afternoon sunlight, a horseman rode through the gateway. The rider wore a broad-brimmed hat, and had a clerical collar. He halted, touched his hat to the marquis and was about to make a polite introduction when he saw Mr Bitton, and his expression became one of astonishment.

'Harry Bitton! Gracious me!'

Harry Bitton rubbed his eyes, which was the wrong thing to do in view of the dust, but when he had pulled a face and let them water, he peered at the dismounting clergyman.

'Septimus?'

The Reverend Septimus Greenham almost threw himself off his horse, and would have greeted Lieutenant

Bitton with an embrace of long-standing friendship, had that gentleman not backed off, declaring himself unclean.

'I may safely assume you two gentlemen are acquainted, then,' murmured Lord Athelney, observing their curtailed transports.

'I should say so, my lord. Septimus and I were at school together. Well I never. I would not have marked you as the clerical type, Septimus.'

'At fourteen, not at all. I did not feel the calling until I was up at Oxford. I was only inducted into the parish the week before his late lordship died, and then I had leave of absence because my own late father's affairs necessitated my attendance. But here I am, and Anne, my sister, also. She is keeping me in good order at the parsonage. And you have survived sea and Napoleon!'

'Might I suggest we continue indoors, gentlemen,' requested Lord Athelney, before Harry Bitton could respond. 'Seeing that there are many years upon which to catch up.'

'I am sorry, my lord.' The Reverend Greenham coloured. 'Of course. In fact, I seem to have caught you at an inconvenient time. Should I . . .'

'If you take your mount to the stables and await us in the library, Mr Bitton and I will make our best efforts to remove the dust of ages from our persons and join you over a glass of wine.'

This plan being put into effect, the three men met in the library some fifteen minutes later. The parson first addressed Lord Athelney upon the reason for his visit, which was a matter concerning the parish clerks, and then his lordship effectively sat back and watched two men peel away the years to their adolescence. It was both interesting and informative. He had known Harry Bitton for three years at sea, known him well, but known the seaman officer, not his background, which had formed him before his naval service. The young parson was an unknown quantity, but he thought it useful to learn what he could about him by simple observation and listening. What he saw, he liked. When Septimus Greenham rode back to his sister, he had an invitation for them both to dine at the castle three evenings hence, since he was engaged for both the following two evenings.

'It is not popularity, you understand, my lord, but a desire among the local squirearchy to see if I am "sound".'

'And are you?' Lord Athelney enquired, smiling.

'That, my lord, depends. On my Biblical knowledge, yes. On my views as to how it should direct our lives, perhaps less so. Charity is, to many, coppers in the poor box. I think it as much an attitude of mind, and a desire to help those whose misfortune is not of their own making. In some quarters that may be seen as revolutionary.' He sounded as if he might find his host one of that number.

'Unlike many of my rank and wealth, Reverend, I have seen poverty and squalor, not just on these shores. Some men bring about their own reduction in circumstances, but others are beaten down by weather or disease, and it is no fault of theirs. I would engage you further upon this, but in principle I see it as sound.'

The parson departed thinking his lordship a capital fellow.

Mr Bitton was given a chamber in the west wing, and the crimson drawing room as a temporary office. He was also instructed to get himself to Shepton Mallet as soon as it was possible and obtain some civilian garb suitable for riding about the countryside. It was at this point that he revealed he was a very novice horseman.

'I think you and I need to go to the next sales in Shepton, take the head groom with us, and find mounts suitable for sailors.'

'Will they tack in a headwind and stand still if there is no wind at all, my lord?' Mr Bitton grinned.

'I sincerely hope not, Mr Bitton.'

A brief conversation with the head groom vouchsafed the information that there were weekly sales of stock in Shepton Mallet, and that they might find horses the first and third weeks of the month. Mr Bitton had therefore to put back his assault upon the garbled ledgers, since sale day was upon the morrow.

It could not be said that either of the naval gentlemen had much idea about horseflesh, but Amos Fittleton more than made up for their ignorance. It was one thing to decide whether a beast was sound in wind and limb, and aged as declared, but another to discern temperament merely from looking at the animals in the yard and seeing them trot up and down. It was a pleasure to him, when all that remained in the stable were four carriage horses and the elderly Sulphur, to select two amenable horses that would give their riders confidence, yet not appear sluggish. Lieutenant Bitton and the marquis watched him at work with a mixture of awe and bafflement.

'I am not sure I understood the half of what he said was wrong with that chestnut mare, my lord,' whispered the lieutenant.

'Nor did I, but it would be better not to admit it.'

'You do realise we are being observed, my lord, on your port quarter.'

'Yes. I have no idea who it might be.'

'Then we may be about to find out, for here they come.'

A gentleman in a curly-brimmed beaver, and a coat with several capes, approached, and hailed Lord Athelney a little uncertainly.

'Do I have the honour of addressing the Marquis of Athelney, sir?' The voice had the merest hint of a lisp, which made the word 'marquis' end with a slight hiss.

'You do, sir.'

'Then may I present myself, Bertram Heigham, a friend of your late lamented cousin, Mr William Hawksmoor. Your servant, my lord.' He made a rather flowery bow. Lord Athelney disliked him on sight. Any friend of Wicked William was unlikely to be a man with whom he would wish to associate, and this specimen was particularly unappealing.

'Mr Heigham.' Athelney nodded, no more.

'I was wondering, my lord, if I might have private,' here Mr Heigham shot the gentleman in naval attire a swift glance, 'conversation with you.'

'I see no need, Mr Heigham.'

'I think you might, my lord, when I reveal the topic.'

'If it has anything to do with Mr William Hawksmoor, sir, it is unlikely to shock me, believe me.'

'Debts of honour, my lord.' Mr Heigham said the words softly, sibilantly.

'I fail to associate my cousin and honour in any way.'

'Would you rather I . . .' Harry Bitton looked uncomfortable.

'Stay where you are, Mr Bitton, if you please.' It was a command. Mr Bitton stood where he was. 'If,' Lord Athelney continued wearily, to Mr Heigham, 'you are going to tell me that my cousin died without paying you money he lost to you at the gaming table or upon the turf, I can only say that I am not, myself, liable for those debts, nor do I care if you shout his iniquity from the church tower.' His lordship did not choose to say that Mr Heigham might apply to the Trustees of the Athelney estate. He looked the sort whose 'debts of honour' were not necessarily come by in an honest fashion.

Mr Heigham looked distinctly put out, but made a recovery. 'Perhaps both of those things are true, my lord, but in view of what else I might reveal, if pressed, you would be wise to listen and reconsider your position.'

'You begin to bore me, Mr Hei—'

'William Hawksmoor's "conquests" in this very

district might lead to great embarrassment, gentlemen pounding upon your door, demanding blood.'

'Well, since he has been buried the better part of two months since, his blood is not available to them, and mine of no possible interest. If you think to threaten, Mr Heigham, I fear you have picked the wrong man.'

'And of course there were "conquests" closer to home.'

'Yes, I heard about his orgy and the depredations upon innocent young women. As I say, there is nothing you can reveal that will shock me, nor indeed incline me to submit to what is little more than blackmail.' He leaned a little closer to Mr Heigham. 'And I do not blackmail, nor do I threaten, but I do give assurances. If you ever as much as enter the courtyard of Kingscastle, I shall take great pleasure in taking a whip to you.'

Mr Heigham turned white. He opened his mouth to speak, and, seeing the look upon Lord Athelney's face, thought the better of it. When Mr Bitton also advanced by a single step, he turned and walked away very swiftly, although Mr Bitton remarked that he did so as if walking upon a tightrope.

'If that is the sort of man whom your cousin accounted a friend, my lord . . .'

'As I said, Mr Bitton, a dashed loose screw. Now, let us see what Fittleton has in mind for us.'

CHAPTER SEVEN

T HEY RETURNED FROM THE SHEPTON SALES with
a neatish bay cob, suitable for a man who might
ride about the district upon his business, and of placid,
if possibly slightly indolent temperament, and a grey
thoroughbred cross that kept the looks of the aristocrat
but the calm pragmatism of its more lowly dam.

Lieutenant Bitton had not even had the time to take
his first riding lesson with Fittleton before he made the
acquaintance of Lady Willoughby Hawksmoor, and
Miss Hawksmoor. He was walking the grounds next
morning, which effectively meant the area bound by the
loop of the river, and was armed with a map. His first
few hours with the books had made his head spin, so
he had decided to take a breath of air. His concession
to his civilian situation was to have replaced his shoes

and stockings with serviceable boots, and he wore his greatcoat, though his pace kept him warm and it was unbuttoned. He had reached the Dower House just as her ladyship was being assisted to alight from her carriage. He halted, touched his hat in automatic salute and then remembered, and removed it with a bow remarkably graceful for one in a heavy greatcoat.

Lady Willoughby stared at him as if he were some peculiar and unpleasant specimen, though her daughter, still within the vehicle, found the young man in the bicorne and blue coat rather handsome, with his fair hair and open countenance.

'Your servant, ma'am. Henry Bitton, lieutenant in His Majesty's Navy.'

He anticipated a formal introduction. Her response astounded him.

'Not another! Are we to be flooded with half-pay officers in the district?' She glared at him.

Whilst he had not expected to be greeted as a conquering hero, he had equally not expected to be regarded as an affliction upon the locality.

'I . . . I do not think that his lordship and myself are enough to be considered a flood, ma'am, and his lordship can scarcely be counted as a half-pay officer.'

'Athelney should be consorting with those of his own rank and class. I shall remind him of it,' declared her ladyship decisively, as one taking on a civic duty.

'I really would not do so, ma'am,' replied Mr Bitton in haste, recalling those instances when those without right had attempted to tell Captain Hawksmoor his duty.

'Really, sir?' Her tone was icy.

Harry Bitton was no coward, and was about to reply as Miss Hawksmoor was handed down from the carriage. He promptly forgot every word. Lady Willoughby, erroneously, thought that she had put him in his place.

He bowed, and made a halting apology for not having observed her before. Charlotte was used to not being observed, and was rather touched. Lady Willoughby did not introduce her daughter, and merely wished the young naval officer a dismissive 'Good day' and whisked her progeny within doors with the command, 'Come, Charlotte,' thereby unintentionally furnishing him with her identity.

The implacable Lady Willoughby filled Mr Bitton with dread, rather, as he later described it to Lord Athelney, like facing being driven onto a lee shore and shoals, but Miss Charlotte was something else, an angelic vision beyond any image of womanhood he had ever even dreamed about.

'She is a pretty little thing, but so cowed by my aunt I could not tell you whether she possesses an opinion of her own on any subject at all, nor whether there is any sense in her.' Lord Athelney recalled the miserable dinner.

'She did look dashed nervous, every time Lady Willoughby as much as glanced at her. Pity.'

'My aunt is a tyrant to all who let her be so, and Charlotte has never learned how to stand up to her. She ought to take a leaf from Miss Burgess's book.'

'Miss Burgess, my lord?'

'Was she not with them? Miss Burgess is Lady Willoughby Hawksmoor's paid, and probably underpaid, companion. I believe her to be some connection of her ladyship's family. She is treated like a cross between a skivvy and a gun-dog, but though she does as she is told, I have seen her, and she is no more afraid of her employer than I am of Sturry. What is more, I think she holds Lady Willoughby in contempt, quite privately, mind.'

'She must be quite redoubtable, my lord,' declared Bitton.

'Redoubtable? Yes, now you mention it, she probably is.' Lord Athelney smiled.

The Reverend and Miss Greenham arrived for their dinner engagement in his lordship's carriage, since Lord Athelney did not think Miss Greenham ought to have to travel in her evening clothes, in November, in the parson's gig. The young clergyman did not look overawed at the prospect of sitting down to dine with the most powerful gentleman in the district, for which Lord Athelney was grateful. The invitations and cards had started to arrive from the upper echelons of local society, and he could foresee many winter evenings spent with people seeking either to impress him or afraid to say anything with which he might not agree. Septimus Greenham was respectful, but not of their number. Harry Bitton had already primed the marquis with details of the parson's background and home life. Although Greenham was two years his senior, they had been friends at school until the youthful Master Bitton had gone to sea. Septimus, he said, had been terribly clever, but not clever enough to keep them out of trouble with their pranks.

'You would not think it, my lord, but he was most inventive and up to every lark, so long as nobody was hurt by it, though. Never saw him pick upon another, though he did come to fisticuffs with an older boy who was making the life of a much younger one perfect misery. Perhaps that was one of the seeds from which his leaning for the ministry grew. He dislikes cruelty and unfairness.'

'Which will set him at odds with Lady Willoughby Hawksmoor in very short order. She is very full of the rights of the "better sort" of person, and thinks parsons are beneath her notice.' Lord Athelney told Mr Bitton about the exchange over Lord Nelson.

'I know she is a relation, my lord . . .'

'Thankfully by marriage, not blood.'

'Indeed.' Mr Bitton gave a small smile. 'But I have yet to see or hear anything appealing about her.'

'I have given up looking.'

'And she might find Septimus hard to swallow. He will not alter to suit her, and if she treats him like a worm, she will find she has the wrong man. Why, his father was a bishop, and his grandfather a belted earl.'

'You know, I look forward to watching their encounters.' Lord Athelney gave a slow smile, and anticipated an interesting evening.

Brother and sister made a comely pair. Septimus Greenham, whilst wiry of frame, had a pleasing countenance framed by wavy, burnished gold hair, and his sister shared both colouring and inches, though her face was delicately shaped rather than with the firm jaw of her elder sibling. Remembering how it felt to be the sole member of one's gender at a meal, Lord Athelney made a conscious effort to include her, but he need not have feared. Miss Anne Greenham was a listener more than a talker, but her attentiveness included rather than excluded her, and those comments which she put forward were sensible and pertinent. Mr Bitton conversed at some length with her upon botany, in which they discovered a shared interest, and the evening was enlivened by anecdotes of foreign climes and minor misadventures. It was held by all to have been a success, and a tentative offer made of dinner at the parsonage in the near future, should his lordship, and of course Harry, choose to accept 'humble fare', which was said with twitching lips.

'Do you know, my lord,' confided Mr Bitton, stifling a contented yawn as he departed for his bed, 'I can scarce recall an evening I enjoyed more. I think coming into Somerset was an excellent thing to do.'

'That, Mr Bitton, is because you have temporarily forgotten the frustrations of my ledgers.' Lord Athelney smiled. 'Goodnight to you.'

It could not be said that Lord Athelney spent as many enjoyable evenings entertaining or being entertained.

Being new to the area and to his position, he had no acquaintance in common, and little local knowledge, so he was concentrating, learning all the time. He almost felt he ought to make notes afterwards. Once he had a wider circle upon whom to call, he could hold dinners with a better selection of guests, and also without inviting deadly foes. Since Lady Willoughby Hawksmoor was of a combative temperament it was not altogether surprising that her presence gave an edge of discord, but he felt he had no choice initially but to invite her to some smaller private dinners, which her mourning did not entirely preclude. He had no notion that at the second such evening he was sitting her at table with a lady who relished a fight just as much. He became aware of a chilling of the atmosphere as soon as the Dower House party arrived, late enough to make an entrance. He was making small talk with Colonel Wilton, but that gentleman took a sudden intake of breath and muttered, 'Oh God, no,' as Sturry announced Lady Willoughby Hawksmoor, Miss Hawksmoor and Miss Burgess. Eyes turned, as Lady Willoughby intended they should, but one pair glittered.

Lady Augusta Wilton was, in general, content to order her husband and her household. 'Yes, m'dear' was even the colonel's nickname behind his back, but when it came to Lady Willoughby Hawksmoor, no quarter was offered or given. It stemmed from precedence. As the daughter of an earl, Lady Augusta ranked immediately above Lady Willoughby as the wife of the younger son of a marquis, and Lady Augusta knew very well what was her due. Lady Willoughby resented that 'the colonel's lady', as she waspishly referred to her, should always be that infinitesimal bit higher up the social ladder. She was not so advanced as to make it easy for her to defer, which would have been the case if she had been the daughter of a duke, and they were not naturally friends, in which case the distinction would have been forgotten on all but the most formal of occasions. Instead it was open warfare, and virtually everybody in the county knew that to invite both to any function of less than fifty people was asking for trouble; everyone, that was, except for the Marquis of Athelney.

Miss Hawksmoor visibly trembled, and Miss Burgess winced. From the moment Lady Willoughby sailed forward with a 'friendly' greeting that might have frozen the sea off the Azores, Lord Athelney realised that there was going to be a very bloody encounter over the turbot and haunch of venison. He had consulted Sturry on the seating plan, and the butler had been very useful in all but warning him of the fuse he was bound to light, especially since it would turn out that the ladies were seated almost directly opposite each other. Whilst this would prevent them conversing directly, each would be sure that the other could hear their conversation. Sturry, seeing that invitations had already been sent out, thought it kinder not to upset his master, and did what he could by placing the largest piece of silverware in the cupboard in their line of sight. It was not a piece that appeared very often, being one which the last Lady Athelney had loathed and which, infelicitously, had open-mouthed griffins at each of the three corners. He had considered asking if his lordship would like Lady Willoughby to act as hostess, and take the place at the head of the table, but thought that might get short shrift.

'My dear Lady Willoughby, what a delightful way you have dressed your hair. I declare that it makes the grey so very distinguished, almost as if you had intended the contrast.'

'Why, thank you, Lady Augusta. When one has a uniformity of grey it does become rather dead. I am so fortunate. I hope Colonel Wilton enjoys his customary good health. Is he still deeply involved with the breeding of pigs? He owns some prize sows, I have heard.'

Lord Athelney gave up. Like it or not, the evening was set to be one where all ears, if not eyes, were going to be on the two protagonists. Miss Burgess managed a brief exchange with his lordship before dinner was announced.

'You did not know, did you?' She glanced at Lady Augusta, puffing herself up like a rooster at a cock fight. 'How very unfortunate.'

'I plead ignorance, yes, but how was I to know?'

'You were not, of course. It is just so well known that everybody assumes everybody else knows. It goes back to when Lady Willoughby first took up residence in the Dower House. Lady Augusta is, by virtue of being the daughter of an earl, marginally higher in rank. Need I say more?'

'No, Miss Burgess.'

'I would say that I am fortunate, being towards the lower end of the table.'

'You are at the head.'

'But that is the position of hostess.'

'It is also the only sensible seating plan, since I need a lady at the head and would not, for any price, give that position to my aunt. I have every confidence that you will be able to sustain the role for the duration of a meal. It is surely not significant.' He frowned, for her face had fallen. 'I am sorry, ma'am, have I said something wrong?'

'No. But, oh dear, Lady Willoughby will assume I am taking precedence to which I am obviously not entitled . . . I shall pay for it.'

'But can you not explain?'

'I could, but have no hope of being believed.'

'Then should I say . . .'

'No, my lord, I beg of you, it would only end up worse.'

'She cannot have you whipped, Miss Burgess.'

'Only with her tongue.' She noted his expression. 'Ah, you think me weak to be upset by it, and in general I am a hardy soul, but when she finds fault and complains day after day . . . Every time I am not instantly there to do her bidding it will be because I am suddenly too puffed up in my own esteem. Every comment I make will be crushed because she has heard my voice too much when I should be silent. It grinds one down.' She sighed, but then smiled. 'Though at least I will be able to take wicked pleasure in watching your discomfiture as the evening progresses.'

'I have every intention, ma'am, of remaining sanguine throughout.'

'You say that now, my lord, but . . . Good luck.'

She turned away, and became involved with a lady in a discussion on the price of dyed ostrich feathers.

Lord Athelney wondered how acid the air had to be to make syllabub curdle. The opening shots had been across each other's bows, but once they were seated, it was definitely broadsides. Lady Augusta had the advantage, because to her left was an elderly and obviously deaf peer, who cupped his hand over his ear and kept requesting that she speak up. Whatever she said was therefore heard by much of the table. Lady Willoughby had no cause to increase her volume, but achieved a very strident tone, which actually reminded Lord Athelney of 'Antoinette's aunt'. That they managed to maintain an exchange of incivilities through third parties was astounding, but seemed endless.

'My poor dear William, yes, such a sad loss. I am only glad that black is so flattering to the well-kept figure. I declare I am not sure how I will manage when I return to colours, for so many shades are far too bright for the matron. One risks looking quite ridiculous,' sighed Lady Willoughby.

Lady Augusta was wearing a gown of deep rose twilled silk, over a striped underdress.

'My daughter, Lady Sompting, is about to be confined

a second time, and has already presented her lord with a very fine son. She has only been married three years, and was swept up in her very first Bath season.' Lady Augusta spared a glance at Charlotte, who bit her lip.

'Bath is not what it was in years past. One no longer encounters the cream of society, and success there is achievable by those with the barest modicum of beauty and dowry. Had Charlotte not been suffering from a nervous complaint this year, her London debut would have been a resounding success.'

'I do not hold with the way young women fancy themselves to be always ill. In my day one dismissed all but the most serious complaints, but nowadays they affect such die-away airs. I would not allow any daughter of mine to quack herself with nonsensical preparations.'

'Sir Henry Halford said he had rarely seen a young lady as done-up as my poor Charlotte.'

Miss Hawksmoor studied her plate, acutely embarrassed and aware that she had never met Sir Henry in her life. Meanwhile, Lady Augusta changed tack.

'The young lady at the top of the table, my lord? No, Lord Athelney is not married. That is Miss Burgess, very good sort of girl. Long ancestry in the north.' Lady Augusta paused, and added, even louder, 'Sort of girl who would make a good marchioness, much like my sister, Hester, who is the Dowager Marchioness of Louth. Character, that is what is needed.'

Eleanor, who had been rather enjoying the contest despite feeling for poor Charlotte, and having resigned herself to suffering in its aftermath, cast a desperate glance along the table. Lord Athelney could only spare her a brief grimace of sympathy.

'It is so often the case, don't you think, Lord Frome, that social mushrooms are mistaken for individuals of superior quality by those who no longer habituate the best circles.' Lady Willoughby spoke with an overtone of pity.

Eleanor ground her teeth, and the gentleman to her left, who had been about to make a remark, addressed himself instead to the compote of plums, in view of her very fierce expression.

Lord Athelney, who had, as he foretold, thus far remained entirely sanguine, looked grim. It was one thing for two middle-aged women to engage in a battle of words, but firstly his cousin, and now Miss Burgess, were being put to the blush. All that he could do was whisper to the Countess of Frome that he thought it might be a good time for the ladies to retire. Her ladyship, recognising that, without a formal hostess, Lord Athelney was reliant upon her, nodded, though she knew that the ladies would be left in the unfortunate position of having to put up with the protagonists continuing their combat in the drawing room. She therefore whispered back that she hoped the gentlemen would be brave and not linger over their port.

Eleanor could not decide whether his lordship had taken pity on his cousin and herself, or was just behaving like a man and hoping that as long as he did not have to listen to it, the argument no longer existed. She saw little respite likely in the drawing room, and so did her best to be 'like a man' and turned a deaf ear to it, choosing to enter into a discussion with Lady Frome about the blending of teas. This proved unfortunate, since that lady thought the best way to keep Lady Willoughby and Lady Augusta from each other's throats was to involve them in a conversation where opinions were unlikely to fray tempers. She did not realise that they could argue over absolutely everything. Thus the merits or otherwise of pekoe, lapsang souchong and bohea became heated. Lady Frome prayed for the gentlemen and the opportunity to request tea, the beverage itself, to be brought in.

When the gentlemen did leave the dining room they were laughing, and all in general accord, which contrasted with the atmosphere in the drawing room. Lord Athelney looked to Miss Burgess. She appeared wearied and shook her head, which had begun to ache.

When the dinner guests finally began to leave, he was unable to speak with her, for Lady Willoughby departed without lingering to say more than was required, and led her daughter and Miss Burgess in her wake. All he could do was bow and wish her goodnight, and look after the departing carriage in a thoughtful manner.

CHAPTER EIGHT

ELEANOR BURGESS'S PREDICTIONS WERE SADLY accurate. The battle with Lady Augusta having ended in neither side surrendering and striking their colours, Lady Willoughby had an unsatisfied desire to sink someone, and Eleanor was her prime target. She began before the carriage door had even closed.

'That was shameless.'

'Ma'am?'

'How dare you take the head of the table, and sit there as if you had the right. I did not know what to say.'

Eleanor bit back the retort that nobody would have guessed. 'I sat where I was directed, ma'am. The choice was entirely Lord Athelney's.'

'He is clearly ignorant of the niceties. You should have declined, and reminded Athelney that he had relatives present to act in the absence of a lady of the house.'

'I think, Lady Willoughby, he was well aware of your presence.'

'And what does that mean, madam?'

'What I say. He did not forget you were there, for we arrived when almost everyone else was present.'

It was true enough, if hardly the whole truth. Lady Willoughby was not appeased.

'You are impertinent, Eleanor.'

'I am merely stating a fact, ma'am. Lord Athelney must have thought about the arrangements, and I was ignorant of them until the last minute.'

Lady Willoughby ignored the sense of this and simply took up another objection. 'I saw you speak to him. I requested that you should not do so.'

'I could scarcely ignore him.'

'What did you discuss?'

'You wish me to report every interchange, ma'am?'

'If necessary, yes.'

'We spoke but briefly. He told me that I would be at the top of the table, and I demurred, but he was quite set upon it.'

'That was all?'

'I do not think I should be required to carry pencil and paper in case I have to note any remarks his lordship might address to me.'

'What you think is of no importance. I am gravely displeased, Eleanor, gravely. I should not have to remind you of your position.'

Yet you always do, thought Miss Burgess, keeping her lips tightly shut and her gloved hands clenched.

It could not be said that Lady Willoughby Hawksmoor's temper improved overnight. Overindulgence in the lobster patties, which her ladyship ascribed to a delicate stomach and which could more accurately be described as simple overeating, led to a disturbed night, during which Eleanor's 'misdemeanour' loomed ever larger to the point of being an intended insult. When her maid drew the curtains upon a grey November day, Lady Willoughby's first instruction was that Miss Burgess should be called before breakfast, to take down her ladyship's note of thanks to Lord Athelney. It had given the dyspeptic lady some comfort in the small hours to construct suitable phrases in her head, and she did not want to find them dispelled by daylight.

Eleanor was awake when the knock on the door came, and the maid entered, with both the command and an apology on her lips.

'I shall get up directly, Martha. Please bring up the hot water.'

While the maid went for a ewer of water, Eleanor climbed reluctantly from the comparative warmth of her bed into the cold of the bedchamber, and scrambled into layers of clothing as quickly as she might. She was dragging a brush through her hair when Martha returned, and within another ten minutes was knocking at Lady Willoughby's door. The command to enter was imperious, and did not bode well.

'Ah, there you are, Eleanor.' The greeting implied that Eleanor had been mislaid, perhaps under a stone.

Lady Willoughby was propped up in her bed with her morning chocolate, a soft shawl about her shoulders and a good fire in the grate, which made her chamber, in comparison to Eleanor's own, seem positively balmy.

'I wish to write my thank you to Athelney.'

Eleanor correctly interpreted this as her ladyship wishing to tell her what to set down. She withdrew a pencil and small notebook from her pocket. The only thing that Lady Willoughby would do would be to sign the fine copy of the missive.

'Of course, ma'am.'

This was not something that had to be done before breakfast. It was therefore obviously some penance for the paid companion.

'Commence with the usual appropriate phrases, and continue as follows. *I regret that your inexperience in matters of social intercourse led you into error with the seating at dinner. Had you but consulted me upon the matter, I would of course have taken the place assigned to the hostess, even without the courtesy of having been invited to do so when invitations were sent out. You need not feel embarrassed to ask me for advice. After all, you have not been in polite society long enough to know . . .*'

'Lady Willoughby, you cannot write this.'

'I beg your pardon?'

'Ma'am, it cannot be taken but as belittling, as well as censure.'

'It is the truth. He was, until my son's untimely death, merely the younger son of a youngest son, and a man who earned his own living as a sailor.' Lady Willoughby said the word as if it ranked with a farm labourer, and he had spent fifteen years dancing hornpipes and reefing sails.

'He is the son of your husband's brother, ma'am, and he had command of vessels in His Majesty's Navy.'

'Boats! And where upon such craft would one find refinement, education, gentility even?'

Eleanor looked into the face of her employer, a woman who, in her opinion, lacked all three of these attributes, and held her tongue with difficulty.

'You speak without knowledge, and without right. Where was I?' Lady Willoughby frowned.

'You were saying that he has not been in polite society long enough to know . . .'

'Ah yes, *not long enough to know the niceties. I will be happy to act as hostess for you upon future occasions.*'

'Until such time, presumably, as he marries, ma'am?'

'Naturally. But Charlotte has been brought up correctly. She will be entirely suitable as chatelaine of Kingscastle.' Lady Willoughby stressed the 'she', and her eyes fixed upon Eleanor as if by glance alone she could depress pretension.

So this was what it was all about. Lady Willoughby wanted to chastise the marquis, yes, but much more importantly she wanted to show Eleanor her place, which was most certainly not at the head of the Kingscastle dining table. Eleanor seethed, both on her own behalf and that of Lord Athelney.

'You may add a paragraph to the effect that he ought in future to ensure that the lobsters he obtains are fresh. Those from Burnham may be recommended. Close as fitting and bring me the fair copy after my breakfast. You may go.'

Dismissed, Eleanor had no option but to withdraw to the yellow saloon, where an escritoire had been set near the window, a window which looked westward, up the hill to the castle. She drew forth a sheet of paper and, with extreme reluctance, began to write in her neat, rounded hand.

Eleanor presented the letter to Lady Willoughby in the breakfast parlour, noting that her ladyship had not had a third place set for breakfast. Charlotte, heavy-eyed and very quiet, sat at her mama's left, nibbling a piece of toast without enthusiasm.

'You have finished? Good. I shall sign it at some point this morning.'

It had been imperative that the letter be written without delay and yet now it might wait. The anger in Eleanor's eyes could not be suppressed, and elicited a smile from Lady Willoughby. Her point had been made.

'Do you wish me to convey it to the castle thereafter, ma'am?'

'No. I have other errands for you today, and I see no

115

reason to send you to the castle, no reason whatsoever. One of the grooms may take it. You are to take a note to Lady Steventon.'

Lady Steventon lived some two miles distant, and beyond Kingscastle. Eleanor would have to walk right past the gates on her way. She had no expectation of Lady Willoughby offering to send her in even the most lowly vehicle from the stables, even though the heavy, glowering clouds portended rain, and there was a brisk north-easterly wind. It would be far better to send a groom on horseback to Lady Steventon, and deliver the letter to Kingscastle on the way, but Lady Willoughby wanted Eleanor to remember her place. There would be days to come of this treatment, Eleanor had no doubt. Her heart sank, but she smiled at her employer.

'I shall be delighted. A brisk walk is just what one needs to prevent stultifying indoors.' Her tone was bright. 'Would you care to accompany me, Charlotte?'

It was really rather unfair to ask Charlotte, since the poor girl would only look to her mama. Eleanor thought that from choice Charlotte would love a walk just to be off the maternal leash, even if the weather was inclement and the outward journey all uphill.

'Charlotte will have more suitable employment this morning.'

Charlotte gave Eleanor a weak smile.

Eleanor set out, without breaking her fast. She was hungry, but admitting to it also admitted her ladyship's victory, so she resolutely refused to seek out even a slice of bread and butter. She wrapped herself in her thickest pelisse and a tippet of rabbit fur that kept the wind from whistling about her neck, donned gloves and a close-fitting bonnet and set off up the hill. The Dower House was almost on the flat, being actually some few feet lower than the river bend, but near the base of the hill which the castle dominated. Once it had done so glowering, but the warmer brick of the later mansion looked down in more benign authority. The trackway led up to Kingscastle, skirting the remnants of what had once been the eastern curtain wall and round the northern side to where it joined the road that approached the castle along the ridge. It was as if the castle had been an immoveable object around which traffic must flow, with the track heading east down to the Dower House and to the south a trackway that was much more a road running down to Sittford Bridge, though it had been constructed merely to end at the castle itself.

She frowned. What would his lordship think when he read his aunt's letter of thanks? It was so blatant. She imagined him screwing her penmanship into a tight ball and casting it into the fire. With a sigh, she turned right and set off along the ridge, with the wind buffeting her so much that even in so tight a bonnet she was compelled to put a hand to it to hold it on. By the time she arrived at Lady Steventon's, she had been walking for almost an hour, which was quite ridiculous for the distance. Lady Steventon offered her refreshment while she perused the note from Lady Willoughby and wrote a response, and Eleanor was glad to accept. Lady Steventon was not a kindly woman, but was quite surprised that Eleanor had walked all the way in such weather. She did not, however, offer to have her conveyed back.

Glancing at the clock in the hall as she set off, Eleanor grimaced. It was gone eleven. The wind had veered more to the north and was now almost at her back, pressing her onward at a pace that was far from comfortable, and after the first half mile it began to rain in driving, nearly horizontal sheets, which soaked through the shoulders of her pelisse and reduced the fur at the back of her neck to a damp, drowned limpness. She shivered.

Lord Athelney was in the constable's chamber, surveying the efforts of his staff to make it presentable. The use of broom and duster, and thereafter polish, had transformed it, though strong winds made the old glazing rattle on the northern aspect, and the other rooms were still to receive a similar spring clean. The rain lashed the diamond panes. He happened to glance out, and saw, very blurred by the rivulets of water, a female figure coming towards the castle.

'Good God, what woman would be out on foot in this?' He peered harder, and Mr Bitton wished he had his telescope that he might identify the visitor.

'Is it not Miss Burgess, my lord?' He paused. 'Yes, for she is turning to port to take the Dower track.'

'She cannot do so. Mr Bitton. Hail her if you will, and

118

have her come in. She can be taken down the hill once we have had a pair put to.'

Mr Bitton sprang to obey this instruction, and was able to make himself heard by cupping his hands to his mouth as he left the shelter of the gatehouse arch.

'Miss Burgess. Miss Burgess. Lord Athelney desires you to come out of the foul weather.'

She turned, and shook her head. 'Thank his lordship, but Lady Willoughby would not want me to be tardy.'

'His lordship would not want you drowned, ma'am. Please come within.' It was more a command than a plea.

She hesitated and then gave in. By the time she reached the gatehouse, Lord Athelney was also standing beneath the heavy stonework of the arch.

'What on earth possessed you to go walking in such weather, ma'am?' He sounded understandably perplexed at her lunacy.

She resented the thought that she might have been so foolish from choice, and her tone was acerbic.

'I assure you, my lord, that I would liefer be sitting by a fire with my stitchery, but Lady Willoughby directed me to take a letter to Lady Steventon and . . .'

'You have been that far?'

'It is but two miles, my lord, and I am not enfeebled.' She sounded out of temper.

'But you surely shall be if you are wet and chilled to the bone. Besides, a note was delivered, or rather a remonstration, by a groom from the Dower House not half an hour since. Why did he not . . .' Lord Athelney halted, seeing the look upon Miss Burgess's face. 'Come indoors, ma'am, and get dry and warm. I shall have you conveyed home by carriage when you are fit to travel.'

He took her by the elbow, and guided her towards the house. He could feel the tremor of the shivering she was striving to contain. Once within the hall he himself assisted her from the heavy, wet pelisse, and held the bedraggled fur tippet at arm's length.

'It is not very prepossessing when wet,' he commented.

'Nor am I, my lord.' She shuddered.

'Your hem is wet also. Come into the library, for I have a very good fire there. Ah, Sturry. Please have these garments set to dry and bring a blanket that Miss Burgess might put about her shoulders. And then, if you please, some mulled wine.'

'Oh no, please do not go to any trouble, my lord.'

'I am not going to any trouble, and my staff will not find those tasks irksome. Now, come into the library and be seated by the fire.'

He was almost peremptory. She put it down to being used to having his commands obeyed in an instant. She obeyed and sat, folding her chilled, white hands in her lap, and resisting the urge to hold them out to the delicious heat. It was a wise decision, but even so, they were so cold that when they warmed they hurt abominably and she winced. Lord Athelney took note of the contortion of her features, but made no comment upon it. He took a chair on the other side of the fire.

'My aunt is an unpleasant woman.'

'My lord?'

'Please, Miss Burgess, do not look as if you do not understand me. I am not slow-witted, and life at sea does not addle brains. I also noted that the signature was different to the hand that penned the thanks I received this morning, so I am assuming yours was the script for the bulk of the communication.'

She blushed, and nodded.

'You will therefore know the terms in which it was couched. Insufferable woman. Her, not you,' he added hurriedly. 'I take it that everything stems from your position at table last night?'

'Yes, she has taken umbrage, as I knew she would,' Miss Burgess sighed.

'Hence you also being sent upon this inadvisable excursion to Lady Steventon.'

'Yes. I must be reminded that I am nobody.'

'I do not think you are nobody, Miss Burgess.'

'Thank you, my lord. Please do not tell that to your aunt or I shall suffer further.'

'I do not see why you remain in her employ, ma'am.'

'I accepted in order that I might no longer be a strain upon my father's purse, my lord. It was the only option available to me.' She gave a wry smile.

Sturry entered, bearing a tray from which a glass of hot wine gave forth an enticing aroma of cinnamon, and with a blanket over his arm. He offered her the tray, warning her that the bowl of the glass was hot, and would have then placed the blanket about her shoulders, but

Lord Athelney took it from him and performed the task himself, and indicated that the butler might withdraw.

She looked up to thank him, and saw that he was frowning.

'My lord?'

'I wonder . . . Have you not given thought to marriage, Miss Burgess?'

'Marriage, my lord?'

'Yes, the wedded state.'

'No, my lord. That is, not since I was seventeen, and smitten with the squire's younger son, who wore dashing scarlet regimentals. But that was not really the contemplation of matrimony, merely the excessive emotions of adolescence.'

'You sound very clinical about it.' He smiled, though wryly.

'I think,' and her brows drew together as she considered the matter, 'that in my situation, to retain any expectation of marriage would be foolhardy.'

'That is suspiciously like Lady Willoughby's dismissal of "romantic" as foolishness.'

'I would not describe love as foolish, for I believe that if one's heart becomes engaged, and if the feeling is reciprocated, there can be no greater joy. My parents, even though now in more mature years, clearly married for love and are most content. Indeed, my mother had to give up many advantages to become the wife of a man of the cloth, and had she not been a youngest daughter, I doubt the union would have been permitted.' She gave what was suspiciously like a grin. 'Lady Willoughby chooses to dismiss me as the indigent nobody, but my mama is her cousin, and the daughter, not of a Gloucestershire baronet, but of a Cheshire viscount. I may rank lower in society, but I have lineage longer and far more grand. Not,' she added, hastily, 'that such things matter, except when one is belittled. It is then that I rest upon the family escutcheon, so to speak. It is wicked, no doubt, but . . .'

'Maintains one's sanity?'

'Indeed, my lord. It does. But I must beg you not to reveal that secret.' She grinned openly.

'Consider it locked in the casket of memory, ma'am.' Her grin was infectious, and dangerous, for it prompted him, upon impulse, to say that which he had intended to keep also locked away for some time to come.

'Would you consider being married to me, Miss Burgess?'

She stared at him, and the colour drained from her face.

'I did not tell you those things to make you pity me, sir, nor to encourage you to play King Cophetua to my Beggar Maid, and if it is a jest, then it is in poor taste.'

'No, I know that you did not. Nor are you a beggar maid.' He spoke seriously. 'And I most certainly would not jest about such a thing. Forgive me, for I have taken you by surprise, but my offer is genuine. You know the stipulation of my uncle's will, and I would not try to hide it from you. I have thought about it. I would not wish to spend my life never sure what the Trustees may

123

permit me to do for the good of the estates, but nor would I marry just any woman to fulfil the requirement. I am not making you an offer because "any lady will do". You find yourself in an unenviable position with a selfish woman. I can offer you position, though I do not expect it to count for much with you, but also comfort and companionship. I cannot deny that I admire you, in your person and character, and we seem to rub along rather well. I think that a good basis from which more tender emotions might spring.'

'Dare you not even say the word, my lord?'

'The word?'

'Love.'

'But,' he looked confused, 'have you not said you do not look for love?'

'I dare not hope for it, my lord, and yet . . .'

'Could it not be that you could come to love me, Miss Burgess, as I truly think I might come to love you? If I suggested that I was even halfway to doing so, after so few meetings, you would dismiss it as falsehood, but I . . . I am not totally sure what love involves. I have no experience of it outside that of son for parent, brother for brother, or the bond between brothers in arms. I have no experience with women.'

He sounded so sincere her resolution almost wavered. It would be so easy to say yes, and for all the wrong reasons.

'I cannot say. My lord, as you say, you scarcely know me, nor I you. If I accepted your offer, it would be from desperation, and unfair upon us both.' She tried to look him in the eye, but blushed and had to turn away, her hand to her pink cheek.

'I have distressed you, and am sorry for it, but be honest with me again, for you have been most honest thus far. In the future we will meet repeatedly, grow to know each other better. If our feelings should become engaged, you would not hold this precipitate declaration against me, would you?'

This time she did look at him.

'I would not, my lord.' She said it as if an oath, her face very calm and serious.

'Then I do not give up hope, ma'am. It only remains for me to assure you that no hint of what has just passed between us need cloud our future encounters. I would wish you to remain my ally when under bombardment from the fortress of stupidity that is my aunt.'

'That alliance, my lord, stands firm, and here is my hand upon it.' She smiled, a tight smile, but a smile for all that, and held out her hand.

He took it, and though a small voice inside him, which he could not explain, wanted him to kiss it, he shook it.

'Thank you, Miss Burgess. Now drink your wine while it is hot.'

When she returned to the Dower House, considerably drier and warmer, Eleanor hoped to have the opportunity of reflecting upon what had taken place, but the moment she arrived Barwell hastened to inform her that Lady

Willoughby had been asking for her the last half hour. She sighed, and went to remove her bonnet. Patting her hair into place before the mirror, she wondered at Lord Athelney's words. He said that he admired her person. What could there possibly be about her that could inspire admiration? Her features were regular; there was nothing obviously repellent about her, but he had actively liked what he saw. She thought he had spoken the truth, but it left her mind reeling. Then she set her own thoughts aside, and went to be berated for having not returned swiftly enough from her task, and hear of the inconvenience this had caused her employer. She did not mention that she had been conveyed down the hill in Lord Athelney's tilbury.

It was only as she retired to change for dinner that she could think at length about what had happened. It seemed unreal. She had received a proposal of marriage. He did not love her, no, but he had said he felt he could, had seemed disposed to love her. He was perfectly genuine, that was for certain, and her answer had been to refuse him. Why? After all, what he had said about her position at the Dower House was true, and oh, the look on Lady Willoughby's face if he stood before her and announced his chosen marchioness was her paid companion. She smiled, but sighed also. That was in part why she had refused. She could not imagine Miss Eleanor Burgess as the Most Honourable the Marchioness of Athelney, and nor would anyone else. They would say he had been trapped, was a fool, had married beneath him and in haste to fulfil a stupid condition in a will. She owed it to him to protect him from that.

She laughed. *Owed it to him to protect him.* What was she thinking? Why did she even want to protect him from his own folly? Surely in her own interests she could assent and be comfortable, more than comfortable, appreciated, find companionship, and even abiding affection. She sighed again. The sad truth was that she liked him too much to accept his hasty proposal, not just out of altruism but because she was greedy. She wanted him to love her, fully, overwhelmingly, not by a gradual slipping into deep affection. It was a mad idea, a bad idea, but it sat there in her heart and would not budge. What she wanted more than anything in the world was to see William Hawksmoor look at her not with appreciation, not fondness, not friendship, but love, and if he did, well, no amount of disapproval from outside would weigh with her.

CHAPTER NINE

Lieutenant Bitton's struggle with the ledgers looked likely to become protracted, although he was generally able to announce at the end of each day that he had made progress. In part it was simply that the latest entries were misaligned. If one could translate what had been set beside the figures, logic could be applied to see if the amount was likely. The operative word was 'if', and the more recent the entry the less likely it was to be legible. Harry Bitton wisely began from the known towards the unknown, studying the accounts for several years before any problems appeared. It was clear that Mitchum was a thorough and honest individual and that any problems that had arisen would not be in any way fraudulent. By learning his style of letters and figures, Harry Bitton was able to decipher the first year that had proved problematic, but that was five years past. Mitchum came and sat with the young man, but his own eyesight was now so clouded that he could not see his own writing, and had to listen to what the naval lieutenant thought likely. There were occasional laughs, the loudest of which attracted his lordship's attention. He popped his head around the door to find Mr Bitton wiping his eyes. He raised his eyebrows.

'I never realised accounting was hilarious.'

'I am sorry, my lord. It was just the only word I could make out seemed to be "cabbages" and in fact it was "cottages".'

'Interesting, but not a source of mirth, surely?'

'Ah no, my lord, except that the sum expended upon these "cabbages" was thirty-two pounds, nine shillings and fourpence ha'penny.'

'That would certainly have purchased an unreasonable number of the vegetable. What, by the way, necessitated the expenditure upon the cottages?'

'I recall that, my lord,' declared Mitchum proudly, as if it were some great feat. 'We had such a wind, a storm so bad it ripped thatch and tile from roofs over half the shire. There seemed no rhyme or reason which dwellings were affected, but damage there was, and through no fault of the occupants. His late lordship knew his responsibilities, whatever Mr Hawksmoor advised.'

'Mr Hawksmoor?' Lord Athelney's eyes narrowed.

'Yes, my lord. Since he was the heir, Mr Hawksmoor thought he ought to have a say in the way in which the estate was managed. He had some schemes he was very keen to see implemented, but his lordship was not so aged in his mind as to agree to the most of them.'

'Most? You mean that some were?' Lord Athelney exchanged glances with Mr Bitton.

'I . . . am not sure, my lord. There was a brief period when I was unwell, winter before last, and Mr Hawksmoor was here, shortly before his lordship sent him packing. I know that Mr Hawksmoor was all for taking some of the money from the wool clip to invest in what he said was another drainage scheme. We never saw no work done, but . . . Nor was it clear what money had been taken. I could not understand the entries, if I am honest, my lord. Very "rob Peter to pay Paul" it seemed to me, but what could I say? Then his lordship sent Mr Hawksmoor off with a flea in his ear after the incident with his riotous friends, and it seemed best not to make too much of it and worry his lordship further.'

'How much was involved, Mitchum?'

'As I recall, about eight hundred pounds, my lord.'

Mr Bitton gave a slow whistle. It was a considerable sum to a naval lieutenant.

'Not insignificant, but not so high as to ruin all, hmmm.' Lord Athelney rubbed his chin. 'I doubt the money went anywhere other than to fund my cousin's debts in the end, even if he had good intentions to begin with, which I doubt. Nothing to be done about the money now, but we ought to address drainage in the spring, I think.'

They were interrupted by Sturry, who announced that Miss Greenham was come to enquire if she might measure the window embrasures in the gatehouse.

'Of course she may, but why? Is she studying historic architecture?'

'Er, my lord,' Mr Bitton coloured, 'she asked if she might assist with the soft furnishings for the gatehouse rooms. Septimus says she is a considerable needlewoman and I thought . . . I know nothing of such things and . . .'

'Will you invite Miss Greenham in please, Sturry.' Lord Athelney smiled at the butler. He returned with Miss Greenham, her cheeks flushed from the climb up the hill and the more so from the westerly wind. She made her curtsey and the gentlemen responded.

'I am but come to see the gatehouse, my lord. Septimus is driving us into Shepton Mallet tomorrow and I thought I might visit the drapers' shops, even the silk warehouse, if I had the sizes. It might be possible to obtain heavy fabrics that would both retain the heat in the chambers and look appropriate. I . . . am unsure as to the budget, though.' She looked from Mr Bitton to Lord Athelney and back again.

'I am sorry, my lord,' murmured Mr Bitton hesitantly, 'I was going to broach the matter with you later.'

'I see no problem, unless you were going to suggest gold-embroidered . . . tapestries.' His lordship had as little knowledge of fabrics as Harry Bitton. 'I am sure you will find what is suitable at a good price also. Have the bill sent here.'

'But should I not show you first, my lord?' Miss Greenham looked concerned.

'I assure you, ma'am, it would not make any difference. Mr Bitton and I are, at heart, simple sailors. You decide, and I, we, are in your debt for undertaking it for us.'

It was Miss Greenham's turn to blush.

'I confess it is a pleasure, to be able to choose without the strictest of economy. Not that I would be spendthrift,' she added hastily.

'We are in your hands, Miss Greenham, and in your debt.' Mr Bitton repeated Lord Athelney's words, and smiled.

'I would suggest that Mr Bitton accompanies you to assist in the task of taking measurements, though.' Lord Athelney had noted the smile, and Miss Greenham's heightened colour thereafter.

'My lord, the proprieties,' murmured Mr Bitton.

'Then take a maid with you also. Sturry, find one who has her wits about her and will understand what is needed, for the measuring not the chaperonage.' He grinned at Mr Bitton.

He watched the young lieutenant follow the parson's sister from the room, and smiled. He could see why Harry Bitton was attracted to Miss Greenham. She was the sort of young woman who would appeal to a practical and decisive man, and was pretty with it. Her features were regular, and her grey eyes very fine, her hair with natural curls that, it seemed to him, could owe little to tongs or whatever women did to their hair to make ringlets. Yes, she was very appealing, much more so than the rather more obviously pretty Charlotte. He might have looked as his lieutenant did, had he not already another lady occupying his thoughts.

Miss Greenham entered the gatehouse with a sense of perturbation. She was a sensible young woman, with no fears, unlike Lizzy, the maid, of skeletons or headless ghosts. She was, however, afraid of spiders. Her arachnophobia annoyed her, and she was embarrassed by it, since she acknowledged the things could not harm her, but it remained, nevertheless, and emerged, like the creatures themselves, unexpectedly. She steeled herself, for she had been warned of the dusty cobwebs.

The door to the lumber room creaked open, and Lizzy squeaked. Anne Greenham gave her a reproving look and trod boldly into the chamber behind Mr Bitton. A rustling in the corner he ascribed cheerfully to a rat. Miss Greenham accepted this with equilibrium, and followed him up the stair to the constable's chamber. The windows had at least been cleaned of the years of grime, and a weak winter sun shone between the chimneys of the main house and into the room. She looked about her. It appeared swept and garnished, and there were no obvious lurking places for spiders.

'Goodness, it is really rather grand.'

'Palatial, I called it, Miss Greenham. It is in sad need of renovation but . . .'

'And those poor chairs!' Miss Greenham's gaze

133

had alighted upon the damaged upholstery. 'I cannot undertake such work myself, but if they were to be taken with us tomorrow, we might have them made good. I could select a suitable material at the same time as the curtains.'

With a woman's pragmatism, and with arachnids temporarily forgotten, Miss Greenham surveyed the contents of the room, and studied the window embrasures. Mr Bitton watched her, caught up in her enthusiasm, and conscious of an unexpected sensation of elation for which he could find no reason.

'Would you prefer a red velvet, or a deep green, or perhaps either colour in a brocade, sir?'

'I . . . er, will be guided by your superior knowledge and judgement, Miss Greenham.'

'A deep red would be very regal, but green, or perhaps even a green and gold brocade, would be more cheering, and less prone to fading, since the main window faces south. We must measure the embrasures, and then I suggest that Lord Athelney have new poles put up upon which to hang the draperies. This room will be habitable in quite short order, you know.'

Mr Bitton did know, and nodded in agreement. Some time was spent in measuring, with Mr Bitton taking the risk of standing upon one of the disreputable chairs, and with the end of the measuring tape tied to the end of an old walking stick to reach the top of the windows. When these measurements were written down in Miss Greenham's little notebook, Mr Bitton indicated the other door from the room.

'There is an adjacent chamber and then more above, if you would care to inspect them, though they are none of them so tidy.'

Miss Greenham smiled, and nodded, though her heart thumped unpleasantly in her bosom. He led the way into the next room.

'Be careful here, for there is a hole in the deck.' He unconsciously broke into naval parlance in this below-deck gloom, and indicated the broken boards. 'The spiral stair in the corner leads up to bedchambers.'

The maid stood as near the wall as she dared for fear of disappearing in a welter of splintered oak. Miss Greenham looked at the chamber with imagination.

'It is perhaps rather a dark room, but might be made quite comfortable if repaired. The fireplace is scarcely much younger than the outer walls in date. What a pity the window looking out along the ridge is so small. Can we reach that in safety, Mr Bitton, or should we wait until such time as the "deck", as you call it, shall have been repaired?'

'Perhaps best to wait, ma'am, but we can ascend safely enough.'

This they did. The upper chamber was much as the one below, but boasted a tall narrow window facing north which showed signs of having been greatly enlarged from what was originally a mere arrow slit. The panelled chambers over the constable's chamber made Miss Greenham exclaim.

'Such fine work for private lodgings! Oh dear, I must sound a perfect bluestocking, Mr Bitton, but you see, I grew up with old churches and ancient buildings. A dust and liberal polishing would make these chambers very cosy. Can you reach the windows? Good. Rugs. You ought to have rugs in these rooms. The fireplace flues must lead into that of the main chamber, so I would doubt they would smoke. Have you a preference for a bedchamber? The south-facing one has better light, of course.'

'Which would you choose?'

'The southern one, because it gives more an air of being part of the castle community as opposed to being in some form of isolation. I . . .' She was about to go on when she saw it, a large-bodied black spider crawling up from a fold in her skirt.

Miss Greenham screamed. Lizzy screamed, not knowing why, but if the lady was screaming it must be worth her doing so also. Then she saw the spider, lifted her skirts and ran from the room.

Mr Bitton blinked. Miss Greenham stood very, very still, her little hands clenched into fists. He followed her horrified gaze.

'It won't hurt you, ma'am,' he reassured her, stepping forward, 'and please forgive me.' He reached out his hand and grasped the spider from what must have been halfway up her thigh. He tried to open a narrow casement, but it required such force that the window itself fell with a crash to the courtyard below. Lizzy, somewhere on the spiral stair, screamed again. The offending spider was cast after the glazing. Miss Greenham did not move.

'It is gone?' she whispered.

'It is gone, Miss Greenham.'

'I am so very sorry . . . the window . . . my fault . . . shamed . . . but spiders, ergh.' She gave a great shudder and then, rather to his surprise, and very much to his horror, burst into tears.

Harry Bitton had led boarding parties, but had never been faced with anything quite so disconcerting as a young lady in distress. He was not at all sure what he ought to do, and so, by default, obeyed instinct, placing his arms about her, and drawing her head onto his shoulder.

'There is nothing to blame yourself over, my dear lady, nothing.' She trembled against him. It was a novel, but not at all unpleasant, experience. 'Might have frightened anyone, a thing like that.'

'It did not frighten you, sir,' she mumbled from against his lapel.

'Never been afraid of them. Mind you, I can't abide the sight of trotters, not on the pig you understand, but as something to eat. Always made me feel distinctly unwell. Not afraid of them, of course, but you see, different people react to different things.'

There was a nervous gurgle of laughter, which was what he had half hoped to achieve, and it was then that Miss Greenham seemed to become aware of the position in which she stood, and pulled back, flustered.

He let her go immediately.

'I am sorry . . .' they began simultaneously.

'You were being noble, I understand that, sir, not taking advantage.'

'Of course I was . . . I mean not noble . . . not taking advantage either . . . comforting.'

'Indeed, and I am grateful for it.' She blushed in the pale sunlight. 'I think it best we forget it, do not you? It might be misconstrued.'

He nodded, but when they stood in the courtyard and parted, both knew that forgetting was the last thing they wished to do.

Whilst the embrace remained a private matter, Mr Bitton did feel it was incumbent upon him to reveal that he had in fact broken Lord Athelney's window. His lordship, when told it had been damaged in an effort to remove a spider, smiled.

'I never thought you had anything against spiders, Mr Bitton. In fact, as I recall, it was you who faced that large hairy one we had to remove from those plantains we bought in the Caribbean.'

'Miss Greenham holds them in strong aversion, however.'

'Ah.'

'I shall of course reimburse you . . .'

'Don't be a fool, my dear fellow. It was an ancient window. Such things occur. You may place the repair bill in the accounts, legibly of course. Now, what, other than making her dislike of spiders clear, did Miss Greenham say?'

'She requested permission to remove the chairs in the main chamber to be reupholstered in Shepton when she purchases material for the curtains, and she recommended that the upper rooms be as thoroughly cleaned as the main chamber. Curtains for the windows in the western chamber will not be made until the decks have been repaired.'

'I see. Then best we obey the lady's commands, don't you think, Mr Bitton?'

'Aye aye, my lord.'

The Reverend and Miss Greenham presented themselves next morning just before nine of the clock. The bedraggled chairs could just about be lashed to the back of the gig, and Miss Greenham said that she would arrange for them to be brought back by carrier when restored. Upon seeing the look that Mr Bitton gave the lady, when he thought he was unobserved, Lord Athelney suggested that his apprentice steward abandon his books for the day and accompany his friends to the town. He might thus keep note of any expenditure, and, he remarked with a grin, restrain Miss Greenham from bankrupting the estate by purchasing the most expensive silks. Miss Greenham coloured and demurred, and her brother laughed, since it would give him the opportunity to see Harry Bitton on horseback. His friend told him that was a very unchristian attitude, since he undoubtedly hoped to see him fall off, and in great good humour the trio set off for Shepton Mallet.

They arrived mid-morning, and first of all sought out an upholsterer, leaving the chairs to be stripped of their ancient fabric while Miss Greenham sought replacement materials. Much of the silk that was produced in the manufactory by the river went direct to warehouses in Bath, but Miss Greenham decided that a visit to the site of production might prove useful. After all, the goods would be locally produced, and there would be no third party to pay.

The silk mill did not in general receive visitors, but the Reverend Greenham's clerical collar and educated tones gained them admittance. The gentlemen were intrigued by the process, but Miss Greenham was interested in the product. What became apparent, however, when they reached the weaving floor was the presence of the children. Of itself this was not a surprise. There were powder monkeys and midshipmen at sea as young as some of those scrabbling beneath the looms, but there were a number whose years seemed too few to be in any employment.

Septimus Greenham frowned. 'Are these children so undernourished that they appear so young, or are they as few in years as they seem?'

'They are all over six years old, sir.'

'On whose authority could one know that? Surely a parent in dire need would tell a falsehood? That boy there. Look at him. You are saying he is six years of age?'

'I can only say that is the age we are told, sir.' The overseer looked uncomfortable but resolute. 'And a younger child would not understand the work. We have turned off some in the past as have been unable to work because they were obviously not as old as their parents declared.'

'It is shameful.' The clergyman was shocked.

'With respect, sir, it is better than starvation. They earn, they eat, aye, and they help pay for younger brothers and sisters to eat. You being a reverend gentleman it is understandable as you should see the bad side, but the world is a hard and, yes, ungodly place, sir. I was no older than these when I started, and out in the fields that was.'

'But the work seems . . . dangerous.' Miss Greenham frowned.

'It can be, true enough. But the small ones work half the day here. Most then sleep while brothers, sisters, cousins, work their shift. You can't keep a nipper of six alert for twelve hours. Decision was made here some years back because of poor work and accidents. They may earn less but are safer.'

'Thank you for your honesty. I cannot but find it terrible that in our modern world these infants need to work just to eat, but your not employing them would not help matters, and you have some care to them. The weaving itself is fascinating.' Miss Greenham smiled sadly, for the bright fabric would never again have the same connotations of luxury in her head.

They were, however, there to purchase on Lord Athelney's behalf, and Miss Greenham brought forth her measurements. They studied the rolls of silks. Many were dress silks, over which Miss Greenham could not but sigh. Her brother did not live upon the stipend alone, but she possessed but three silk gowns. The heavier brocades and velvets were even more expensive. Miss Greenham flinched at the prices, but knew them to be cheaper than in a draper's shop. With a little input from Mr Bitton, she selected a silk velvet in a colour that seemed green from one angle, and gold from another, and a heavier version for the upholstery, to be sent on to the upholsterer. Mr Bitton was very taken with a plain mulberry slub silk, which she purchased for the room he had chosen as his bedchamber, once the window, as he noted wryly, had been replaced.

'I think elsewhere we should restrict ourselves to linens for draperies. After all, this is not for Lord Athelney's own quarters. It actually feels very decadent having ornate fabrics at all.' He sounded guilty.

'But the main chamber is in many ways a public room. People, tenants, will come there. It proclaims status, not only his own, but that of his steward. It shows you are held in esteem by him.' Miss Greenham sounded very reasonable.

'I hope he continues in that view,' sighed Mr Bitton ruefully, thinking of the ledgers he had abandoned for the day. 'I shall be happier with more simple hangings elsewhere.'

They therefore adjourned to a private parlour in one of the posting houses for luncheon before visiting the largest of the drapers' shops in the town. The meal did much to raise Mr Bitton's spirits, since it gave the opportunity to discuss old times with his friend, and also the chance to be close to Miss Greenham. They emerged later from the draper's with parcels of fabric, which were placed beneath the seat of the tilbury. The wind had got up, and Miss Greenham drew her pelisse more tightly about her person, and wrapped the rug about her knees. They parted from Mr Bitton at Kingscastle with Miss Greenham promising to send word as her sewing neared completion. Mr Bitton dismounted, still with an air of relief that the day had not been marked by him falling off his horse.

CHAPTER TEN

Anne Greenham was not a young woman given to fanciful thought. She was, however, guilty of idle daydreaming as she cut out the new curtains for the gatehouse, and it was not concerning the potential splendour of the rooms. She was twenty-three years old, and had never seen herself as anything beyond housekeeper and support to her father, and now her brother, in whose intelligence and humanity she saw an unconscious channelling of her own beliefs. Their father, long a widower, had been first the precentor of a cathedral and then a bishop, and she had grown up within a clerical society. His demise at the time when her brother was coming to the end of his curacy meant that she naturally moved from one clergyman's household to another. Meeting her brother's erstwhile schoolfriend, Lieutenant Harry Bitton, had given her something to think about beyond the sermon on Sunday and Septimus's ability to wear out the heels of his clerical stockings. Her offer to assist in the refurbishment of the gatehouse had not been made with any conscious thought that it would enable her to get to know Mr Bitton rather better; she had seen a job that needed doing and knew herself capable of taking it on. Her Christian duty was therefore to offer her needle and time. As a consequence, however, she had been thrown into close proximity with the young naval officer, whose sunny disposition and ready smile, not to mention his decisive way with spiders, brought him often into her thoughts. It was pleasant, she lied to herself, to have expanded her narrow circle of friends. In the village, where she was 'the parson's sister', she was treated with deference, but not offered friendship. Lady Willoughby Hawksmoor clearly looked upon her in much the same light as she did Miss Burgess, above the status of an upper servant, but below that where one might display friendship. She was thus so far limited to her distant correspondents and the wife of a neighbouring incumbent. Miss Burgess might prove an ally, but she was rarely seen apart from Lady Willoughby. Mr Bitton, and, to a small degree, Lord Athelney, seemed unconcerned about the social position of the parsonage residents. Yes, to have new friends was a delightful surprise.

As if to chastise her for her falsehood, the needle she was plying pricked her finger, and she rubbed the pinhead of bright blood away with a small frown of discomfort. Septimus, hunting for a note he had scribbled to himself when inspiration had struck for the sermon for evensong, put his head around the door of the dining room, where Anne had unfolded the materials.

'Have you seen my pencilled note, the one I wrote before breakfast?'

'No, dear brother, I have not. You had it in your hand at one point, because you nearly spread butter upon it. I remonstrated, remember?'

'I did!' He grinned. 'You have an idiot for a brother, Anne. I need only recall where I went immediately afterwards.' He noticed her still rubbing her finger. 'Should I tell Lord Athelney that you are going so far as to bleed for his furnishings?'

'Septimus, really! It was my own fault, for I was not paying attention. Now, you set your mind to remembering where you set down your note.'

'I shall.' He turned to leave the room, but as he did so, mentioned nonchalantly, 'Oh, and I thought I might invite Harry to take luncheon on Sunday with us.'

He did not see the slight blush upon his sister's cheek as she assented to the scheme.

Eleanor tried not to show how much her treatment following the dinner at Kingscastle irked her. There had been spells like this before, when Lady Willoughby Hawksmoor took out her ill-humour or frustration upon her companion. Eleanor thought she understood what

146

it must have been like to be a whipping-boy. There was no logic to any of it, but Lady Willoughby and logic were barely acquainted. Anything that Eleanor did was insufficient, took too long or was even simply ignored. When Eleanor received a letter from her mama, she was conscious of feeling desperately homesick.

The letter contained the exciting news of Mary's betrothal to Richard, elder son of Sir George and Lady Langley, and the plans for the wedding in the spring. Mama hoped that Lady Willoughby might be prevailed upon to give Eleanor leave of absence to attend the nuptials. Reading this, Eleanor pulled a wry face. Mama might hope, but all depended upon Lady Willoughby's mood. It was understandable that Mama should feel elated at the successful establishment of her daughter, for the young man was both pleasant and clearly enamoured of the beautiful Mary, and his family were of note in the shire. Mary could look forward to a life where watching every household bill would not be vital, and with a decent man. If the Reverend Burgess was less interested in his social position than his character, then that, declared Mama, was as it should be 'for I do not hesitate to tell you that it is we ladies who must oftentimes be the most pragmatic, when it comes to matrimony'. Eleanor read the words and wondered what Mama would have said if she knew her second daughter had refused an offer of marriage from a marquis.

The other news was more homely. Margaret had completed a quilt she had been working upon for the past twelvemonth, Emily had had a putrid sore throat but it was now much better, and the oldest resident in the parish had died at the grand old age, at best guess, of ninety years.

It was these details that brought the lump to Eleanor's throat. She recalled Margaret's first stitch upon that quilt, and had oftentimes visited Old Margery with her father, when the old lady had been keeping to her cottage in poor weather. Somerset felt like exile.

Lady Willoughby was not a woman of intellect, but her female intuition was not at fault. Whatever Eleanor Burgess might say, she could see attraction when it reared its head. That her nephew had, most reprehensibly, and with no thought for his rank, been attracted to the girl, was as obvious as if he had put out flags, and the Nobody did not rebuff him with any show of willingness. Well, it would not be allowed to continue. Every effort must be made, and she would do so for her daughter's right to be the next Marchioness of Athelney, and for the good of the family, to ensure that no deeper relationship should be given a chance to grow. The first and most obvious way to achieve this would be to keep Eleanor away from the castle and Athelney's company. It was also quite simple. She picked a time when Charlotte had been sent upon an errand that her mother knew would result in a fruitless search, and then fixed her basilisk stare upon her companion.

'Now, Eleanor.'

'Surely I could have gone . . .'

'I wish to speak to you, without interruption, Eleanor.'

Eleanor's heart sank.

'You will attend to what I say, and you will do as I command. I have, frankly, no faith in your protestations that you only converse with my errant nephew out of politeness, and I have even less faith in his understanding of his responsibilities as the Marquis of Athelney. You shall therefore not accompany me, or Charlotte, when we visit the castle in the future.'

Eleanor, still reeling from the description of Lord Athelney as 'errant' in view of Lady Willoughby's son's blatant immorality, raised an eyebrow.

'Will that not occasion remark, ma'am?'

'Why should it? You are merely a paid companion. If I do not require your companionship at such times, it is my decision, and mine alone.'

'But if the invitation is inclusive . . .'

'Pah!' Lady Willoughby shrugged in a dismissive gesture. 'Besides, we do not dine there so frequently that it may not be glossed over with the excuse that you have the headache for the first few occasions.'

'And if I should encounter Lord Athelney and he asks after these frequent indispositions?'

'I have said that you will not encounter him.'

'Short of cooping me up within the house, ma'am, I cannot see how you can guarantee such a thing.'

'Oh, it is quite simple. Should it reach my ears that you have broken my commandment,' Lady Willoughby drew herself up very straight indeed, 'you will find yourself upon the stagecoach back to your disappointed parents immediately, without any future reference, and with my letter explaining your disobedience, your irresponsible wilfulness, to your poor mama. I dare not imagine how it may prostrate her.'

She made it sound, thought Eleanor, as if her word ranked with that of the Almighty. Having said which, her power over such a being as a mere companion might just seem comparable. Mama would be disappointed, certainly, but if Lady Willoughby thought that Papa would believe her poisoned words over those of his daughter, she was very wide of the mark.

'So, since you are so frank with me, Lady Willoughby, let us be perfectly clear. If, even through no intent of my own, I should so much as pass the time of day with Lord Athelney, I shall be dismissed without character.'

'Yes.'

Eleanor fought the very strong instinct to simply resign with immediate effect and take the mail coach from Wells of her own volition. She was not entirely sure why she did not. That there might be a reason in the form of Lord Athelney himself, and that she had no wish to leave his proximity, even if she was forbidden to speak to him, she ignored. It would be foolish. She had no feelings for him, nor he for her. All this was from the warped mind of Lady Willoughby. In reality the only bond between them was of genteel acquaintanceship. She cast from her mind his proposal and the desires of her heart, at this juncture, as not helpful to her argument.

'Then, for the sake of my position, ma'am, I must hope that his lordship vacates Kingscastle and sojourns at his other estates as soon as possible. If that is all, for the moment, I shall do as you requested before luncheon, and go to write your invitation to Lady Bryanston to bring your grandchildren to visit at New Year.'

It appalled Eleanor that Lady Willoughby did not write to her own daughter in her own hand, but she no longer even made representations that Lady Bryanston might find it awkward that her mama communicated via the blatant scribing of another. She gazed without any sign of perturbation at her employer, though she seethed within, and, after a moment in which they stared at each other, Lady Willoughby inclined her head. The interview was concluded.

Harry Bitton adjusted his neckcloth. He need not, he knew, stand upon ceremony with his friend Septimus, but, he told himself, it would not look right to attend church looking less than neat as a new pin, since he was Lord Athelney's acting steward. If the face in the mirror that looked back at him seemed to dissolve into that of Miss Greenham, he could not give a reason for it.

It was a foul day, and it did not take much persuasion for Harry to relinquish the idea of striding down the hill and risking mud over his boots, and accept Lord Athelney's request to keep him company in the carriage.

'I know I must seem to have become a paltry soft

fellow, but the truth is that the villagers expect me to act like a lord, not a sailor and so . . . One day I shall go out in a really good storm and just stand there being battered by the elements for old times' sake, but I must ensure I am not observed or like as not they will think me destined for Bedlam.' Lord Athelney smiled.

Mr Bitton grinned back. 'I shall not be returning with you, though, my lord, for I am invited to the parsonage for luncheon.'

'You reject my table for religious discussion?' Lord Athelney raised a quizzical eyebrow.

'No, no, my lord. I would run aground pretty fast if I dared. Septimus invited me, for old times' sake. I shall return after evensong this evening, and walking will suffice me then.'

'Since you only return to this ramshackle hovel?'

'You are determined to rake me, my lord. I protest it is unfair.'

'Mightily so. Then go with my benison.' Lord Athelney's lips twitched, and then he laughed out loud.

He had hoped to have Harry Bitton play a few rubbers of piquet in the library, but resigned himself to an afternoon of solitude with a volume of Ovid, which was about as erudite as he could manage with his rusty Latin. It would be a good discipline.

The carriage bore them down to matins, where his lordship insisted that Mr Bitton share the Kingscastle pew, much to the dislike of Lady Willoughby, which was an additional reason to do so, as he explained later. Miss

Burgess, who seemed very subdued, and barely lifted her eyes from her prayer book or hymnal throughout the service, did, he noted, suppress a smile at the huffing going on to her left. He wondered why she was so very mousey, and frowned so much during the sermon that the Reverend Greenham asked him at the church door if the tone of the sermon had offended him.

Lord Athelney did not reply with the truth, which was that at least half his mind had been inattentive to the parson's carefully chosen words. Thankfully, enough of his attention had remained for him to applaud an apposite analogy. Having allayed Septimus Greenham's concerns, he departed, with the briefest of exchanges with the Dower House ladies, surmising that any word to Miss Burgess would be cause for her to suffer thereafter, and he would be damned if he would converse with his aunt and cousin and ignore her completely.

Mr Bitton hung back, and awaited the emptying of the church. Miss Greenham, who had been shielded from his view for much of the service, was engaged with one of the villagers. He watched her, the earnest expression on her face giving her a maturity beyond her years. Her hair was barely visible beneath the modest poke bonnet, unadorned but for a band of black grosgrain ribbon that matched her pelisse. Nothing about her cried out to be admired, and yet he was conscious of admiring her.

When the parishioners had all departed, Septimus came in from the cold porch with a wry grin, and, rubbing his hands together to get the blood back into them, then went directly to the vestry to remove his surplice, and take up both hat and cloak. They then formed a trio who trod the few yards to the parsonage briskly. Conversation would be far better in front of a good fire.

Anne disappeared to check that everything was ready for luncheon, and to brush her crushed locks. Vanity was a sin, but looking unkempt was no virtue. She resolutely refused to wonder whether Mr Bitton might find her high-necked gown too old. After all, she was still in mourning. She sighed, guilty of wishing she might wear colours. Folded neatly in tissue paper, she had several gowns that had drawn admiration in the cathedral close. She went downstairs, in time to hear Mr Bitton's laugh, and halted upon the threshold of the neat, square parlour.

'I am sorry, my dear, we were reminiscing about our old mathematics master.' Her brother turned to his friend. 'We must not go on forever over luncheon about our schooldays, or my sister will be heartily bored with the pair of us, and have Cook hold back the curd tarts, which I happen to know have been prepared especially.'

'You happened to mention they were a particular favourite of yours, Mr Bitton, when we dined with you and Lord Athelney,' murmured Miss Greenham.

'They are, ma'am, but I hardly expected you to recall such a thing.' He coloured slightly, as did she, and she dropped her gaze.

'Anne has a remarkably good memory. I, alas, am lacking in that useful asset, and frequently resort to cudgelling her brains, rather than my own, when things go astray. Only the other day I mislaid the sermon I was writing for evensong tonight, and only found it by working from when Anne had seen me with it last.'

'And by asking the maid which rooms you had visited after breakfast. You claim too much credit for yourself, brother mine.'

'Ignore her, Harry. Brother and sister as we are, she chides me mercilessly.'

Miss Greenham spluttered, and would have responded to this calumny, had her brother not grinned at her.

Harry Bitton enjoyed an excellent luncheon, even before the delights of the curd tarts. Anne would have withdrawn after the meal to permit them to converse in private, but was prevailed upon to remain, and sat with some stitchery, hemming the cuffs of a new shirt for her brother, while the gentlemen failed in their attempt not to spend the afternoon in anecdotes, though they moved on from school to Septimus's life as an undergraduate at Merton, and Harry's rather more risky existence at sea. Miss Greenham could not but exclaim at some of his descriptions of storms and actions, for which he apologised, saying that he had so far forgot his surroundings as to have recalled things unsuitable for a delicate lady's ear.

'I am not delicate, sir, but I confess your recollections are described so vividly as to make me feel almost seasick. I crossed to the Isle of Wight once, and suffered not at all, but such weather as you describe . . . Oh dear.'

'My dear Miss Greenham, forgive such a foolish

gabster as I am. I should perhaps tell you instead of my inadequacies as a horseman. They are manifold.'

'If they are, then I fear I shall exchange a fear of *mal de mer* with sympathies for bruised limbs.'

'I have taken the odd tumble, but the tyrant of the stables assures me that such events will improve me, and that I shall learn to fall off much better. Strangely, I do not find this heartening.'

By the time the clock struck the hour that required Septimus to return to his duties in the church, all three persons had spent a most entertaining afternoon, and if the wind nearly whipped his hat from his head, and his boots, and indeed his breeches, were spattered with mud upon his arrival back at the castle, Mr Bitton cared not a whit, beyond hastening to change before dinner.

CHAPTER ELEVEN

Lady Willoughby's charity was, as Eleanor had previously informed Lord Athelney, designed to be seen and talked about by the lower orders. It did not extend to going out in the cold to play Lady Bountiful. Having been made aware of the indigence of the Dower House's old housemaid, she felt it imperative that her generosity be obvious as soon as possible. She had little doubt that the Reverend Greenham would thereafter mention it from his pulpit.

She herself viewed the items sent in the basket, as if surveying them imbued them with her graciousness. There was a cold brisket, some potted meat, a dozen eggs, some leeks, carrots, a jar of honey and a pound cake.

'You will be sure to tell . . .' Lady Willoughby paused,

having completely forgotten the name of the old servant.

'Grace Malling, ma'am.'

'Yes, Malling, of course. You may tell her that I will ensure that another basket is delivered before Christmas, if her nephew is still unwell and unable to provide for her.'

Since the nephew in question had very recently broken his arm and was the local wheelwright, it was highly unlikely that he would be working in only a few weeks.

'I shall do so, Lady Willoughby.' Eleanor looked past her employer and out of the window. The bare branches of the chestnuts swayed, buffeted by the gale. At least the rain had stopped, though it was just possible that she might not have been sent on foot if the downpour that had commenced the previous morning, and then had continued all day and through the night, had continued today. Lady Willoughby followed her gaze, and sighed.

'Yes, it is quite a windy day, is it not?' The sigh was merely an expression that she found the weather depressing to the spirits, for she would be remaining warm within doors. 'Make sure you do not linger.' She smiled at Eleanor, but not in a kindly way, and added, lest she think the concern be for her person, 'I want you to sort my tapestry silks before tea. I cannot think how they managed to become so muddled.'

Eleanor murmured an assent, and went to wrap herself as best she might against the elements, and to put on her stoutest ankle boots.

The wind buffeted her even as she left the house, and

she made her way along the muddy path to the nearby Sittford Mill bridge, for the alternatives were to trudge all the way up the hill and down into the village by the road, or follow the river loop round to the stone bridge, which was shorter but without any path, and now extremely muddy. At least a track led from the mill to the village, and she would take the opportunity to ask after Mrs Flowers, whose baby was surely due.

Sittford Mill was accessed by a wooden bridge that ran nearly flat across the river on wooden supports. The rain and high level of the water made the planks slippery, and she kept her gloved hands on the rails on either side. Once, her left foot slithered, and she gripped ever more tightly, but reached the far side without any major mishap. Mrs Flowers had not as yet presented her spouse with another babe, but had the look of a woman yearning for the relief from the discomforts of late pregnancy.

Having established that all was well, Eleanor trudged into the village, and delivered the contents of the basket to the aged Grace Malling, who was suitably grateful to her ladyship for her kindness and generosity. Eleanor stayed with the old woman for some time, providing her with a selection of news that her nephew would have thought idle gossip, and then, mindful of the tangled silks, began to retrace her steps. A young Flowers waved at her from the mill, and Eleanor took a deep breath and essayed the bridge once more.

She viewed it with the deepest foreboding. The water

raced beneath it so close to the walkway that she feared her feet might get damp. She stepped onto it rather gingerly, and as she did so saw Lord Athelney striding down the hill towards her, his hat clamped to his head and the skirts of his coat flapping about his legs in the wind. It was as she reached a little over two thirds of the way across that it juddered beneath her, and she staggered, grabbing the wooden railing. There was a rumbling, creaking sound accompanied by the splintering of wood; the structure gave an enormous heaving motion, and disintegrated. Eleanor was cast into the tumbling waters with a curtailed scream.

There was a moment suspended in time that seemed to go on for ever, though it was but the blinking of an eye. Lord Athelney threw off his heavy overcoat, ran to the edge of the bank as close as possible to where Eleanor had disappeared, and jumped into the water, unsure as to its depth. It was immediately chest deep and his feet were swept from under him. The flow tugged insistently upon him, and planks from the tumbled structure jostled him, hitting him upon the arm and head. The cold hit him more acutely, and he gasped. With a ball of panic in his chest he realised that he could not see Miss Burgess at all, and then there was a cry and a flailing of arms, and he struck out, trying to swim to her.

An ability to swim was not standard in the naval service, and many men drowned who would otherwise have survived accident or battle. Midshipman Hawksmoor, having seen men die within fifty yards of safety, had decided that was a fate he would try to avoid. He had learned to swim in the warmer waters of the Mediterranean, and swim clothed, but here both the current and the cold impeded him. He knew he was taking too long, was even struggling a little himself, and then his hand touched cloth and flesh and he grabbed at it wildly.

Eleanor Burgess had no notion of how to swim, and her thrashings were but the consequence of instinct and fear. The water was abducting her, dragging her from life itself. The flow pulled her downstream and down into the cold depths, like grasping, molesting hands, drawing her skirts about her legs so that she could not even move them freely. She went under, struggled again to the surface, only to be recaptured by the force of angry nature, and every submersion she knew sapped what little energy she still possessed. She was so cold, was swallowing water, her actions losing coordination; even the panic-strength, the urge to survive, was being sapped from her to leave only an acceptance that she was going to die.

Then something, someone, touched her, grabbed her shoulder, pulled her. Her stupefied brain saw it as some watery, intimate dance as she was grappled close, twisted, turned, given the chance of air, and a view of the leaden sky. Instead of giving herself up to death, she gave herself up, semi-conscious, to the arm about her.

Lord Athelney had his 'prize' but was not sure he could make it to the bank. The down-current was so strong and their combined clothing so heavy that the few yards seemed hundreds, and he knew his own strength was limited. He grew angry with himself, and this fired him to greater endeavour. He would not let the water claim them. It would be too foolish to have survived years at sea to succumb to a little river with ambition to be a torrent. It was an illogical thought, but it spurred him more. Besides, it was not just his life, but hers.

He could hear his own voice in his head, encouraging, berating, commanding as if on his own quarterdeck in the smoke of battle. Then his boot touched mud, and he was scrabbling to get purchase. Twice he was swept on, but the third time he managed a pace and thereby escaped the greatest flow. Then it was sheer determination and endurance.

He dragged himself and the limp form of Miss Burgess from the water and onto the bank where there was a shallow and more gravelly 'bay', of some four or five yards. His limbs failed him then and for a minute he could do nothing but cough, and attempt to get more air into his straining lungs. Gradually he forced awareness of his own body to the back of his mind, and looked to the inanimate form beside him. She lay on her side, facing him, her eyes half open. She breathed, but shallowly, erratically. He struggled to a sitting position and dragged her into his arms. She was like a rag doll, and a dead weight. He sat her up, facing from him, an arm about her waist as she lolled forward, and thumped her hard upon the back with the heel of his hand, making her cough. Then she made a retching sound and quivered. He moved her so that he would be able to lift her. Her eyes fluttered open, and stared at him uncomprehendingly. The quiver became a shuddering. She was cold, too cold. He looked about him, not knowing how far they had been swept downstream. His coat lay upon the bank somewhere, and surely they had not come more than a few hundred yards. At least it lay in the direction that they must take to reach the Dower House. He wished he had a better idea of the distances other than upon a map.

He scrambled to his knees. Eleanor was still coughing, and struggling for breath. She gazed at him, her eyes gaining focus slowly.

'It broke,' she whispered. She sounded as if she could not quite believe what had happened.

He nodded.

A shudder ran through her. They were both soaked to the skin, and the easterly wind ripped into them. Summoning the energy to stand and go on was immeasurably difficult, but he did so. It was imperative that he get her home, and into the warm. He slipped his right arm beneath her and lifted her into his arms, and thence struggled to stand without slipping on the mud of the bank. She lay passively in his hold, her head resting against his chest, looking up at him. She gave in to inertia. There was nothing else she could do. In truth, the shock of what had happened to her made her tremble almost as much as the cold, and his broad shoulder, however damp, was good to lean against. She felt immeasurably safe. For some minutes she closed her eyes, and when she opened them moved her head a fraction that she might see his profile. His nose was very slightly aquiline, chin and jawline firm but not blockish, his cheeks perhaps a little lean, and streaked now with water and mud.

'I am afraid you have lost your hat, my lord,' she whispered.

'I did not care for it much, ma'am, and in the scale of things, it matters not at all. It is more important, however, that I find my coat, which should be at least a little dry.'

He looked down at her pinched face, in which the eyes were still a little wide from the shock and fixed upon him as if he were solidity in a swirling world. Her bonnet had been pushed back from her head, and dangled by its strings over his arm. Her hair, darkened by the water, was plastered to her wet forehead; there was mud on her cheek; her clothes clung to her and she was shivering; yet he did not think he had ever seen anyone more beautiful. It was not intended, but he was buoyed by adrenalin, his heart still pounding in his chest, so very much aware of being alive, and of how close to death they had been. He bent his head and kissed her, a kiss he felt was not stolen although not exactly requested, briefly but firmly.

Eleanor stiffened in his arms. As a decent young lady she ought to slap him, but her arms felt too leaden, and part of her was not at all offended. She ignored that part.

'Just like your namesake . . . after all,' she gasped.

'I am sorry.' He winced as if she really had hit him. 'It was the impulse of a moment – most reprehensible and wrong but quite utterly overwhelming. I do beg your forgiveness. You see, you looked so beautiful, and I was so glad you were alive, we were both alive. I assure you my intentions are completely honourable. Will you marry me?' The wince twisted very slightly into a most uncertain and contrite attempt at a smile, which did not survive her response.

'And your wits . . . have gone begging also.' Her reply was instant, and tart. 'I would not marry you . . . out of desperation, my lord, nor will I . . . marry you out of gratitude. Even,' she added honestly, 'if you have just saved my life.'

'I would prefer that you married me because you rather liked me.' He sounded disappointed but not unhopeful, like a puppy hoping for praise despite a mistake. 'It is not, perhaps, the most propitious time. I ought to be patient, but just here, and now, it has been borne upon me just how very, very much I like you.'

The cold, she decided, must have seeped into his brain. It was up to her to remain sensible.

'Set me down, my lord, this instant.'

'You cannot support yourself, you know.'

'I demand that you put me down, sir.'

He lowered her feet to the ground and intentionally loosed his hold upon her. Her knees gave way, and she crumpled at his feet. He looked down at her, sitting in the mud.

'I said you would fall down,' he remarked mildly.

She made a frustrated growling noise. He let her sit there for perhaps half a minute, and then bent and lifted her again, his voice now quite firm.

'You have shown your independence, ma'am. Now you will behave like the sensible woman I know you to be, and let me carry you home before you catch your death of cold. And please do not struggle, because I will be forced to carry you the less dignified but easier way, over my shoulder.'

She sought refuge in silence. The ground was heavy, squelching beneath his boots, and he was concentrating upon not slipping and casting his already sodden burden back into the mud. Progress was steady but slow, and it seemed an age before he espied his coat.

It lay, an abandoned heap, some yards from the bank by the splintered, ragged remnants of the shattered bridge, which looked as if it had been charged by a stampeding herd of wild beasts.

She felt him alter the disposition of her weight slightly.

'Am I very heavy, sir?'

'Not at all, Miss Burgess.' He spoke the truth, but the additional weight of water and mud in her clothes had added enough pounds to make his arms start to ache. 'I only apologise for the slowness of our progress. It is almost like crossing a quagmire.'

'The castle was of course built on high ground but around the Dower House the gardeners always complain that the ground is too wet. And this weather is exceptional.'

'Ah yes, of course.' He laughed, with just a trace of bitterness. 'We might discuss the weather without any embarrassment.'

'I did not mean to offend . . .' She frowned.

'No. I am sure that you did not. Now, I will set you down a moment to collect my coat and wrap you in it, but I will retain a firm hold about you.'

He did just as he said, and she was content to be submissive. He wrapped her, lost in the voluminous coat, and swung her back up into his arms, gave her a brief, encouraging smile, and set off in the direction of the Dower House.

Eleanor wondered vaguely about what reception they would receive, and she was silent until they were almost at the front door.

'You really must put me down now, my lord. Lady Willoughby will . . . Oh, and I have lost her basket! That, for certain, will be deducted from my wages.'

'I shall not put you down yet. You have suffered an accident, and she should be glad you are still living. Why were you out on such a day, and down by the mill, by the way?'

'Lady Willoughby is very keen to be seen as fulfilling her obligations to the sick and poor. An old Dower House servant lives with her nephew, the wheelwright, who cannot work and earn at present, for he suffered an accident the week before last and his arm is broken. Lady Willoughby required me to take them a basket of provisions – meat, some vegetables, a cake.'

'So her charity does not extend to visiting these people herself?'

'Oh no, not unless she can be driven there and remain outside so that those receiving her bounty may come out into the street and everyone see how generous a lady she is.' Eleanor was so used to this that she spoke without any conscious irony.

'You really do not have an enviable position, Miss Burgess.'

'On the contrary, my lord. Unlike the woman I was intended to visit, I have plenty to eat, warm clothes, when they are not wet, and no fear of destitution.'

'That was not quite what I meant.' He was frowning.

'It is the only way to approach the matter. I am one of six daughters, unlikely at my age to marry, a burden upon my father's finances, for his stipend is not large, and would otherwise face indigent spinsterhood.'

'For which you have exchanged drudgery, at the beck and call of a selfish woman.'

'Comfortable drudgery, my lord.'

'And you do have the chance to marry, do not forget. Would it be so very bad?'

'Please, my lord, do not pursue this.' She coloured, and he pulled the bell.

Barwell opened the door, and stared in amazement at the sight of the bedraggled pair.

'My lord!'

'The bridge by Sittford Mill has collapsed. Miss Burgess

168

nearly drowned, and is very cold.' Lord Athelney spoke even as he entered the hallway. 'She needs both dry attire and warmed blankets about her as soon as possible.' He looked down at Eleanor. 'You must strip off those . . .'

'My lord!' A voice of outrage was heard from the top of the stairs, and Lady Willoughby Hawksmoor began to descend, bosom heaving. 'How dare you speak such indelicate . . .'

'Your pardon, ma'am, but this is not the moment for niceties, and I was suggesting that Miss Burgess strip off her wet clothes, not,' he paused for a second, 'that she should be stripped.' He did not add 'by me', but there was a dangerous twinkle in his eye.

Eleanor stiffened. She hated the effect his presence had upon her employer, for she always bore the brunt of its aftermath, and, in view of the injunction upon her, thought Lady Willoughby might even refuse to permit her to so much as to change her sodden clothes and simply cast her out as she was.

'Please put me down now, my lord,' she whispered, but he ignored her.

'Which is Miss Burgess's bedchamber?' He advanced towards the staircase.

There was so much authority in the marquis's voice that Barwell, regardless of his mistress, hurried ahead to direct his lordship to the appointed chamber, and even opened the door.

Lord Athelney set Eleanor down in the chair by the fireplace.

'A fire is to be lit immediately, and a hot brick brought for Miss Burgess's feet. Send a maid to assist Miss Burgess into dry clothing, and send up warmed blankets as soon as possible.'

'This is not your house, my lord.' Lady Willoughby stood in the doorway. 'I shall arrange matters as I see fit, and if I think Eleanor needs a hot brick I shall direct one to be brought.'

'With respect, ma'am,' and Lord Athelney's voice held none, 'I have had experience of what immersion in cold water can do, and if you value Miss Burgess, at all, you will ensure my commands are obeyed.' His tone brooked no opposition.

Lady Willoughby blinked, and shooed Barwell from the room, telling him he might do as he was bid. She was about to say more to Lord Athelney, but he was already addressing Eleanor.

'I am perfectly serious in what I say, Miss Burgess. It is imperative that you get warm. I shall leave you now, so that you may disrobe, but be sure that I shall send to find out how you go on tomorrow.'

'But you also are chilled and wet, my lord.' Eleanor thought perhaps the cold had got to her brain, for it seemed to be working very slowly. 'And I have not thanked you properly for . . .'

He raised a hand to halt her words. 'It is but a swift walk of seven or eight minutes to the castle, and I am used to being out in poor weather, ma'am. Do not concern yourself over me, nor thank me for what were the actions of instinct.' He paused, then added, rather pointedly, 'I would rather that you forgave me for them.'

He bowed, favoured Lady Willoughby with a rather more peremptory nod of the head, and left. As he closed the door, he heard Lady Willoughby demand to know what had happened to the basket.

He strode up the hill at his best pace, and in a confused frame of mind. She had refused him, again, but there was something intangible between them, and he felt it markedly. Yet it was as if some barrier had been placed quite suddenly between them, and she was trying to deny the bond. Should he have told her more? Should he have told her that for a few desperate moments in the water he thought she was lost, and that nothing had ever seemed so hard to contemplate, or that holding her in his arms made his blood race?

He stopped suddenly, and stood stock still.

'I am a fool,' he announced loudly, sending a wood pigeon flapping from the branch of a bare elm. 'I love her.'

He was filled with an exultant glow, which warmed the physical chill of his body, and almost cast away the niggle of worry about what Miss Burgess felt kept her from accepting him. It was a remarkably cheerful peer of the realm who grinned at his butler as he entered the house, and declared himself in need of the hip bath yet again.

'You need not think it contrived, though, Sturry, because I miss water. The Sittford Mill bridge is down. I daresay the increased flow of water has washed at the central support and undercut it.'

'We haven't had so much rain in I don't know how many years, my lord.' Sturry shook his head. 'Not that it would worry us up here, but there was bad flooding better part of a score years back, long before her ladyship came to the Dower House, and into the village too. Five people, including a child, drowned, and quite a few livestock.'

Lord Athelney frowned, his personal happiness forgotten for a moment. 'Then best I send to make sure they have taken precautions.'

'Precautions, my lord? It is surely a matter of fate?'

'Well, the flood itself cannot be prevented, if it comes, but one can attempt to lessen the damage. Door frames can have channelled posts affixed to the outside, into which a panel of wood may be slotted, and if there are then bags of sand or earth placed in front, that can keep out much of the water, as long as it does not come too high.'

'There are some as might do that, my lord, but for others even that cost . . .'

'The estate owns the village. They are my tenants. Since it protects my property, I see it should be covered by the estate.' He sighed suddenly. 'Though I suppose after the event I will have to argue my case with the Trustees.' He shivered. 'Hot water, Sturry, since I do not

172

want to expire before dealing with this matter.'

He handed the butler his damp coat, removed his wet boots and padded, with small squelching noises, up the oak staircase.

CHAPTER TWELVE

ELEANOR WAS TOO MUCH OVERCOME BY the shock of what had happened to respond to Lady Willoughby's questions about the basket, or indeed about what had occurred, beyond repeating, 'The bridge gave way beneath me.' She sat shivering more from the shock than from cold, as though her brain was as numbed as her body. The arrival of maids with warm blankets and the hot brick effectively ended the interrogation. Lady Willoughby could see that she would learn nothing at present, and that Eleanor was indeed incapable rather than obstructive. She therefore gave obvious commands about what should be done, and withdrew, having shown, to her own satisfaction, that she was a most considerate woman.

The maids fussed over Eleanor, though she hardly

registered their presence. She let them remove her wet garments, rub her dry and sit her well wrapped by the fire with a hot brick to her feet, and another, in several layers of shawls, upon her lap for her white hands. She stared into the hearth, and continued to shake.

'There, miss, you sit quiet like, and Emily will bring you hot, sweet tea. You are safe now, miss, safe and warm. Poor miss.'

She mumbled a thank you, and they withdrew, shaking their heads over so near a calamity.

The tea helped, though Eleanor needed both hands to hold the cup, and it chattered against her teeth. Her mind was a maelstrom, like the swirling water, and she tried to grab at thoughts, only for them to spin away. She had been so close to drowning, so very close to death. Her own mortality had never seemed as imminent, and it left her shaken. He had saved her. Without him, she would have been lost. He had risked his own life for her, and then . . . That kiss, it had seemed so meaningful and yet must have been the exuberance of survival, the sheer rush of life. And afterwards, he had not seemed put out by her refusal, not at first. Perhaps it was before it had sunk in, or rather he might have become more distant from choice, realising that his outburst had been a thing of madness, of the moment. He had not meant it; he could not have meant it.

It was amazing how she could lie to herself so successfully.

A lethargy came over her as the shaking lessened. She

was too tired even to lie upon the bed, and fell asleep in the chair, which was where a maid found her some four hours later. She was still very pale, evinced no interest in food, and, though despising herself for such weakness, asked only for assistance to her bed and to be permitted to sleep again. When Lady Willoughby rang to ascertain whether Miss Burgess would be in attendance upon her during the evening, Barwell, with the faintest hint of surprise, declared that Miss Burgess had been helped to her bed, and was now asleep. The look of displeasure upon his mistress's harsh features sent him away to complain to Cook that her ladyship lacked even an ounce of the milk of human kindness.

'You would have thought she would be delighted that the young lady was returned to us alive, but she looked so put out that Miss Burgess could not dance attendance on her I almost expected her to order me to go up and wake the poor soul from her slumbers.'

''Tis not natural, Mr Barwell, and she is as harsh with Miss Charlotte, who is her own flesh and blood. Ice in her veins, that is what she has, nasty, cold ice.'

The next morning Eleanor awoke with a dull headache, and a desire to do nothing. She was aware, however, that she would no longer be allowed the luxury of indisposition, and that Lady Willoughby must be faced. She therefore appeared at the breakfast table, decidedly pale, but in full possession of her faculties. She realised that to Lady Willoughby what had occurred might be seen as designed purely to inconvenience her, and so anticipated any carping on her ladyship's behalf by apologising for her own near death, which Lady Willoughby accepted, graciously, if with some show of reluctance. Eleanor could have laughed out loud. The sheer selfishness of the woman enabled her to view the apology as heartfelt, though it was so ridiculous.

'I shall endeavour not to discommode your ladyship further by any watery mishaps,' she murmured, her eyes downcast to hide the look upon her face.

Barwell, commanding the presentation of eggs and toast, was forced to clear his throat to disguise his grunt of surprise. Charlotte, who was nibbling a slice of bread and butter, frowned very slightly.

'You frequently discommode me, Eleanor. However, on this occasion I accept that you can have had no intention to do so. I sent one of the stable boys to the bridge this morning, as soon as I had arisen, and he confirms that the bridge is entirely gone.'

The implication that the story of the bridge had to be proved made Eleanor clench her hands into fists beneath the table.

'The river was very high when I began to cross on my way to the village, ma'am, but I had no thought that it might suddenly be swept from beneath me. I dimly recall that Lord Athelney was walking down the hill, some distance away, then . . . I did not speak to him, afterwards, with wilful intent to disobey your injunction, ma'am. I believe I said the bridge had given way, which was, of course, patently obvious, but my mind was disordered. Thereafter I may have spoken disjointedly, but my recollections are dim.'

The woman deserved no more than the lie.

Lady Willoughby watched her closely, but could not detect a falsehood.

'In view of which, you shall not be dismissed. The circumstances were unique.' She contrived to sound magnanimous.

'Dismissed, Mama? For falling into the river? I cannot—'

'Finish your breakfast, Charlotte.'

Charlotte's frown remained, though she said no more. It was later in the morning, when Eleanor was on an errand to find a particular shawl that Lady Willoughby desired to protect her from the cold, that she met Charlotte on the stairs, and that damsel eyed her with sympathy.

'I may not be privy to Mama's thoughts, but she cannot have considered sending you away for suffering an accident. There is more. It was because he rescued you. She is still hoping that my cousin will offer for me, isn't she? I do hope he does not. It is not that I dislike him but . . .'

'But?'

'He is very serious, and not in a way I comprehend. Oh, I do not mean that I do not understand what he is saying, but why he should be so. I mean, the Reverend Greenham is very serious, but he must be, being a parson, and giving moral advice. I listen most assiduously every Sunday.'

Eleanor, the daughter of a parson, suppressed a smile. Her dear Papa was indeed a serious man in matters of faith and morality, but was renowned for being far from serious when playing spillikins, or writing acrostics for his daughters to solve. She also did not see Lord Athelney as depressingly serious; indeed, he often appeared to her to have a streak of humour remarkably close to the surface.

'You think that a naval officer ought not to be serious, Charlotte? He has had command of many lives, led men in battle. Such things are serious.'

'Yes, but . . . but he is now Lord Athelney, not a naval officer, so he need not be serious any more.'

Eleanor thought it would take far too long to even try to explain either that one's degree of seriousness was not a garb worn according to profession, nor that Lord Athelney was still a naval officer in attitude and outlook, regardless of his new circumstances. It was tempting to ask her if she felt that a marquis ought to be frivolous. She merely smiled, and would have passed on up the stairs but for Charlotte laying a hand upon her arm.

'I am not clever, Eleanor, nor am I strong enough of will to stand up to Mama, but it does not mean I do not *feel* for you.'

Eleanor was amazed, and also deeply touched. She had never really considered that Charlotte had any insight into her own position as her mother's companion.

'Thank you, dear Charlotte. That is . . . a comfort to me. Now, I really must hurry to fetch your mama's claret paisley shawl, or I shall be in further trouble.'

The collapse of the bridge gave Lady Willoughby much food for thought. That Athelney would have done nothing and watch a woman drown was most unlikely, from what she had come to know of the man, and of course, she reasoned, he was used to water. However, that such a rescue would engender feelings in both rescued and rescuer seemed unpleasantly possible. Eleanor was bound to feel a great degree of gratitude to the man who had saved her life, and it might easily lead to her disobeying her employer's explicit commands. Athelney, whose partiality she did not doubt, would be increasingly dismissive of his duties to his name, and the unthinkable loomed. Forbidding contact to Eleanor could not guarantee, as events had proved, that they should not meet. It was therefore incumbent upon her, for the sake of her daughter's future, and the family name, to make sure that Athelney would dismiss the lowly Eleanor Burgess from his mind once and for all. She set her mind to this admirable task, and found the solution, one which she was sure would work. It only needed her next encounter with her nephew to begin putting the plan into effect.

This was not as swift as she had assumed. Lord Athelney, though keen to find out how Miss Burgess fared following the accident, was conscious of not wishing to seem too pressing, and did not come in person the next day to ask after her well-being. With the groom he also sent an invitation for the Dower House ladies to dine with him at the end of the week, by which time he assumed Miss Burgess would have fully recovered from her misadventure. He himself wanted to get down to the site of the bridge with Mr Bitton and the local carpenter as soon as possible, to assess how long it would take to replace the broken structure.

The carpenter shook his head, and then, as if to stress his point, sucked his teeth.

'My lord, with the winter as it is, I would not care to try and get a span across until a good spell of fair weather. Would be downright dangerous to attempt it.'

'Could you prepare it, ready to assemble as soon as the poor weather abates?' asked Mr Bitton, frowning.

'I could make a fair start, but it would mean paying for something you could not see, if you understand me.'

'That is not a problem. What is a problem is having no bridge here, and anything that will lessen the time we go without will be worth the price.'

'As you wish, my lord.'

'And in the meantime could we arrange a boat ferry, a punt even?' Mr Bitton was thinking hard.

'It would not get enough use to make it viable, Mr Bitton sir, surely? Who would run it?' The carpenter sounded dubious.

'Do we have a craft of any sort, in the village?' Lord Athelney wondered. 'Are there those who fish, perhaps?'

'Them as do, stand upon the bank with rod and line, my lord, and Mr Bitton here should have their names, since this stretch of river is your lordship's and they needs permission.'

The thought ought to have occurred to him, but it had not.

'When there was bad flooding here, years back, how were the villagers rescued?'

'Rescued? Those that could, and had an upstairs room, took themselves up there, aye, and took in neighbours where they could; some went to the bell loft in the church, or to the mill, for there is space there. They went while the water was low enough to wade through, but there was no rescue.'

Lord Athelney frowned. It was not a matter for the carpenter, but, as he and Mr Bitton began to climb the hill again, he voiced his thoughts.

'I own this village. It sounds autocratic, but it is true. I may as well own the occupants, in some ways. The river is very high, and the power of it in spate has already been proven. If the winter is wet, or hard and then there is a thaw, who knows what will happen. They will think me mad, no doubt, and the Trustees will wonder at it, but I want two small boats, they need not be larger than a captain's gig, and we will keep them at the castle, away from too many prying eyes. If needed they can be taken by cart down to the river.'

'There is the stone bridge, though, my lord.'

'Yes, but even such as that may fail, and I am thinking

more of taking those that are stranded to safety. I have already learned of the lives lost last time the village flooded. I want flood boards provided, which can be slotted before every outside doorway, in case there is flooding that does not become too deep, and I would advise your friend at Sittford Parsonage to make contingency plans for the church, to protect anything of value that is susceptible, vestments and the like. Sittford is my responsibility now. Make it so, Mr Bitton.'

'Aye aye, my lord.'

If Lady Willoughby had to wait to set her plans in motion, the waiting meant that she refined them. Her nephew did not like her; she accepted this with equanimity. After all, she did not much care for him either. If she were to simply present him with the full 'facts' he would, quite probably, deny their veracity. Far better she should begin by a drip, drip of insinuation, deft hints that there were things he did not know about Miss Burgess, and combine it with keeping her well out of his way. By the time she was likely to be abroad alone, upon her ladyship's business, the full story would have been revealed, and he would shun her. It was all rather neat, and it was with a feeling of unusual pleasure that she received Lord Athelney in the afternoon, two days after the accident.

'Show him in, Barwell, and tell Miss Burgess I shall not be needing her for the next hour. She ought to lie upon her bed.'

'Yes, my lady.'

Lady Willoughby smoothed a crease in her gown, and sat ramrod straight, for the 'audience'. Lord Athelney entered and made his bow, observing that Miss Burgess was not in her customary attendance.

'I fear she is still far from recovered. She appears robust, but . . . poor child . . .' She left the phrase hanging. 'I know I do not remember often enough, since she puts such a brave face to the world, even to me . . . But there, she would not have pity; she is too proud for that.' If she had sounded unnaturally caring, the last phrase had a genuine bitter edge that lent truth to the whole.

Lord Athelney looked justifiably confused, but gathered that whatever he might ask would be considered inappropriate. Trust a woman, he thought, to say nothing of substance. He therefore made a vague reply, hoping that Miss Burgess might soon be restored to health. He assumed that she had perhaps suffered some illness in the past that left her prone to debility. She certainly struck him as the sort of woman who would dislike having sympathy for what she would account as weakness. It made sound enough sense. He was disappointed, since he had hoped to see her for himself, even if he was unable to exchange any words in private with her. He could not admit that finding out her condition was the prime motive for his visit, though he gauged Lady Willoughby realised that it was so. He therefore launched into details, which he knew would mean little to his hostess, about the reinstatement of the bridge when circumstance permitted, and concluded by repeating his invitation to the Dower House ladies to dine with him three days hence, on the Friday evening, by which time he assumed Eleanor Burgess would have taken up her companion duties once more. He could not see Lady Willoughby doing without her for longer than completely necessary. He left no better informed than at his arrival, and did not see the smile, one which lengthened the thin line of Lady Willoughby's lips, as the door closed behind him.

'That, my boy, was not the seed of doubt, but merely a tilling of the ground into which it is to be sown,' she murmured, well satisfied. 'Men have so little guile.'

When the clock indicated that Eleanor had enjoyed her hour of repose, Lady Willoughby requested that she come downstairs to take tea, and called also for her daughter. Both answered the summons out of habit and without pleasure. Eleanor, surprised to have been given an hour off duty, could have profitably taken a second, and Charlotte, who had ostensibly been embroidering slippers for her mama for Christmas, even though she knew they would receive cool thanks, be set aside, and never touch that lady's feet, had in fact curled up on a sofa in the former nursery, and read, most avidly, the opening chapters of a Gothic romance, lent to her covertly by Lady Steventon's elder daughter. Her head was still swimming with images of ivy-clad ruins, and a heroine of saintly, if cloying virtue, who was on the point of being ensnared in the trap of a villain of such turpitude that she had actually shuddered, and wrapped her shawl more tightly about her person, despite the cosy fire.

'There you are, at last.' It was not clear which of the two young ladies was being addressed, or if, indeed, it applied to them both. 'You may pour tea, Eleanor, and less milk than last time. I am not a cat.'

The thought occurred to Eleanor that she was more of a serpent, but she nodded and obeyed the instruction, passing the delicate china to Lady Willoughby and then to Charlotte before pouring herself a cup with a hand that, she noted with annoyance, had the slightest of tremors.

'Athelney has paid a call, my love, to invite us to dine at the castle on Friday. I hope that mark to which I drew your attention on your black silk has been removed.'

Eleanor felt that the 'us' did not include her, but it was unclear.

'Yes, Mama, I had Dorothy attend to it as soon as I took it off the other evening.'

'At what time do you want the carriage ordered, Lady Willoughby?' Eleanor enquired.

'A quarter to six, if you please. We shall not be back very late, I am sure, but I do not need you to wait up for me.' Lady Willoughby smiled, and the smile said everything, except for one rather vital point. Eleanor was left wondering whether Lord Athelney had specifically not invited her, or whether Lady Willoughby had chosen to act as if that was the case.

CHAPTER THIRTEEN

HAVING INVITED THE DOWER HOUSE LADIES to dinner, Lord Athelney panicked, and decided that an evening with only Mr Bitton for support would not be likely to permit him the opportunity to speak with Miss Burgess. Lady Willoughby would be sure to do everything to keep him from speech with her. As a private dinner it would be difficult to invite a man without a wife, and he knew of no useful widowers in the vicinity. He might just help the odds by inviting the Reverend Greenham and his sister. There would be more conversation, and the numbers would still be too small to necessitate speaking formally only to the persons on each side, which would mean him talking solely with the two Hawksmoor ladies, which was an unpleasant prospect.

He was fortunate in that Miss Greenham was on her way to the castle with a package containing the curtains for Mr Bitton's bedchamber. It was actually rather heavy as she toiled up the hill with it clasped to her bosom. By the time she arrived she was very pink of cheek and said bosom was heaving slightly. Mr Bitton, mulling over a knotty problem in the constable's chamber and looking down into the courtyard, saw her appear almost beneath him, and hurried down to meet her and take the load from her.

'Miss Greenham, surely you have not come up here carrying such a burden?' He sounded shocked.

'I assure you, sir, these are the small curtains for your bedchamber, and if it had not been so windy and damp, carrying them would not have been a hardship.'

'You are therefore admitting that it was. Let me have them, ma'am.'

He held out his arms, smiling at her in a way that increased her heart rate far more than the ascent of the hill. She blushed, and handed over the parcel. He faked it being exceptionally heavy, half staggering, and she laughed softly.

'Really, Mr Bitton. You must not think me what I am not . . . Weak and feeble.'

'I do not think of you in such a light, Miss Greenham. I think you . . .' He gulped down the sudden words that came unbidden into his head. 'I think you industrious, and far, far too kind to an undeserving sailor.'

It was more than he really ought to say, and far less

than he felt at that moment. She looked up at him, a little shyly, but a dimple peeped.

'But, sir, I do it for these ancient walls, and to put me in the good graces of the local seigneur.' She gave the lie to the words with her deepened blush.

Harry Bitton, standing in the castle courtyard on a damp, cold December day, felt as if bathed in the warmth of a balmy summer. They stood, lost in a very private moment, in a far from private place, and only the arrival of Lord Athelney under the arch broke the spell.

'Miss Greenham, do you read minds?'

'My lord?'

'I was but thinking that you and your brother ought to dine with us again. Would Friday be too soon? At six? I will send the carriage again, of course.'

'I . . . I am sure we would be honoured, my lord. I do not believe we have any other engagements, for we rarely go out. I must ask my brother, of course, but I think I may say that unless he sends to say it is not possible, then we will be pleased to dine.'

'Excellent, I am most reliev—delighted.'

'Relieved, my lord?' Miss Greenham quizzed him, as he looked uncomfortable. 'Have you inadvertently ordered the roasting of an ox and fear to be overwhelmed by food?'

'Worse, Miss Greenham. I have invited Lady Willoughby to dine and dread the idea of myself and Mr Bitton here facing her all evening on our own.' He smiled ruefully. 'Cowardice, undoubtedly.'

'I have never seen myself as a shield. How novel!' Miss Greenham did not appear affronted in the least. 'It is clearly my duty to defend you helpless gentlemen.'

A gust of wind brought her hand, instinctively, to her bonnet.

'This is no place for you to stand and become chilled, ma'am.' Mr Bitton was concerned. 'Do you wish to go into the house with his lordship and . . .'

'I came with curtains, sir. I wish to complete my task and see them hung and check I have them right. Old windows are often not quite true, and the illusion of being level is very important. I made them square enough, but that may look all wrong.'

'Then may I suggest a compromise, ma'am,' interposed Lord Athelney. 'By all means go and see that they hang true, but then both of you must come and take refreshment in the morning room. You have been in your eyrie since early this morning, Mr Bitton, for I saw the light of candles in the chamber above, it was so gloomy.'

He made his bow again and strode off across the courtyard. Mr Bitton ushered Miss Greenham into the gatehouse, and took up a short ladder from the lumber room. The constable's chamber was positively welcoming. The newly upholstered chairs, the smart hangings and the presence of the steward's ledgers, maps and books upon the great refectory table and in a deep bookcase, and a good fire in the hearth, made it, if not homely, at least very lived in and alive.

'What a transformation, is it not, Mr Bitton?' Miss

Greenham could not quite keep the edge of pride from her voice.

'Remarkable, ma'am. Is it just as you envisaged it would be?'

'Better, I assure you.'

'Well, the credit is all yours. I feel most at home here, and look forward to being able not just to work, but live within the thick walls.' He opened the door on the far side of the chamber. 'You will see that the holes in the floor have been mended. You might hold a dance here in safety.'

'Do you know, I have never attended a dance where one worried about falling through the floor,' she confided. 'It would have added a certain excitement, do you not think?' She wondered at herself, being so merry. 'It will look very different furnished. Whilst never the lightest of chambers, it could become quite cosy. If the furniture is placed well, the narrowness compared to length will not seem so obvious.'

Harry Bitton watched her, unselfconscious, imagining. In the gloomy chamber she seemed to have a glow of vitality that lit it. After years at sea, in confined, dark quarters, and with little personal space, he would be quite content to have warmth, a comfortable chair, a small table, and light. He looked at the four thick walls and saw a chamber; she saw a home. He thought it charming, sweet.

'The upper chamber is likewise made good. Ma'am, the curtains for my chamber . . . Should you feel it improper to be there, with only my presence . . . I would, if you prefer, take them and hang them, and report back so that you might go up alone?'

'I . . . Mr Bitton, do you think me wicked if I say there is no reason why I might not in trust enter the same chamber with you? I trust you, sir. Where there is no evil intended, surely there can be no wrong. Now, lead on, sir, and let us see these curtains in their rightful place.'

'Aye aye, ma'am.'

He led the way, and in the bedchamber, which he reassured her was spider free, he stood upon the ladder rungs and hung the curtains as she directed. She stood back, eyes slightly narrowed as she assessed the horizontal.

'They will do, yes, very well. You know, I am really most pleased with them. There is now but the need for a counterpane for the bed to match them and this will indeed be fit, though I think the fire should be lit here when you are working below, and it will make the room so much the better. I think you will be half here, half there, in the main house, a little longer.'

'I do not expect to be here until after the Christmas period. Lord Athelney has said I might go to Shepton and choose some furnishings, and a new mattress. I . . . Perhaps if your brother is free, you and he might accompany me there. I was never any good at shopping. I usually enter a shop, ask for such and such an item and hand over the money. If I am required to choose . . . There's the problem. It is a great advantage of naval uniform.' He smiled, and she smiled up at him.

'You might get down from the ladder now, sir. I only say so, because otherwise my neck may ache with gazing upwards.'

'Oh, yes, yes of course.'

He stepped down, though the ladder wobbled slightly as he did so, and she instinctively held out her arm to steady him. His hand lay upon it only for a moment, and in that moment their eyes met. Then both became embarrassed.

'I shall ask Septimus about a trip to Shepton. He should be able to give an answer on Friday, Mr Bitton.'

'Friday, yes, Friday.' He stumbled over the words as if confused. 'Now, let me escort you into the house, and you can be warm again, and his lordship will have you conveyed back to the parsonage in the tilbury.'

Lord Athelney found himself urging the clock to advance the hour more quickly as Friday afternoon dragged by. Dressing for dinner, he felt even more than normally clumsy when tying his neckcloth in an accepted mode, and paced the drawing room before the first of his guests was announced. Mr Bitton watched and wondered. The signs he saw were of his captain in agitation. The frown that creased his lordship's brow lifted as Sturry opened the door, but the smile of welcome lost its warmth as Lady Willoughby Hawksmoor and Miss Hawksmoor were announced, and those two ladies entered the room.

He wanted to ask the most important question

immediately. Where was Miss Burgess? There were, however, the polite and insincere formalities that had to be gone through first. It was therefore some minutes later when he, with every appearance of mere casual enquiry, asked why that lady had not accompanied them up the hill. Before Lady Willoughby could answer, the door opened once more and the Reverend Greenham and Miss Greenham were announced. Lady Willoughby bristled, and cast her host a look of reproach. That she and Charlotte had been invited to dine was perfectly fitting, but that it should be in the company of the village parson and his pert sister was an affront. She smiled graciously, but her eyes looked daggers.

Mr Bitton, failing to take his eyes from the beauty of Miss Greenham, saw that young lady lift her chin and give back a gaze that was both composed and unimpressed. *Good for Miss Greenham*, he thought.

Lady Willoughby utilised the time before the announcement of dinner to direct a monologue at the parson, indicating her displeasure at the recent egalitarianism of his sermons. Mr Bitton treacherously took post at Miss Greenham's side, and Lord Athelney, the concern at Miss Burgess's absence still gnawing away at him, attempted to engage his cousin in conversation, but found her monosyllabic, and with her eye upon her mama and the reverend, presumably lest her mother cast her dreaded gaze upon her. It was only as Lady Willoughby took his arm for him to lead her into dinner that he repeated his question about her ladyship's companion.

'La, of course, I was about to tell you, was I not, when your other guests,' she dropped her voice disapprovingly, 'arrived. Poor Eleanor said that she really did not feel up to mee—going out, just yet. She said she had the headache still, though she appeared much recovered yesterday.' Lady Willoughby sounded perplexed by the sudden relapse.

Lord Athelney said nothing. She could not face him? Why? Had his proposal, when looked upon calmly, seemed so outrageous? Had the stolen kiss assumed the enormity of a crime? He wanted to see her, explain to her, and both were denied him. The evening's pleasure, which had foundered upon the reef of disappointment from the moment of her non-appearance, now became a torment. Yet as host he had to maintain the veneer of hospitality and interest, even as his mind worked itself into knots.

Lady Willoughby and Miss Hawksmoor were seated on either side of him. Septimus Greenham was placed on her ladyship's other side, opposite his friend, and Miss Greenham sat next to the lieutenant. With great presence of mind, Sturry had rearranged the placings when it had become clear that the number was to be even. It was an easier and more pleasingly symmetrical arrangement, but Lord Athelney, whenever he glanced along the table and saw Miss Greenham's open, intelligent face, saw in his mind Miss Burgess, as she had been at the fateful dinner.

On this occasion, Lady Willoughby did not make

mention of the seating, since it suited her very well to be opposite her daughter, commanding with her steely glare, and even a well-aimed foot, to make appropriate conversation with her cousin. Since his lordship was, despite his best attempts, preoccupied, she found this extremely difficult.

The Reverend Greenham, observing her patent discomfiture, first attempted to distract her ladyship in conversation, which earned him a grateful look from Miss Hawksmoor, and a snub from Lady Willoughby, and was then bold enough to speak across the table to the nervous Charlotte. Miss Hawksmoor had been warned not to 'waste her breath' upon Mr Bitton, 'that hapless sailor', but had not been specifically commanded not to converse with the parson. In a daring move, for which she fully expected to pay thereafter, she answered his question upon the idea for a Sunday school at the church, and Anne Greenham, finding her brother pressing his foot to hers beneath the table, immediately joined the conversation. Lady Willoughby and Lord Athelney were left to desultory speech while the younger members about the table exchanged anecdotes of their own youthful experience of the scriptures. Mr Bitton might be said to have won the day with the tale of how, at the age of six, the governess had sat down to teach him and his three brothers about the appearance of the Lord in the locked room after the Resurrection.

'She told us the story, and then asked how we thought Jesus got into the chamber when the door was locked shut. My younger brother, James, said it was simple, and that Jesus had climbed through the keyhole.' This had drawn scorn from his older brothers, the elder of whom had just returned from his first term at school, who denounced Jimmy as a fool because Jesus could not have got through the keyhole if the key was in the lock. He had taken his younger brother's side, largely out of habit, and shortly afterwards, a fraternal fight ensued. 'We did not have a governess long after that.'

Septimus grinned at his friend. 'What a pack of heathens you were.'

'Not at all, my dear fellow. We were simply continuing a very theological discussion in . . . a physical way.'

'Remind me not to enter into a theological discussion with you from the pulpit. No doubt you will bring out a grappling iron, climb up into the pulpit and assault me.'

'Not I,' declared Harry Bitton, looking virtuous, 'for I distinctly remember being told that grappling irons are, like swords, not permitted in the church. I would have to leave it in the porch.'

Miss Hawksmoor giggled softly, and Lady Willoughby, attending with half an ear, and both annoyed and a little out of her depth in the face of this gentle banter, brought the conversation back to the present, in a firm tone.

'If there is to be Sunday school, and I have to say I thought that such a thing was the invention of non-conformists, then Miss Burgess, as the daughter of a clergyman, and being older than Miss Greenham, ought to take it. I shall inform her that it will be part of her duties from henceforth.'

Charlotte Hawksmoor opened her mouth to say something, but thought better of rebelling twice in one evening, and merely gave the parson a look of apology.

Lord Athelney, in an increasing repressed atmosphere, could only be glad when Lady Willoughby decided that the ladies would withdraw, and once the gentlemen were safely alone, heaved a great sigh of relief.

'I assure you it is with the deepest sincerity that I paraphrase the Litany and say, "From terrible aunts, and the caustic tongues thereof, good Lord deliver us".'

'Amen,' came the answer in unison.

Looking back upon it, Charlotte Hawksmoor thought she had learned so very much from the evening, not least that her mama could be faced with equanimity. Anne Greenham was not bound as Eleanor Burgess was, with the threat of dismissal an ever-present sword of Damocles above her head. Only her sense of Christian duty and good manners kept her from treating her ladyship with coolness bordering upon disgusted disdain, but she remained entirely unmoved by Lady Willoughby's display of rudeness, and rose above it with aplomb, which left Charlotte marvelling. That her mama had acted beyond the bounds of civility made Charlotte wince. The three of them had sat in the drawing room, and whilst Charlotte would have loved to have enjoyed chatter with a young woman her own age, Lady Willoughby had obviously decided that Charlotte should be kept from forming any friendship with Miss Greenham, and first interrupted, then effectively suffocated, their nascent conversation.

'Charlotte will make changes here, once she has the running of the castle.' It was a bald statement, intended to surprise. 'I hear you are acting as a seamstress for the steward's quarters, Miss Greenham. You would be advised not to waste your energies upon any changes within the house.'

'I assure you, Lady Willoughby, I have no intention of doing so.' Miss Greenham did not rise to the bait.

'I suppose you have had to undertake needlework out of necessity. Did you make that gown?'

'Yes, for I did not choose to go out in the aftermath of my father's death, and it was good occupation. It is also simple, and I know my limitations. Most of my gowns would be beyond my skills.' She smiled innocently.

Without saying anything specific she had informed Lady Willoughby Hawksmoor that she did not habitually wear homemade dresses. This was true, but there was a caveat that she did not reveal. The dresses of which she spoke had been purchased while she was 'the bishop's daughter'. As 'the parson's sister', she would not be visiting stylish modistes. Her inheritance was, at her father's instruction, to be her dowry, and she did not want her brother, who would no doubt one day have a family of his own to support upon his stipend and his own inheritance, paying for what she termed 'fancy furbelows'. The pretty gowns she had folded neatly in tissue paper would emerge once she left off her mourning, but would not be augmented by fashionable purchases. This, Lady Willoughby need not know.

Lady Willoughby's eyes narrowed. She was not fooled by word or look. Miss Greenham held herself far too high; how dare she look her so boldly in the eye.

'You should have seen the gowns my dear Charlotte wore last year at her come-out. Provincial dressmakers are all very well, but for the most fashionable attire, London is the only possible place.'

'Yes, indeed, ma'am. Did you prefer Madame Fanchon or Madame Corneille? My Aunt Eliza recommended the former for her cutting, and I think she was quite correct. Decoration can be altered, but a badly cut gown will never work.'

Charlotte bit her lip so hard it hurt.

Lady Willoughby knew she ought not, but could not resist enquiring. 'Your Aunt Eliza?'

'Yes. I do not suppose you are acquainted with her, are you? She is now, alas, the Dowager Countess of Winterburn. My poor uncle died last year.' The innocent look was now even more pronounced.

Lady Willoughby looked sour. She did not know Lady Winterburn, but had been in her own first Season when that lady had become betrothed. She therefore knew just who Miss Greenham's connections were.

Miss Greenham's eyes danced, though she kept her countenance. Lady Willoughby was so easy to read.

Charlotte was in awe. She would not have the courage, or the quick wits, to say such things, but it did her good

200

to know that Mama could be bested.

It was at this point that the gentlemen rejoined them. Septimus Greenham observed his sister closely. Her smile as she turned to him had a brittle quality that he knew from childhood. An eyebrow was raised a fraction, and the smile lengthened.

'Here you are, brother dear.'

He knew for sure. Her tone was the final proof. He looked at Lady Willoughby. Her cheeks flew two slightly heightened spots of colour. Lord Athelney was also observant, and secretly applauded Miss Greenham. Mr Bitton was only interested in Miss Greenham, and would have applauded her simply for handing him the cup of tea, which she did when that beverage was brought in a few minutes later.

Charlotte retired as soon as she and her parent reached the Dower House. Lady Willoughby was too engrossed in going over the events in her mind, and rerunning the conversations in her mind but with her very clever responses trumping those of the impertinent Miss Greenham.

Charlotte let her maid undress her without comment, claiming tiredness, though in fact she was feeling most awake. In recent days she would have not blown out the candle until she had read another chapter of her borrowed novel, but tonight she did not want to read it. She had no interest in the dark-haired, brooding hero, or the simpering heroine. She had been in the presence of the clever Miss Greenham, and her brother, who had seen her under pressure and come to her aid, a true hero in the real world. He was a man of principle, of high morals, and rather nice, wavy, golden hair. She sighed, and closed her eyes, while smiling.

Eleanor Burgess would have enjoyed her evening of peace, had her employer been dining anywhere else. As it was she had taken supper in her room, and retired early to lie in her bed, and not sleep. Instead she lay there, wondering why she had not been invited, for that was the impression that Lady Willoughby had given. It seemed unlike Lord Athelney to be petty. Had he reflected, and been hurt more than he had shown, by her reaction to his offer? She would like to explain to him, except she could not explain to herself. It was thought-provoking, and sleep-depriving.

CHAPTER FOURTEEN

THE MORNING BROUGHT NO LIGHT UPON that matter, but at breakfast Lady Willoughby informed her that she was to go to the parsonage and be told by the Reverend Greenham about his plans for the Sunday school. Eleanor, who liked the parson, felt even more left out when she discovered he and his sister had been dining at the castle.

'I immediately put you forward, since you are eminently suited to the task, Eleanor. An education in the scriptures is a good foundation for even the most lowly and otherwise uneducable of children. That way they gain morals, and learn their place in the world, the place into which the Almighty has set them.'

Having heard Septimus Greenham's sermons, Eleanor thought that this was far from his intention, but kept quiet.

'It is not raining so very hard this morning, so you may go before luncheon.'

'May I accompany her, Mama?' enquired Charlotte.

Lady Willoughby blinked at her daughter in surprise. 'What on earth for, Charlotte? You will get damp feet, and you have nothing to do with such things.'

'Should I not have some knowledge for the future, to see how things should be done? In case I should be in the same position as you, Mama, at some point.'

'I ought not need to remind you, child, that you are to be the Marchioness of Athelney, and since the provision of a Sunday school here will have been established by those of suitable degree, there is no possible reason for you to go out. You may continue to work upon the embroidery of my slippers.'

Charlotte cast Eleanor a look of mingled regret and apology. When Eleanor was upstairs, putting on her pelisse and bonnet, she knocked upon her door, and entered shyly.

'I am sorry I cannot go with you, Eleanor. Whatever my position in life, I think I ought . . . But . . . Please tell the Reverend Greenham that I would have come, had it been permitted. It was so interesting, at dinner, listening to him, and Miss Greenham, who is clever and oh, if you had heard her with Mama . . .' She giggled. 'She said nothing impolite, but Mama was bested at every turn when we ladies withdrew. Mr Bitton and my cousin were both impressed, for they heard the latter part of their interchanges when they joined us. I wish I had the cleverness, and the courage also, to be brave with Mama, but I have not.' She sighed. 'I had best get downstairs quickly, or she will berate me for being slow. I do so wish . . .' She smiled, and closed the door behind her.

Eleanor toiled up the hill to join the road by the castle, for the path that ran about the bottom of the hill past the Dower House and to the stone bridge and road was now easily more than ankle-deep in mud. She glanced through the archway of the gatehouse as she passed, but saw nobody. The journey downhill was easy and swift, with wind and drizzle in some part kept from her by the wood on the westerly side. She arrived at the parsonage at a little before eleven of the clock, and tugged the bell, listening to its jangling echo through the passages. The manservant came to the door, and, on hearing her request to speak with the Reverend Greenham, informed her that he was not yet returned from a visit to one of his parishioners, but that Miss Greenham would surely be pleased to entertain Miss Burgess in the morning room if she would kindly follow him. He showed her into the cosy, square chamber, with its cheeringly crackling fire, and she warmed her hands before it until Anne Greenham, who had been counting the jars of pickled beetroot and other preserved items in the larder with Cook, had removed her apron, patted her hair into place, and entered with a smile. She greeted the visitor, sent the servant for tea, and invited Miss Burgess to seat herself by the fire.

'I do not think my brother expected you, I am so sorry. There was no suggestion last night that the Sunday school would be started immediately, although I am sure Septimus would be delighted if it commenced before Christmas. I should add that I believe he brought up the subject merely to assist Miss Hawksmoor, who was making heavy weather of conversing with Lord Athelney.' She frowned. 'I do not know why that should be so, for he always appears to me to be a very approachable gentleman, never one to flaunt his rank, with a fine sense of humour, and most generous.'

While Eleanor was in complete agreement with this reading of his lordship's character, she felt illogically piqued that it should also be the view of another young lady.

'You know, I feel rather guilty, Miss Burgess, for it is I who ought to take Sunday school. My brother would have asked me to do so, but Lady Willoughby was so determined that you should have the running of it, and you are, of course, the more senior. She said your father is a man of the cloth?'

'Yes, a parish in Cheshire.'

'Then we are both "daughters of the rectory", so to speak. I . . . I hope we may become good friends, Miss Burgess. There are few ladies of our own age in the vicinity, and it is clear that however much I might also care for friendship with Miss Hawksmoor, her ladyship views me as a social mushroom, and will do everything to keep our contact to a minimum.' She smiled wryly.

'Lady Willoughby Hawksmoor brings out all that is least charitable in me. Perhaps I ought not to say so to you . . .'

'Oh, do not think that I should be offended, Miss Greenham. Circumstance places me in her household, not choice, and I perfectly understand.'

'One ought to turn the other cheek, and be generous of spirit.'

'One ought, but it is, I assure you, almost impossible. She is my employer, and thus I should limit my comments upon her character, but be sure that I do not hold her in esteem in any way. Had I any other choice of employment . . .' She halted, as the voice in her head reminded her that she had twice been offered an alternative. *Being a marchioness is not employment*, she told herself sternly, to which the voice replied with a sigh that it was not indeed; it was infinitely more appealing. 'Miss Hawksmoor, who wished very much she might accompany me this morning, reported in great delight that you had, and I quote, "bested" her mama.'

'Oh dear, was it that obvious? I really tried not to say anything other than the truth.'

'The truth can be unpalatable, especially to one with so little interest in it as Lady Willoughby.'

Encouraged by Eleanor's frankness, Anne Greenham recounted the words that had passed between herself and Lady Willoughby Hawksmoor after dinner. Eleanor could not but smile, but Miss Greenham's concluding comment was less welcome.

'It is clear poor Miss Hawksmoor is being almost

thrown at Lord Athelney, but equally obvious that she would not suit him nor he her. He is every inch the naval officer, and I cannot see such a man liking indecision. Miss Hawksmoor seems sweet-tempered, but I am sure you will say she has been allowed no liberty to develop a character of her own. I came across militia officers, when I was younger, but there is something about a naval gentleman that is different, a quiet self-confidence rather than arrogance. Even their garb is less showy, and yet elegant.' She blushed slightly.

Eleanor felt as if something was being snatched from her – in fact, two things. She would like to be this young woman's friend, and yet here she was extolling the virtues of Lord Athelney, clearly interested in him, and had not Charlotte said how he had been impressed with her manner when faced by Lady Willoughby? The woman she wanted as a friend was greater than just a rival. Would not her own faint-heartedness, on top of her double refusal, mark her as no longer worthy of regard? Yes, he had offered marriage, but not from some deep passion. In such a case, why should he not focus upon a better woman, a woman unafraid? She told herself she had no right to feel as if he was hers in any way at all, and yet here, and now, she claimed him in her heart, when it was too late. She could not go to him, fall upon his chest and say she had been foolish to refuse him, say that she had done it for his own sake. She had, in fairness, to stand back, and let another woman into his heart, but she did not want to be fair. She wanted to make him want her again, even if it left him torn. She most certainly did not want to stand back and be noble.

'Miss Burgess, are you unwell? You look quite pale.'

'No, I am . . . Had you not heard that when the Sittford bridge collapsed, I was in the middle of it? Lord Athelney saved me from drowning. I am perhaps a little . . . fragile still.'

'He . . . oh, I had not heard. That must have been why you were not at dinner last night. Lord Athelney did not mention it, but then, as I say, it would not be his manner. How brave! How daring! How fortunate that he was there! And yet you came all this way this morning. Poor Miss Burgess. I shall tell Septimus he simply has to drive you back.'

'Oh no, please, I did not say that for sympathy, merely to explain.'

Miss Greenham was, however, clearly shocked at the news, and would not rescind her decision.

Septimus Greenham came into the room a minute or so later, solemn-faced, for his pastoral duty had been to a sickbed that showed every likelihood of becoming a deathbed within the next couple of days. He smiled, a little perfunctorily at first, as his sister explained Miss Burgess's visit.

'The Sunday school. Yes, of course. My apologies, Miss Burgess, for I had not thought you would be so quick to become engaged in the project.'

'Lest you think me a woman with some mission, sir, I ought to say that while I have taught a scripture class in Father's parish, at times, and I support your idea, the swiftness of my arrival upon your doorstep is entirely due to the fact that Lady Willoughby instructed me to come this morning.'

'Oh dear. She is rather dictatorial, is she not.'

'"Tyrannical" would be my preferred term, but yes. However, if a Sunday school is to be established here, then it might as well be commenced as soon as possible, even if it is only with me telling religious stories to the children. It would take place before matins?'

'Yes, that would be my intention, Miss Burgess, with the class seated together for the service.'

'Are you intending that it be moral instruction alone, or some practical education in letters and counting also?'

'Well, I think it would be a splendid thing if every child in this parish could sign the register when they marry, as opposed to leaving their mark, at the very least. Ignorance is not a state in which those who are not born fortunate, as we have been, should be forced to remain.'

'You had best not say that to Lady Willoughby, or my services will be withdrawn in an instant. I am sure she sees it as instilling a sense of their lowly position and how to respect their betters.'

'She indicated as much.' He nodded.

'But, forgive me, the most important voice will be Lord Athelney's, and he is most unlike her ladyship in attitude,' Anne Greenham interjected. 'His career has brought him into contact with the common sailor, who is largely ignorant. He has far more experience of the poorly educated than most gentlemen of his rank.'

'And from what he has said to me, I think he would be whole-heartedly behind a scheme that would enable self-improvement. But you are quite right, Anne. I ought to discuss the details with him as soon as it is convenient. The teaching of biblical stories is a start that will be quite unexceptional. If I were to pass the word about the village, might we begin this very Sunday, an hour before matins? I could have a bell rung, and everyone could meet here, or rather in the study. I do not think it would be too crowded.'

'Yes, I . . . Yes, of course. Do you wish to set the text or story for the week?'

'Since it is the third Sunday of Advent, perhaps you could talk about John the Baptist.'

Eleanor wondered how she might do this for an hour, but kept the thought to herself.

'Miss Burgess, if her ladyship could spare you on Tuesday, we might . . .'

'Not Tuesday, Septimus. You forget that Tuesday we are going to Shepton to help choose furnishings for the castle.'

'Oh yes, let us say Wednesday then. In fact, rather than you have to travel here, perhaps I might come to the Dower House and discuss plans with you. That will mean that I have time to see Lord Athelney on Monday, or at worst on Tuesday.'

Eleanor agreed, and said that she ought to be able to give a time and confirmation on the morrow after church.

What was swirling in her head was that Miss Greenham was helping to choose furnishings for the castle. Lord Athelney was already so much at ease with her that he felt he could ask for her assistance in the decoration of his own home.

Lady Willoughby was feeling very pleased with herself. Her prime reason for pushing Miss Burgess forward as the Sunday school teacher was to remove her from the box pew where she might be in dangerous proximity to Lord Athelney. When Eleanor returned from the parsonage looking preoccupied, she came to the half correct conclusion that his lordship was the cause. However, she believed it to be because Eleanor had realised that she was to be kept from him, when in fact she was facing the more unpalatable thought that whatever place she might just have held in his affections was being taken by a woman she could not even have the satisfaction of legitimately disliking.

From misery, Eleanor moved to anger. If he thought so highly of her that he had asked for her hand, how could he so swiftly place another on such a footing? Women were accused of being fickle, but this . . . She roused herself from gloom to righteous wrath, and it was a good thing that the Sunday school theme was not 'turning the other cheek'.

Lady Willoughby, when the gentlemen from the castle joined the Dower House ladies in the pew on Sunday morning, saw the sudden realisation of Miss Burgess's absence strike her nephew, and smiled in a most unpleasant way.

'Dear Eleanor has charge of the children this morning, of course. She will be bringing them in to sit at the back of the church. My only real concern is that being so close to them might bring infestation into the Dower House. I certainly would not do as the Reverend Greenham has done and invite the peasantry into my home. I hope he has removed all valuable items from view.'

Her opinion of the villagers was patently that they were disease-ridden and of dubious honesty. Lord Athelney did not vouchsafe a response, and Mr Bitton, who knew his moods very well, saw the way he stiffened and grew distant. From his position it would be impossible for Lord Athelney to see the Sunday school group enter the church without looking back over his shoulder, which would be very obvious. Had he done so he would have seen a very erect young woman with an unusually serious expression. Throughout the service he was aware of her presence, and hoped to have the opportunity of at the very least a few words with her at its conclusion, but, unusually for Lady Willoughby, who normally wanted to delay everyone by giving her distillation of the sermon back to the clergyman, she whisked her party to her carriage with barely a nod to the Reverend Greenham. He caught Miss Burgess's eye for one fleeting moment, and where he would have expected to see humorous mutual understanding he found only a cool acknowledgement. He returned to the castle in uncommunicative mood, and withdrew to his library to brood.

Mr Bitton had not had more than a few words with Miss Greenham or his friend, but was cheered by the news that they would be happy to go to Shepton on Tuesday, and he, at least, could contemplate his luncheon in excellent spirits.

The Reverend Greenham had hoped to pay a call upon Lord Athelney on the Monday, but was called back to the bedside of his ailing parishioner. When he and his sister arrived at the castle on Tuesday morning, he got down and left Harry Bitton talking to his sister, and went to at least arrange the chance to talk to the marquis in the near future. His lordship, having heard the arrival, was in fact on his way out to assure Miss Greenham that she need not be excessively cautious in her purchases for the gatehouse. When he and the parson met, he listened and made a swift decision.

'I have nothing pressing today. In fact, I have far too little most days, truth to tell. I shall come to Shepton with you, which will enable you to discuss the Sunday school with me, and if I am present, Miss Greenham may secure my approval for her selections without worrying if she has made the right choices. Come into the house, briefly, while Fittleton puts the horses to, and the stable boy can put your equipage in the stables.'

This was seen to be an excellent plan, not least by Mr Bitton, who shortly found himself facing Miss Greenham, and making conversation with her all the way to the town, while parson and landowner discussed education. He had expected to have to ride beside the parson's gig. This was so very much better. She was in the happiest of moods, since being able to select furniture and furnishings was undeniably exciting to a young woman who had for years lived with what was in situ, even if this was not for her own home.

'Mr Bitton, you must tell me your preferences. You will, won't you? I would hate to find myself making choices that I like, but that you find objectionable. Please say that you will tell me.'

'I cannot think that view could be worth having, ma'am. You forget that I have not had to choose anything in the way of household stuffs. I am used to blue, you may say that.'

'So when it comes to rugs, I may say, "That one please, since the colour will be familiar"?' Miss Greenham bit her lip.

'You may, with pleasure.'

'And do you have any preferences in chairs and tables?'

'I like them to have four legs, and not to rock.'

'That will undoubtedly limit us, sir.'

They smiled at each other.

The conversation between her brother and Lord Athelney lacked levity, but was most constructive. Athelney listened as Septimus Greenham expounded upon the ignorance in rural communities.

'Lady Willoughby would no doubt see education

as dangerous, since if the poor gain learning they may aspire to being more than their forefathers, and lose sight of their position in the "natural order".'

'My only doubts would be that for those who did not achieve those aspirations there might be discontent and disappointment, but then is not disappointment one of the things we have to learn to face in life? No, giving opportunity to the youth of Sittford is an excellent notion, and if, upon occasion, there is a youth who shows real promise, I might offer a scholarship to the school in Wells.' Lord Athelney paused. 'You say Miss Burgess will take the class every week?'

'Yes, though my sister would happily share the task, I know. We shall see how it develops.'

Lord Athelney thought a division of the labour a good idea, not least because it would at least place Miss Burgess back in the pew more regularly.

'If this Sunday school is to be schooling in a regular manner, then you will need a blackboard, slates and chalk. We can arrange for their provision in Shepton, at my expense. And for every child that learns to read, to the satisfaction of the teacher, there shall be the reward of a book.'

It was in happy accord that the party arrived in Shepton Mallet.

Lord Athelney was not particularly interested in the choosing of furniture for his steward's private quarters, but knew that if he approved the expenditure, Miss Greenham would be spared any feelings of guilt.

He was more interested in watching his erstwhile first lieutenant in the throes of love. What amazed him was that Septimus Greenham seemed unaware of what was clearly a mutual attraction between his sister and his friend. Miss Greenham was circumspect. She did not give in to the temptation to focus all her attention upon Mr Bitton, but he did see the half smile play about her mouth when she watched him in conversation with her brother, and the spark between them when they had occasion to talk together. He had both liking and respect for Harry Bitton, and thought it a good match in character and personality, though her ancestry and his current position might seem to make it an unequal one. However, from what little he had read about the advances in agriculture in the last thirty years he could see that the management of an estate the size of Kingscastle, making it more efficient and profitable, and using it to best advantage, was not a menial position, and ought to be one of greater weight. Seeing Miss Greenham selecting household goods made him wonder if, in the back of her mind, there lurked the hope that she might live amongst them in the not-too-distant future.

They went first to purchase a Wilton carpet and several rugs, and Lord Athelney found himself so appreciative of one that he bought it for his drawing room. This extravagance was so unusual he almost apologised for it. Then it was on to select a table suitable for dining, some chairs, side tables, a chest and a fireside chair. When Lord Athelney suggested that one was insufficient, Mr Bitton looked horrified.

'But, my dear fellow, if I should come to discuss matters in your own apartments, I refuse to stand all the while, nor would I take your chair. You need two wing chairs, and in my opinion, a small sofa.'

'A sofa, my lord? I am not some fainting miss. What use could I have for a sofa?'

Out of the corner of his eye, Athelney saw Miss Greenham colour slightly. She at least had imagination.

Harry Bitton let himself be swept along by the current of enthusiasm shown by his employer and nascent love. He had not put his mind to the need for candle sconces and twisted oak candlesticks, 'for the chambers are a little lacking in natural light', nor fire irons, or a mirror for the dressing chest deemed necessary for his bedchamber. He blinked, and nodded, simply delighted in seeing Miss Greenham happy.

The final purchases were of a mattress for the bed, and suitable linens. Miss Greenham managed the latter without blushing, but absented herself from the choosing of the mattress. At the conclusion of this exhausting round of purchasing, it was agreed that the gatehouse would soon be fully habitable excepting cooking facilities. A carrier was arranged to bring the goods to the castle by the end of the week, and Mr Bitton secured Miss Greenham's promise that she would come and assist him in the placing of the furniture about the chambers. The gentlemen all agreed that shopping was remarkably tiring, and were suitably impressed by Miss Greenham's stamina.

The Greenhams would have set off immediately back to the parsonage, but Lord Athelney, having enjoyed a day of company, invited them to take pot luck with him, and sent a lad to advise the parsonage cook that dinner would not be required. When they finally drove home, a little after eight o'clock, Miss Greenham was feeling the effects of the day, compounded by a good dinner, and sagged a little against her brother's shoulder. He smiled, but said she had done too much.

CHAPTER FIFTEEN

THE CARRIER WAS BRINGING 'MISS GREENHAM'S trophies', as Mr Bitton declared the results of the shopping expedition, on Thursday. The drop in temperature and ominous clouds, which old heads shook over and declared harbingers of heavy snow, left her in some agitation the day before, lest the journey be made impossible. The weather, however, held off long enough for her to brace herself against the northerly wind and reach the castle some time before the carman and his cart. Mr Bitton greeted her with what he termed a 'direct order' from Lord Athelney that she was not to be left in the cold, but brought into the warmth of the house and provided with refreshment until such time as the vehicle appeared.

'You have had quite a struggle just to reach us,

ma'am. Your cheeks look frozen cold, and I speak as one who has seen men with ice upon their beards in northern waters.'

'Mr Bitton, this is Somerset, not the Baltic.' She shook her head. 'I must seem so weak a creature if you think that a winter wind would be the end of me?'

'Not at all, but . . . ladies . . . delicate frames and all that.' He blushed, inadvertently thinking of Miss Greenham's very appealing frame.

'I would be most obliged to Lord Athelney, however, for a cup of coffee, and so accept his hospitality.'

She was ushered into the house and thence the morning room, where his lordship soon joined them.

'Good morning, Miss Greenham. Very noble of you to have come up to officiate over the disposition of furniture. Bitton here would probably place everything in a line down one wall.' He grinned at Mr Bitton, who feigned affront.

'Indeed not, my lord. I would place them randomly, for effect. The trouble would be what the effect might be.'

'You seem to have great faith in me, gentlemen,' murmured Miss Greenham. 'I only hope that I come up to your expectations.'

Mr Bitton could not imagine how she could fail to come up to every possible expectation, and gazed at her with what Lord Athelney privately thought was the expression of a devoted spaniel.

'Since our expectations of our own abilities are so

low, ma'am, you cannot but . . .' Lord Athelney stopped, realising that what he was saying might seem to be damning with faint praise.

Miss Greenham gave way to mirth. 'Ah, I now see, my lord. Alas, poor deceived soul that I am! That will teach me the dangers of pride.'

'I did not mean . . . oh confound it, you may take that grin off your face, Mr Bitton,' he admonished his friend, who had also given up any attempt at keeping a straight face.

Sturry came in with coffee, and fresh biscuits, and found all three persons in what he later termed 'a state of mild merriment'.

'The drawing-room furniture has been moved, my lord, to facilitate the laying of the new carpet upon its arrival.' There was a vague air of disapproval, since Sturry could not imagine the need for a new carpet, however threadbare and faded the present floor-covering had become.

'Thank you, Sturry.'

'I am sorry there is so much upheaval, my lord, but you will be very pleased with the final result.' There was the slightest hint of uncertainty in Miss Greenham's voice.

'Oh, I have no doubt of it, Miss Greenham.'

There was another knock at the door, and a maid announced that the carrier had arrived. There followed a busy half hour. The carpet for the drawing room was brought in to be rolled out under Sturry's stern gaze. At first the brightness of the fresh colours made him blink, but he later admitted it to be a very fine carpet. Getting the furniture up into the gatehouse took several men, and even though there was now a new key to the door of what would become the kitchen, the spiral stair from that side made it necessary to ascend via the straight steps and traverse the constable's chamber. Lord Athelney and Mr Bitton stood to one side as Miss Greenham, with all the calm of a general making dispositions of troops for battle, had each piece placed just so, to best advantage, a little to the left, a little nearer to the window, as appropriate. Manhandling the mattress up to the main bedchamber, and removing its predecessor, proved problematic, since the only access was via the upper part of the spiral stair, and Miss Greenham wisely covered her ears for much of the process, since the language involved was most unsuitable for a lady's hearing.

Eventually, however, the three of them stood alone in the main private chamber. It certainly looked like a home, albeit in need of a roaring fire and some personal items. The stone walls were unsuitable for pictures, but, as Miss Greenham commented, the panelling in the bedchambers would allow for any paintings that were currently gathering dust in the main house, and a display of martial implements might be appropriate on the bare stonework.

'Surely there are halberds and axes, or other such weapons, stored in a castle?'

'Since the constable's chamber must once have also

been bare stone, we could always panel at least part of these rooms,' suggested Lord Athelney.

'But that would be yet more expense, my lord, and as it is you have just purchased everything in this room. I feel quite guilty.' His acting steward looked worried.

'You would think me happy to leave you mouldering as if in some mediaeval dungeon?'

'No, no, of course not. I . . .' Mr Bitton floundered, and Miss Greenham took pity on him.

'Panelling might be nice in the upper chamber if a larger window embrasure was made at the courtyard end. It would then be logical to panel that wall at the least. The only awkwardness of these rooms is the available daylight for writing, and embroidery and . . .'

'Do you do much embroidery, Mr Bitton?' enquired Lord Athelney, with a smirk.

'Cannot say that I do, my lord,' responded that gentleman, grinning. 'Sewing on a button is about the limit of my skills with a needle.'

Miss Greenham went bright red.

In a small rural community like Sittford, such a thing as the delivery of a cartload of furniture, and shortly thereafter the removal to the gatehouse of a court cupboard, a blanket chest and several pictures that had been gathering dust in unvisited rooms in the house, were bound to be commented upon, and Miss Greenham's part in it assumed an even greater role as fact and supposition blended. The news reached the

Dower House, and passed from Charlotte's maid to her mistress, who could not resist mentioning it at dinner. She knew it must be unwelcome news to her mama, but if her cousin was showing interest in another it was, as far as she was concerned, all to the good. That it might depress her other auditor did not occur to her.

Lady Willoughby nearly aspirated a forkful of pheasant, and coughed, making her eyes water. 'Ridiculous, Charlotte. Why on earth would Athelney seek advice from the parson's sister?'

'She chose the furnishings, including a carpet for the drawing room, and I remember you complaining that it was appallingly threadbare, Mama. He also called for his chaise and, quite unexpectedly, joined Miss Greenham, with her brother and Lieutenant Bitton, on the expedition to Shepton, giving her free rein to decide upon what should be bought.' Charlotte was adamant.

Her mother remained openly dismissive of the truth of these 'foolish rumours', but, privately, was shocked. Having set in motion a masterly plan to ensure Athelney did not consider Eleanor Burgess as a possible bride, she was now faced with the equally horrifying prospect of Anne Greenham. Her dislike of that young woman had grown since the dinner the week before. She had initially been ignored as beneath her ladyship's notice, but the evening had given Lady Willoughby cause to re-evaluate that position. Whilst clearly too lowly by virtue of being merely the sister of the local incumbent, Anne Greenham might lay claim, as Eleanor Burgess could also, to a lesser degree, to having ancestry which raised her standing. She was obviously not in awe of the marquis, and had a disgraceful boldness to her manner, which presumably Athelney mistook for confidence. While watching the steady retreat of one threat to Charlotte's assumption of a marchioness's robes, Lady Willoughby acknowledged that another had crept dangerously close without her recognising it. She set her mind to work.

Eleanor, for her part, felt her heart sink the further. She had heard, from Anne Greenham's own lips, her patent admiration of naval officers, and the ease which had enabled her to mention the trip to choose furnishings without it sounding an earth-shattering event. As her heart sank, Eleanor's anger rose as if in compensation. How dare he transfer his affections, however shallow, so very fast. Why could he have not asked her own opinion on furnishings, weeks ago? (She conveniently ignored the fact that had he asked for her assistance, Lady Willoughby would have found an excuse to prevent her giving it.) Well, she would not waste any more of her life being miserable about a man who was so . . . annoying, inconstant, arrogant in the assumption that he had but to ask for her hand and she would fall at his feet. Let Anne Greenham fall for his appealing manner; she would not.

It was a small but insistent voice within her that reminded her that she had already fallen.

While the weather held off long enough for the carrier from Shepton to make his delivery, thereafter it showed every indication of making up for that generosity. It snowed; large feathery flakes fell from a laden sky so thickly that a man's footprints were obliterated within minutes of his passing by, and the strengthening wind began to pile the whiteness into drifts. By Saturday evening it was a blizzard.

Lord Athelney and Lieutenant Bitton spent a convivial evening playing backgammon, though Harry Bitton was surprised to win so often. His lordship was a little distracted perhaps, though good-humoured enough, and laughed when his conqueror remarked that it was a pity he had not suggested the wager of a florin upon each game.

'I might have made a tidy profit this evening.'

'Content yourself with the honour of victory and good claret.'

'That I do, my lord.' Mr Bitton yawned. 'Upon which thought I shall retire to bed, with your permission.'

'By all means. I do not suppose Miss Greenham will be able to visit for some time if we are snowed in. She mentioned cushions the other day, did she not?'

'She said that there was sufficient velvet remaining for a couple of bolster cushions for the parlour. I shall continue working in the gatehouse, and have fires in the hearths while there, to keep whatever warmth in the place. Miss Greenham advised it.'

'And Miss Greenham knows best on these matters, no doubt.' Lord Athelney watched the slight blush rise, and smiled. 'I have no doubt she will have all the bolsters and counterpanes and draperies ready for when the weather eases. Perhaps we should have given your friend Greenham a signal book and then we could have hoisted messages by flag from here to the church, and thus remain in communication as long as there is no low cloud.'

Harry Bitton went away laughing, and dreamed of Miss Greenham making cushions in the manner of flags. Lord Athelney remained alone by the fire, idly making piles of the backgammon pieces and frowning. His wooing, if so it could be termed, was going very much awry. He had not been cocksure, surely, for Miss Burgess had met his first clumsy protestations with rejection born, he was certain, of surprise rather than horror. She had continued friendly, cheerful, and with that air of understanding existing between them right up until that fateful muddy embrace. That she viewed it in so despicable a light that she now feared to meet him at dinner, that her looks, when perforce they were near each other, were antagonistic yet defensive, confused him utterly. He had no experience upon which to draw, and was mystified as to how he should now proceed. If she did not wish to see him, how might he advance his cause once more, how might he even crave her forgiveness for any perceived insult? How could he make right, when he did not understand what was wrong?

The weather now colluded with her to keep him distant. He had little doubt there would be the better part of a foot of snow before dawn, and that was without the drifting. Here was he, in his castle, besieged by the elements, besieged by doubt. He was so used to knowing, if not the outcome of situations, then at least how they must be tackled. This was like being becalmed in fog. When he did at last retire to troubled repose, those banks of fog swirled through dreams of unexplained disquiet.

The last few days up to Christmas lacked any festive anticipation. The white world might appear magical, but its realities were harsh. Kingscastle was isolated, but had at least plentiful supplies of food, and wood for heat. For those in the village, unable to work and earn, and finding even the potato clamps hard as iron to dig into, the prospect for Yuletide was far from cheerful. The final Sunday before the Nativity found empty pews in the church. Those in the village could struggle through the snow, but those in outlying farms had no chance of attending the services. This also applied to the Dower House inhabitants, and to those up on top of the hill at Kingscastle. The Reverend Septimus Greenham surveyed his depleted flock, commended those who had made it to church, and invited prayers for those left stranded in their homes by the snow.

Miss Greenham knew she ought to be thinking of those facing hardship, but the image in her head was of Lieutenant Bitton, seated before the fire in the constable's chamber, poring over maps and ledgers in solitary state. It gave her a warm glow of pleasure to be working upon the cushions and curtains for the gatehouse parlour, even though it might be weeks before she had the opportunity to deliver them. She was an honest young woman, and now freely admitted to herself that her feelings were engaged. She was thus far only dreamily hopeful that the same was true of the gentleman, and therefore preferred to keep her dreams to herself. If her brother noticed a change in his sister, he too was saying nothing, but Septimus Greenham, for all his philosophical depth, was not blind, and had a very fair idea what was in the wind but said nothing. For his part he thought it only a matter of time before his friend approached him about making Anne an offer, and assumed it was only the temporary insecurity of his post that held him back. However, he also believed Harry Bitton would make a great success of the stewardship of Kingscastle and indeed increase the standing and importance of the position. Lord Athelney obviously held him in the highest esteem, quite rightly. He was a man of good temperament, unimpeachable honesty, and diligence, and he would make his sister very happy.

His assessment of Harry Bitton's situation was accurate, though not complete. For all that part of him felt that his prospects were not so good as to make it proper for him to contemplate the married state, the inexperienced lieutenant was also assailed by the fear that he was misreading the acts and gestures of a generous, open and naturally happy young woman for something pertaining just to himself. After all, they had known each other barely two months. How his life had changed in those weeks. For his own part he did not doubt that he was in love. There were times, as he made a register of works done upon the estate and identified their location on the map, that his mind wandered, and field boundaries with relaid hedges, new gates and deepened ditches faded at the thought of Anne Greenham's entrancing smile, the ready comprehension in her laughing eyes, the sweetness of her voice. Could such a woman entertain the most tender of feelings for him? His lack of self-conceit made him doubt it, even as the small signs that he had read in her demeanour made his heart beat faster. He wondered if he might seek, as soon as he felt he could see his future clearly, a serious interview with his friend Septimus, and take soundings, hoping that his prospects did not appear too lowly to one who had grown up in episcopal grandeur. Like it or not, he was currently a half-pay lieutenant, and an estate steward, and that did not sound nearly grand enough. What he could not know was that, like at Kingscastle, the grandeur had been mostly of scale, and that worn carpet, faded furnishings and outdated furniture had been as common as in the house in which he now sat to breakfast each day. His own childhood, as a squire's younger son on a prosperous Cambridgeshire manor at the edge of the fens, had been more cosy. His mother, a most redoubtable lady, had ensured that if her husband would from choice have spent every penny on seed drills and prize rams, sufficient was put by to keep the Hall decorated to a standard on a par with that of all the local estates.

Only last week Harry had written to his father

for advice upon the management of land prone to inundation, in the belief that the combined knowledge of Mitchum and his sire would enable him to propose a plan of spring works to Lord Athelney, rather than simply collate information on the estate as it stood when the marquis inherited. From what had been discussed, casually over the course of evening in the library, this would meet with Lord Athelney's approval and support, for idleness was not in his nature either, and simply watching the rents come in would not be in his style at all. The only squall on the horizon was then having to traipse to the estate's trustees to obtain the money to pay for what was needed.

CHAPTER SIXTEEN

I<small>T CONTINUED TO SNOW, BUT IT</small> became desultory by Christmas Eve. Lord Athelney contemplated his first Christmas at Kingscastle, and decided that being absent from the Christmas morning service was not a good way to establish himself in Sittford. He stood at the library window with his hands linked behind him, gazing down the hill towards the bridge and the village beyond, the church spire visible through the scattering of shielding trees.

'Mr Bitton, what say you to attempting to reach the village tomorrow?'

Harry Bitton looked up from perusing a week-old copy of the *Bath Chronicle*.

'On foot, I take it, my lord?'

'Yes, on foot. A carriage would find it impossible, and

I would not trust either a horse or my horsemanship, but if we took stout sticks and set off in good time, the trudge ought to be perfectly feasible. I would not demand that the servants make the attempt, though any who wish might accompany us.'

'I think reaching the church the easy part, though. Climbing the hill afterwards looks more likely to end in a tumble.'

'Then we must hope we are not observed, at least by any who might choose to regale their friends at our expense.' Lord Athelney gave a small smile. The expedition had a touch of adventure that his life had recently lacked. He would not, of course, see Miss Burgess, for it would be impossible for Lady Willoughby's carriage to reach the road, but he would be among people who looked to him as an example, and would see his efforts to be present for what it was, an expression that he was also one of the community. 'Assuming it does not snow again this evening, I think it best we allow an hour and a half for the journey. I would far rather be early than arrive embarrassingly late.'

'Indeed, my lord, and if we should make especially good time, I am sure we might warm ourselves at the parsonage.'

Mr Bitton was not entirely able to curb the pleasure in his voice. He had accepted that there would be a period of absence from the charms of Miss Greenham, and would not be so foolish as to mope over it, but the opportunity to see her upon Christmas Day was an unexpected Christmas gift.

'What an excellent idea.' Lord Athelney's smile grew. 'I wonder I had not thought of that.'

Mr Bitton hid behind the periodical.

Fortunately for their plan, the snow had not been augmented by Christmas morning. The two gentlemen set off early, accompanied by the stable lad and a footman, who both saw an opportunity for some adventurous fun, rather than being impelled by some insatiable desire to hear the Reverend Greenham's Christmas sermon. Muffled up to the eyes, and in the thickest coats they possessed, with galoshes, and then sacking wrapped about their boots to the knee, the quartet set out with Sturry shaking his head at the foolhardiness of the young.

The courtyard had been swept of snow so it was only when they emerged from beneath the gatehouse arch that they faced the reality of their task. The snow had an icy crust, but beneath was still soft and giving. They found themselves floundering, above knee deep, testing the depth with their sticks, taking it in turns to lead and expend the greatest amount of energy. There were tumbles, and snow seeped within collars to send icy rivulets coursing down backs and draw forth surprised expletives. As the slope fell away before them, keeping a footing became more difficult, and the truth of Mr Bitton's comment about how much harder it would be to climb the hill on the return was brought home to them. The exertion was such that even in the severe cold they felt hot, and the mufflers about their mouths became damp with their condensing breath. As they reached the flat ground before the bridge they paused, after slip-sliding and taking irregular strides down the steepest part, and tried to regain a regular trudge. The snow was deeper upon the western side of the bridge, and there was a degree of shelter in the lee of the eastern wall. Close in, the snow was barely a foot deep. Upon the far side it was but a hundred yards to the first dwellings of the village, and it was evident that householders had tried to at least clear snow from their doorsteps, and those exposed to the drifts had shovelled it from beneath window sills lest it cut out what light there was. The Kingscastle party ploughed on to the church. At the lychgate it was seen that only the upper portions of the headstones poked out of the snow, but that the sexton and his lad had cleared a path to the church porch for all who had reached the sanctuary of consecrated ground to have easy passage to the celebration of the Feast of the Nativity.

Lord Athelney consulted his watch. It lacked a good half hour before the service. He sent the servants ahead to the church and looked to his lieutenant.

'Shall we see how surprised the good reverend is to see us this morning, Mr Bitton?'

'I think so, my lord.'

The pair followed the churchyard wall to the path that led up to the parsonage. The trees, branches weighed low with snow, had given sporadic protection and the depth was patchy. The last few yards had been cleared. Lord

Athelney pulled upon the bell and waited. The servant who opened the door could not have looked more surprised if there had been an angel upon the doorstep.

'My lord!'

'Good morning, and,' added his lordship in a spirit of seasonal goodwill, 'a happy Christmas to you. Mr Bitton and I were wondering if we might warm ourselves before the morning service, if Mr Greenham is not at his breakfast.'

The servant blinked and stood back to bid them enter. 'Breakfast is put away, my lord. If I may show you into the morning room, I shall fetch Miss Greenham. She was with Cook but a minute ago.'

They bent to remove the protection from their legs, had assistance in removing their wet coats and then were shown into a room with a welcoming fire, where they stretched cold hands to the warmth. Miss Greenham entered, and they turned, smiling, and now with pink cheeks, to face her.

'I would lay odds you did not expect to see us this morning, Miss Greenham.' Lord Athelney watched her amazement.

'Lord Athelney, Mr Bitton.' She made her curtsey. 'Indeed not. Surely no vehicle could . . .'

'We have walked, Miss Greenham,' declared Mr Bitton with just a touch of pride.

'Goodness me! You must be so very cold. I will call for coffee, for there is time before the service. My brother is composing himself. He likes to have some minutes of secluded contemplation before we prepare for departure, and I believe he has just shut himself in the study for that purpose. If you will accept my meagre company in his stead . . .'

'Charming company it is, Miss Greenham.' Lord Athelney smiled at her, and she could not but respond.

'Happy Christmas, ma'am,' added Mr Bitton, not to be outdone.

She laughed softly, and wished them also the compliments of the season, then rang the bell, and called for a pot of coffee to be brought immediately.

Twenty minutes later, fortified by hot coffee, and, in Mr Bitton's case, the presence of Miss Greenham, the two gentlemen accompanied the parson and his sister to the church, Mr Bitton especially solicitous that Miss Greenham did not slip, and nobly offering her his arm for support. The presence of the two Kingscastle servants meant that the marquis's arrival was not a total surprise, but nonetheless a rustling whisper passed through nave and aisles. Lord Athelney gave every impression of a man whose journey to church had been no different from usual, and acknowledged several greetings as he and Mr Bitton went to the Kingscastle box pew. It was there that the morning lost a little of its snowy sparkle, for he and Mr Bitton felt isolated, and he could not but imagine Miss Burgess in her accustomed position.

Despite this, he sang forcefully enough, his baritone contrasting with Mr Bitton's tenor, and the familiar Christmas ritual was played out. He recalled Christmases spent at sea, where he had conducted the service himself on a spume-sprayed deck, or, in earlier years, standing head bowed, listening to his captain read the service, and wondering about his family back in England. It brought it home to him that there was no family remaining now, and a small part of him imagined this pew filled by a new generation of Hawksmoors trying not to yawn through the sermon, or be seen goading a sibling.

Mr Bitton remained happy throughout, even though Miss Greenham was hidden from his view, excepting the top of her bonnet. He had seen her, wished her a happy Christmas, received her smile and kind words. It was more than enough to keep him contented. At the conclusion of the service, Lord Athelney joined Septimus Greenham in the church porch to give all his tenants and neighbours Christmas greetings, and his stock among the locals rose thereby. Eventually the church emptied, the parson drew his cloak more tightly about him, and the Kingscastle men contemplated their climb up the hill. Miss Greenham was apprehensive.

'I assure you, ma'am, we shall not get lost, nor freeze entirely to death, and if luncheon is delayed, so be it.' Lord Athelney smiled wryly.

'I just hope none of you catch a chill, or get frostbite, that is all, my lord.'

'We shall go at our best pace, never fear, and not dawdle. Now all we need do is collect our sacking bindings and be upon our way. It was worth it for the sermon, Greenham, and for the coffee too, ma'am.'

Watched by brother and sister from the parsonage windows, a few minutes later they set off. The wind had dropped, but it was still bitterly cold where snow met clothing and clothing passed the cold to flesh. Until the hill steepened they made swift progress, but then relied increasingly upon their sticks to gain purchase. Progress was painfully slow, even though their track from the descent had created a vague path and patches where the snow had slid away.

It was two hours after the service ended that four men, conscious of a good effort, though tired, entered the castle portals and were greeted with patent relief by Sturry. A change of raiment, a good fire, hot food and a brandy certainly rejuvenated the marquis, and he even won several rubbers of piquet before dinner that evening.

It could not be said that Lady Willoughby Hawksmoor greeted news of her nephew's exploit with pleasure. That a peer of the realm, and a Hawksmoor, moreover, should have walked through the snow like some peasant, appalled her. To this was added the fear that the thought of seeing Miss Greenham, rather than piety or the more acceptable determination to show the villagers that mere snow would not deter their lord from his duty, had sped his footsteps.

In this latter thought she was, silently, joined by Miss Burgess, for whom absence from the Christmas service had been a blow. She had never failed to attend services on Christmas Day from the moment she could walk, and for all the impossibility of reaching the church, she still felt a weight of guilt. That Lord Athelney had managed to do so made it worse, though logic should have told her there was a vast difference between gentlemen in boots and breeches struggling through deep snow, and a lady in skirts. Could it have been that he simply felt such a need to see Miss Greenham, perhaps even to give her a gift? So she added guilt to feeling angry, not jealous of course, for he meant nothing to her, but angry at his swift change of feeling. This in turn made her blame him for giving her such unchristian thoughts in the season of goodwill.

The only person cheered by the revelation was Charlotte, who said that the Reverend Greenham must have felt very much appreciated when the most important gentleman in the district put himself out to such a degree to listen to his sermon.

Lady Willoughby admonished her daughter, telling her that her brains were addled, and bemoaned the fact that the poor weather would almost certainly prevent her elder daughter, Lady Bryanston, and her family, from fulfilling their promise to come for the New Year.

It was four days later, when there had been some signs of a thaw, that she was able to see Athelney for herself, and assess whether he looked like a man on the verge of a declaration. He had decided to throw caution to the winds and visit his aunt, ostensibly to check how the ladies had fared during their snowy imprisonment, and would then ask to speak to Miss Burgess alone. He felt that, as a sensible young woman, she could not but applaud him being open, honest and forthright with her. He would tell her how he had missed her, missed the chance to apologise if she felt he had behaved badly, and would then renew his offer, humbly but with passion. He therefore appeared to his aunt a little bright-eyed and exactly as she imagined he would be, a man in love and eager. She was genuinely shocked. He made his bow to her and to Miss Burgess, to whom he strove to send a signal in a single look, though she acknowledged his presence but then dropped her gaze and continued her task of winding a hank of wool. Lady Willoughby regarded him balefully, and cast about for a reason to send her companion from the room. While Miss Greenham now appeared the greater threat, she would not make the mistake of discounting Eleanor Burgess entirely.

She almost brushed aside his polite enquiries after their healths, and watched very carefully his response to her own questions.

'Yes, yes, we are quite well and passed Christmas quietly but without suffering any undue annoyances, other than not being able to attend church. I am glad that you at least were able to represent the family, Athelney.' She managed to make it sound as if he had done so at her request. 'No doubt the parson and his . . . sister,' she said the word in the same way she might have enunciated 'serpent', 'were astounded to see you.'

'Oh yes, but they greeted us most hospitably. Miss Greenham has a very pragmatic mind, and once over the

242

surprise ensured that we had a hot drink and the chance to dry ourselves a little before going to the church itself.'

'Pragmatic, hmm. I would say she certainly knows how to get the best from a situation.'

Lord Athelney frowned, which she saw as disapproval of her view but was in fact perplexity. Why Lady Willoughby should take Miss Greenham in dislike he could not fathom, beyond the fact that the lady did not fawn before her or regard her opinions as Delphic. He looked at Miss Burgess, but that lady showed no sign that she was aware of him. Lady Willoughby gave a theatrical shudder.

'I fear the draught in this room has become unbearable. I shall almost certainly develop a stiffness in the neck. Eleanor, go up and find my cashmere shawl, the black one with the embroidered roses upon it.' Since she knew she had given it to Charlotte to darn a small moth-hole, for Charlotte had the neatest and most delicate of stitches, this hunt ought to take far longer than the duration of the visit.

'Of course, ma'am.' Eleanor seemed, to Lord Athelney, unusually subdued. She rose, made him her curtsey and was gone without him having the opportunity he so wanted. His eyes followed her as she left the room, and Lady Willoughby decided that the final blow ought to be administered to remove any threat from that quarter once and for all.

'Ah, poor Eleanor. Anniversaries are so very hard on one.'

He looked puzzled. He thought her parents still living, and she had denied any romantic attachment in her life.

'Ma'am?'

Lady Willoughby, most unusually, dropped her gaze. 'It was at Christmastide last year. William often came home in November and remained until the New Year, even after his uncle so cruelly denied him access to the castle, which was by far the most suitable place for him, as the heir, rather than in this little place with his poor, widowed mama. He enjoyed the hunting, and some shooting of course, but he could not entertain his friends here.' She did not say that this was because she had forbidden him to do so with his sister, young, beautiful and innocent, within the walls. She sighed. 'Of course, poor boy, he did get rather bored in the evenings, with nothing better to do than play patience while we sat with our embroidery, and some nights he did linger rather too long over the port. If only his poor dear father had lived to guide him, but will a son listen to his mama as he would his sire? No, sadly he will not.' She put her shapely, pale hands together, and rubbed one over the other in a gesture that struck her nephew as reminiscent of the action of Pontius Pilate. There was a pause, a heavily loaded pause, and then she continued.

'My poor, fatherless William was a very naughty boy. It pains me to say so, but I am honest. Of course young gentlemen are undisciplined with menials, that is to be expected, but he should have recognised that my companion was not simply a servant wench. Poor

Eleanor; for all that I find her wilful and at times difficult, I would not send her back to her family in shame, not after . . .' She closed her lips tightly.

He wanted to say something, but all the words stuck in his throat. He could not ask her to be more explicit; it would be too embarrassing for her, and might even be betraying a confidence. He wanted to say that he had had no inkling of any distress or revulsion when he had first broached marriage to Eleanor Burgess, but admitting that he had asked her might lead to more unpleasantness. He therefore said nothing beyond blatantly changing the subject to hoping that the weather might improve and that if there was anything which his aunt required he would be pleased to obtain it and send it down to the Dower House. He then made his bow and left, with no thought to ask Barwell if he might have a few words with Miss Burgess.

Lady Willoughby Hawksmoor twisted a sapphire ring upon one long, elegant finger, and smiled. She remained smiling so long that a trace of it lingered even when Eleanor returned twenty minutes later after a fruitless search for the shawl.

CHAPTER SEVENTEEN

LORD ATHELNEY MADE HIS WAY UP the hill oblivious to the cold wind, or the snow melting in drips from the trees, even when a chill droplet went straight down the back of his collar.

Not after . . . The phrase left hanging had sent his mind into a whirl like the vortex of a whirlpool. What had befallen her? Had William seduced her, led her to think that he would marry her, for her breeding was good enough, then cast her aside like a used cravat? Had he broken her heart? Or had he broken her by force? Both alternatives revolted. Lord Athelney was tormented. He loved Eleanor Burgess, without any doubt, without any reservation. He wanted to protect her, and the thought that any protection was too late was unbearable. That the cause of her distress was a man named William

Hawksmoor made it so much the worse, if that were possible. While he had seemed merely a friend, when he had first proposed, perhaps she had for a moment considered the option of acceptance to avoid her downtrodden state. She might have thought a marriage of convenience based upon mild affection would work, and then he had mentioned it becoming more and she had declined him. His calm self told him that had she found his mild attentions unpleasant she would not have been as open, as happy in his company, as she had been thereafter. The lover in him riposted with the unpleasant fact that when he had kissed her, kissed her with a passion born of the thought that he had almost lost her, she had recoiled. 'Just like your namesake after all,' she had said. What greater condemnation could there be? And since then she had avoided him completely.

Then another ghastly thought assailed him. How had Lady Willoughby found out? Eleanor Burgess did not act like a young woman who would make open complaint about something that declared her ruin, especially to an employer such as Lady Willoughby, who was both a callous woman, and the parent of the very man who had brought about that ruination. To do so would have been rash in the extreme. Nor was William Hawksmoor likely to have confessed his misdemeanour to his mother. There remained another way in which Lady Willoughby might have found out. 'In shame', she had said. Did that mean . . . She had said that whatever had occurred had been last Christmas. Had she found out because of the consequences of the seduction? Sanity told him that Lady Willoughby would have simply cast her out immediately, and accused her of entrapping her beloved son, and yet . . . If Miss Burgess had miscarried, before any signs were patent to the world, his aunt might have thought it safer to keep her close and under scrutiny, with the threat of revealing her fall to her parents. What torment must she have gone through if that was the case. It might account for her acceptance of the mistreatment meted out by Lady Willoughby, the slights, the constant reminders of her meaning nothing. Well, she was not nothing to him; she was swiftly becoming everything, and yet he could think of no way in which he could prove that to her.

Logic said that he was creating this horrifying scenario based upon the hints of a woman he despised, disliked and distrusted, but Lord Athelney was a man in love, deeply so, and prey to his emotions. The despairing lover in him could also add that Lady Willoughby's hints were corroborated by those with no reason to denigrate Miss Burgess.

He arrived back at the castle and shut himself in the library, with a curt request that he not be disturbed.

The fop Heigham had mentioned 'conquests' that were 'close to home', and he had simply assumed that he was referring to William Hawksmoor's unsavoury and immoral pursuit of the castle skivvies, but what if Wicked William had boasted, in his cups, of something far worse, in terms of the family? That might indeed have given Bertram

Heigham cause to believe he could use blackmail. He felt suddenly rather sick. He had told Heigham he might say what he pleased, and nobody would take any notice, but if that unpleasant individual so much as breathed a word to the dishonour of Miss Burgess . . .

Lord Athelney had never thought much of duelling, considering it for the most part foolish exaggeration of something that could be far better resolved by a hearty bout of fisticuffs and a bloody nose. He had seen men die, far too many, and the reality of death was not as a noble thing, not to be faced for some childish dare. In this case, however, he would have no qualms whatsoever about putting a bullet through Mr Bertram Heigham's rather narrow chest to protect Miss Burgess's good name. He could, would, do that for her. It seemed so little, and he could not speak to her about it. It would be this immense void between them, and he wanted what he had thought possible with her as with no other woman: unity of thought, a togetherness that did not need words to be felt. Today he had gone out in the expectation of offering for the hand of the woman he loved, and now it seemed painfully likely that he might never have the opportunity to do so. If she so much as hinted that she was hanging back because of this black deed that had befallen her in the past, he would tell her, without any hesitation, that it did not change his feelings, or his intent, but that could only happen if she broached the matter. He could not, and recent events indicated that she was unlikely to throw herself upon his chest and say, 'I would marry you, gladly, but . . .'

He sat in the glow of the fire, without candles, as the gloaming became full darkness, and the unsuspecting maid who came in to light the branches in expectation that the gentlemen would spend the evening in the library screamed in surprise when there was movement in the dark room. He would normally have been apologetic, but on this occasion showed little sympathy for her.

Sturry, ushering the slightly hysterical girl from the room, wondered for a moment if his employer had been drinking and become jug-bitten, but there was no glass by his elbow, and nothing beyond his grumpy behaviour to indicate that this might even be a possibility. He pondered whether he ought to warn Mr Bitton, but gauged that that gentleman knew him better than any and would be swift to sense his mood and act accordingly.

Harry Bitton had seen his lordship grow more taciturn over recent days, but tonight he was positively monosyllabic. Conversation withered, and an uncomfortable silence replaced it. Mr Bitton was dwelling in the rosy glow of falling in love, and now found it very hard to imagine how anybody could not be as happy as himself. He made a few unsuccessful attempts to instigate a discussion, and then simply enjoyed the dishes set before him. Lord Athelney could not have said what was offered; he might as well have been on hard tack and salt beef.

He excused himself to Mr Bitton after dinner and went to his room, where he stared for a long time down the hill to where faint points of light indicated the Dower

House. She was so close and yet might as well have been in the Antipodes.

He slept badly. His dreams were haunted by an image of his cousin laughing at him, though he had no real idea of how his cousin had looked as a man. He just knew the mocking laughter was his, the same way he knew that the image of her smiling face was cast into black shadow by the malign presence of William Hawksmoor. Yet when he heard the anguished whisper, 'I hate you, William Hawksmoor,' it was directed at him, and though he tried to cry out that it was not him, no sounds came.

The midwinter dawn found him tetchy, almost morose. Cottam, who had been congratulating himself upon finding so easy-going an employer, was briefly disappointed, but then realised that it was some disorder of spirits that affected him. He hinted as much to Sturry, in the privacy of that individual's little sitting room.

'It might be the weather, and him being cooped up, Mr Cottam. Having had all those years at sea might make house living, with little to engage him out of doors in this foul weather, cramping to his soul.'

'Perhaps so, Mr Sturry, perhaps so, yet I do not deny I wonder if it has not some other cause. Confinement would not deprive him of his rest, and I swear that is so. He was heavy-eyed when I attended him this morning, not for the first time, and his bedclothes were disordered as if he had been agitated.'

They looked at each other, and then into the fire.

* * *

The thaw continued sufficiently for Miss Greenham to be driven up to the castle, with the fruits of her labours neatly folded upon her knees, upon the second day of the new year. Septimus Greenham frowned at the level of the rushing water beneath the Sittford bridge, and took the opportunity of discussing the likelihood of flooding with Lord Athelney, while his sister let Harry Bitton carry the curtains to the gatehouse, and directed him, and the maid, in putting them up.

'The cushions must wait for another day, sir, for they were rather bulky, and could not be balanced safely upon the curtains.'

Mr Bitton was delighted that there was further reason for Miss Greenham to visit, since he had foreseen that the completion of her needlework would see her up at the castle far less often. He had decided that he would simply have to visit the parsonage much more, but since he would ostensibly be visiting his old schoolfriend, time with the enchanting Miss Greenham would be at a premium.

'Dear ma'am, cushions are most cumbersome . . . not that I have ever carried them about with me. I would not want you to put yourself to any trouble. Are you sure it might not be better to bring them one by one?' He then thought this sounded as if he was too lazy to collect them, and added, hastily, 'I would be happy to collect them myself, but their disposition would be far better in your hands.'

'Mr Bitton, I am sure you have made far, far more

important decisions than where to place a cushion.' Her eyes twinkled.

'At sea, yes, Miss Greenham, but we are not at sea.' The laughter was in his own expression as he stood back to survey the final effect of the new draperies. 'You have achieved a transformation, ma'am, truly you have.'

On impulse, he took her gloved hand, and kissed it. She looked up at him shyly, her cheeks tinged with colour, and it took an iron control of his will not to succumb to the urge to kiss her. The presence of the maid, and the knowledge that if the maid were absent, he would be betraying trust, held him back. His mind was flooded with the memory of her in his arms, trembling, after the spider incident. He yearned to hold her like that again. His voice, when he mastered it, was a trifle thick, and barely more than a whisper.

'Thank you, for everything.' He was not really thinking of curtains, and she knew it. Her fingers squeezed his, very slightly. It was one of those moments that remains memorable.

'Begging your pardon, sir, but is I needed any mores?' The maid, the possessor of a lively imagination who found the gatehouse 'creepy and ghosty', brought them back to the mundane.

'No, Sarah, thank you.'

The young woman bobbed a polite curtsey, and disappeared down the spiral stair to the parlour level.

'You should . . . We should . . .'

'Yes, we should, Mr Bitton.'

Never had 'should' been invested with more 'but not from choice'. He preceded her down the spiral stair, lest, he said, she should miss her footing, and turned to take her hand as she reached the bottom steps. He retained it right across the parlour and constable's chamber, and then, reluctantly, let it go for her to descend to the courtyard. For two people who had, without words, confirmed their deep mutual attraction, their faces were remarkably inscrutable as they entered the house.

They found parson and landowner in serious mood, and making contingency plans. The young cleric had already decided to move the registers and vestments to the upper floor of the parsonage. Lord Athelney, whose face she thought unusually grave, seemed to consider some flooding inevitable as the meltwater from the thaw on higher ground added to the volume of water in the river. His only doubt appeared to be the severity. On hearing this, Miss Greenham asked about those items in the parsonage that would suffer irreparable damage: her spinet, pictures and furniture.

'I am sorry to sound alarmist, Miss Greenham, and hope I am proved wrong, but I would advocate moving everything that is portable to the upper storey, despite inconvenience. If it comes, then it may well come fast and leave little time to secure items you treasure.'

'Oh, I know one should not set store upon worldly goods, but . . . The spinet was Mama's and there is Papa's portrait and such things.'

'You will need all hands, Septimus, if you are to

prepare in time, if this thaw continues. Let me come down with you and lend what assistance I may.' Harry Bitton was frowning. He did not want Miss Greenham upset by the loss of precious family items.

'Thank you, Harry, I will be delighted, if you can be spared from your duties here.' Septimus Greenham looked from his friend to Lord Athelney.

'Oh, this takes priority over bookkeeping. While you are in the village, go about and check that the householders are also warned, and that the measures I wanted are set in place, the boards at doorways for example. I do not mind if I am laughed at if proved wrong. Oh, and I think I will send one of the boats down in a cart, to be stored in the church below the bell loft, if that is not considered irreverent. It will mean rescues can be effected far more quickly. Arrange for certain men to act as boat's crew, Mr Bitton. I trust you to select the most able.' Lord Athelney paused. 'I should go to the Dower House and warn my aunt. It lies on the low ground before the slope of the hill and if the banks burst will most certainly be inundated below stairs. The reception rooms are raised several feet, if you think of the steps to the front door, but I am not sure even that will be enough.'

Septimus Greenham frowned. This all sounded melodramatic and unlikely, but if Lord Athelney thought the parish and parishioners at risk, he could not in any way ignore it. While Harry Bitton went to saddle his horse, he arranged for the delivery of the little boat to the church. His sister, who had felt almost lightheaded, and certainly lighthearted, but a few minutes earlier, grew solemn. The gig and accompanying cob were soon heading down to the village, and Lord Athelney, his face a grim mask, set off down the hill to the Dower House, with utter disregard for whether he should arrive windblown and with muddy boots. This, after all, was not a social call.

Barwell opened the door to him in some surprise. Eleanor was at that very moment crossing the hall, and looked sharply towards the door at the sound of the familiar voice requesting admittance. She stood very still, conscious of the very loud thumping of her heart within the confines of her chest, and resentful that she should feel suddenly eager to see a man who had clearly dismissed her from his mind. The gentleman whom Barwell relieved of his heavy coat was not as she had expected. He was frowning, almost scowling, and his mouth was set in a grim line. She had never seen his lordship so cold and unapproachable. He spared her but a glance and bow, and followed the butler to the yellow saloon where her ladyship was lecturing her daughter upon softheartedness towards the undeserving. She could not know that it had taken all his resolve to stick to his duty.

He made his bow curtly, and immediately set out the reason for his visit. Charlotte put up a hand to her cheek and went pale. Lady Willoughby, on the other hand, had fixed upon the state of his attire and paid no attention to his actual words. As Eleanor slipped into the room, she was stridently berating him for appearing before her 'as if from a cow byre'. Charlotte stared at her mother, and then, rather to her own surprise, interjected loudly, 'Mama, Lord Athelney is here because we face danger. His dress means nothing. Listen to him.'

Lady Willoughby stopped mid-exclamation, and blinked at her daughter as if at a changeling. Giving his cousin a brief smile of thanks, Lord Athelney repeated the reason for his call.

'I fear, ma'am, that this house, its contents, and indeed its occupants, stand in very real danger. The river is in spate and now the thaw upriver is seeing meltwaters add to the flow by the hour. I am of the firm belief that unless it abates overnight, this house, and the village, are likely to be inundated before tomorrow, or at best the day after, is out.'

'But this is the Dower House, not some peasant hovel.'

'The status of the building is immaterial to the flood, ma'am. I am telling you that in all probability the river will burst its banks and it is entirely possible that this house could be flooded within ten minutes. If you do not prepare in advance, the damage, and the risk, is likely to be far greater.'

'You think that not only below stairs will be flooded, cousin?' Charlotte had a look of concentration upon her face.

'I cannot be certain but you must be prepared for it, yes.'

Lady Willoughby looked from her daughter to her nephew in disbelief. 'This is ridiculous.'

'No, Mama, it is not.' Charlotte turned to her mother, and seemed several inches taller.

'There has been no flooding here since I have lived in this house,' declared Lady Willoughby defiantly, as if she had forbidden such a thing.

'I believe the last flooding was some years before you took up residence. There were deaths in the parish. I do not come here to raise false fears, ma'am. If I am proved wrong, then I am glad of it, but I doubt that I shall be.'

'What do you recommend that we do?' Eleanor Burgess found her voice, and it was calm and cool, much to her own surprise. He turned, having been unaware of her presence.

'The same as I have just recommended to Miss Greenham at the parsonage. Remove all items of great value, in monetary or sentimental terms, to the upper floors. S—'

'You warned the parson before me?' Lady Willoughby latched onto this piece of information.

Eleanor's mind turned it more to: *You warned Anne Greenham first. You thought of her safety above all others.* She felt as if her heart had petrified and was now just a heavy stone.

'I did not travel to do so, ma'am, for he and his sister were at the castle.'

This did not make things any the better to either Lady Willoughby or to Eleanor. Lady Willoughby raised a

258

supercilious eyebrow.

'Indeed?' she enunciated witheringly.

'I would recommend that you send your horses up to the castle stables, and that you accompany them.'

'To the stables?' Lady Willoughby's eyes bulged. Charlotte choked.

'No, to the castle, with all your servants also. We have plenty of room, and . . .'

'With the servants? Are you mad? Their duty is to protect my belongings. Charlotte and I will accept your offer. Eleanor, you will take charge of the servants. One cannot trust menials in times of calamity. You will keep the waters from reaching this level.'

'I am not King Canute, ma'am. I cannot command them to limit their advance.' Eleanor blinked at her employer. 'Not,' she added, 'that he was trying to do so, but rather show that even a king cannot command the elements.'

'You will do as I bid, or face the consequences. Athelney, you will have the green drawing room made ready for my use, and Charlotte and I will take the bedchambers in the west wing, directly above it.'

Lord Athelney opened his mouth to assert that the offer was not simply to the Hawksmoor ladies, but Eleanor pre-empted any declaration by saying simply that she was quite prepared to remain, although she could not, in all truth, guarantee the outcome being as Lady Willoughby directed. He frowned at her. She was a sensible young woman, but this was not a sensible decision. Eleanor gave him a challenging look, and withdrew. He watched her close the door behind her, and remained staring at it until Lady Willoughby called his attention back to her. She was organising his life, his house, and whilst he ought to have demurred his brain was distracted by the peculiar behaviour of Eleanor Burgess. When he left, a few minutes later, Barwell, his normally inscrutable face pale and worried, was directing the footmen in moving a Dutch marquetry cabinet. Eleanor Burgess stood partway up the stair, staring at the front door as if she could predict how high the waters might reach. He looked up at her as he was assisted into his coat and, upon impulse, took the stairs two at a time to reach her before she might avoid him.

'This is madness, you know it is.' He spoke in a low whisper.

'I have my duties, my lord,' she replied in a flat voice, and did not look him in the eye, 'and you have yours. Best that you attend to them.' It was a dismissal, but he ignored it.

'My duty is to protect the people of Sittford, and this house . . . My people.'

'I do not belong to you, sir.' This time she did look at him. 'Now, if you do not mind, I . . .'

He took her by the wrist. 'I do mind. What cause I have given you, I . . .' He faltered, and took refuge in a statement of intent. 'I do not care what you say, Miss Burgess. If I deem it necessary for your safety I will remove you from this house, which is my property, by

260

force if so required. Understand that.'

Her eyes widened a fraction, her gaze dropped, and he let her go and left without another word. All the way up the hill he chastised himself for not commanding that everyone leave the house, over Lady Willoughby's head. He would have done so, had Eleanor Burgess not effectively volunteered to remain. Had she done it because it was preferable to sharing his house?

CHAPTER EIGHTEEN

THE RAIN EASED, BUT THE SLATE-GREY clouds to north and east showed that further upstream there was no respite, and by the dinner hour the rain was once more rattling the leaded panes of the Kingscastle windows. Harry Bitton had returned, and was making a full report of his time in the village. Lady Willoughby Hawksmoor had declared upon her arrival that she was too 'distraught at being forced from my home' to dine, and that she and Charlotte would eat in their rooms. She also gave Sturry a detailed menu of what Cook should prepare for her. Charlotte, while looking rather more genuinely concerned for those left in the Dower House, appeared in no way too overwrought to join the gentlemen for dinner, but could not put herself forward without any form of chaperone, and contented herself with giving her cousin an apologetic look. Lord Athelney was more than a little surprised that Charlotte had risen to the occasion and actually shown sense and spirit, and wondered if he might have to revise his opinion of her. He was wondering far more, however, about Eleanor Burgess, preparing as if for a siege, and his faithful lieutenant had to repeat himself to get his attention.

'I was saying, my lord, that Septimus and I do not think there will be room for everyone in his parsonage, so we went to Flowers at Sittford Mill. He thinks the banks will burst and has already moved all he can to upper floors. He has such a brood, though, that he cannot take more than about half a dozen folk, so we went to his nearest neighbours, an old widow, and Seth Coombes, who has a wife and three infants, and arranged that as soon as Flowers thinks the breach imminent, he will call them in. Even so, we wondered if we could ferry some of the villagers to the hill and get them up here. I could provide shelter enough in the gatehouse, as long as the kitchens could feed them. I thought perhaps two dozen or more, if needed, could sleep in the constable's chamber and what A— Miss Greenham calls my parlour next door. With your permission, of course.'

He saw the look on the marquis's face. There was no smile accompanying the nod he received. Perhaps accommodating Lady Willoughby was already proving tiresome.

'I saw Miss Hawksmoor upon the stair when I arrived back. She said that Miss Burgess was remaining down in the Dower House to oversee the securing of goods and chattels. When will she join us here?' He asked the question innocently, thinking to distract his lordship, but the grimness increased.

'When I go and fetch her,' answered Lord Athelney, and there was determination in his eye.

The following morning brought no lightening of the sky, but did see the arrival of Miss Greenham, much to Mr Bitton's surprise, handling the reins of the parson's gig. Septimus Greenham had risen early and gone to the Sittford bridge. There was virtually no gap between the torrent and the underside of the stone structure. He estimated they had but a few hours before the inevitable occurred, for the meltwaters and heavy rain were combining to dangerous effect. He also thought of his transport. The gig, the little chestnut that pulled it, and his elderly riding horse, had nowhere safe. He cursed himself for not sending at least old Jeremiah back with Harry Bitton the night before. However, he might just safely send Anne up the hill and it had the advantage that she could remain there. He returned to his parsonage, wrote a note for Harry Bitton, and went to his sister, who was arranging for trivets and kettles to go upstairs so that some form of cooking and heating water might continue if the kitchen were denied them. The downstairs of the house looked denuded and, he feared, abandoned to its fate. Carpets were gone from floors, mirrors and pictures from the walls, everything portable had been moved to what he hoped was safety. Anne turned as he entered the kitchen. It was unusual for him to enter this domain.

'I am not sure how we will cope, you know, for keeping people fed and clean, brother. If the water does not subside within a few hours, overnight perhaps . . .' She shook her head, frowning.

'If the inundation persists, I have asked if we may take refuge up at the castle. I have written to that effect in my letter to his lordship, and have no doubt he will agree. There is space, I am sure. In fact, that is why I came to you now, for I have a favour to ask, my dear.'

'Oh.' She still looked preoccupied.

'Old Jeremiah. I would hate to lose him, and the pony and gig also. I ought to have thought of it sooner, but . . . I think we have little time. I must remain here but might you drive the gig, with Jeremiah tied to the tail, up to Harry at the castle?'

'Yes, but if there is little time . . .'

'Anne, I think it safer if you are there, so do not risk yourself returning if it is too late. The boats will be needed for ferrying the rescued. You have done so much here, but I can manage, and we may end up joining you.' He came and took her hands. 'I am putting my faith in the Almighty and in Harry Bitton, my dear. Promise me you will not do anything risky to return?'

'But . . .'

'Some parishioners will, I am sure, be taken straight away up to the castle, to the gatehouse, for safety. Harry and I agreed it yesterday. Having a woman there, and I do not mean Lady Willoughby Hawksmoor, may be very advantageous. The parish may be split, and we, as a pair, might be better able to minister to the people in practical ways, by being apart.' It was not quite a lie.

She looked at him, and tears sprung to her eyes, but she bit her lip and nodded. 'I understand, Septimus.'

'Good girl.' He kissed her upon the forehead. 'Make sure you take a few essentials with you in case you must remain.'

She went and packed her toilet necessaries, a brush, comb, toothbrush and tooth-powder, a clean tucker and shift, a warm shawl. Armed with these things, and her brother's blessing, she drove determinedly up the hill. She had not driven very often, and had the most rudimentary driving skills, but Septimus Greenham thought her unlikely to suffer an accident on the short journey to the castle. However, she arrived looking drawn, and a little scared, and half fell into Harry Bitton's arms in the courtyard.

'I have brought the horses, and Septimus thinks the river will breach the banks very soon and . . .' she said in a rush. Her lip trembled, and her face was so full of distress that Harry Bitton forgot all propriety, and held her close.

'Sssh, it will be all right, you see.' He paused, trying to control the urge within himself. 'I did not know you could drive.'

'I cannot, not really.' Her voice sounded very

youthful, and caught on a sob.

'My dar—dear Miss Greenham, do not be distressed. You are safe with me. Here, I mean.'

She clung the tighter, and only by the most determined effort did he not kiss her. There was no kiss, and yet . . . They stood in the drizzle for a minute or so, cocooned in a private world. Then his hold loosened a little. She looked up at him, total trust upon her face.

'I . . . Septimus sent you this letter.' She drew the sealed paper from within the bodice of her pelisse. He was conscious of a frisson as he took it because it had lain against her heart.

'Let me get you inside and in the dry, then I shall read it.' He smiled, and called for Fittleton to see to the horses.

The letter was brief and to the point, giving the situation as the parson saw it from down in the village. It ended upon a more personal note, however.

I have persuaded Anne to deliver this and get the horses and gig to safety. I think she may be able to do more up with you if we have villagers seeking refuge at Kingscastle, and I think she will be safer too. She will certainly be in the best of care, my dear friend, for I know how you treasure her. Keep her safe, and free from worry about me and I shall be eternally in your debt. If you would come down at your earliest convenience upon receiving this, however, I think there is work for the boat. You will then be able to report back that we are not all floating away.

Anne does not think the house will be able to support many folk for long, crammed in upstairs. If the flooding persists, would you request his lordship to permit me to ferry those from the village to the castle side and come and join you up there? Space is plentiful, even if in the stables, and cooking and sanitary conditions infinitely better able to cope. I am confident that Lord Athelney will take in 'the waifs and strays' of which number I shall be one. Logic may say we should simply do this from the start, but if the flooding does not persist I think many villagers would wish to remain as close to home as possible.

'I must get down to the village.' Harry Bitton spoke almost to himself, but then looked up. 'Forgive me. My duty today is with your brother but I shall return with the news by nightfall. His lordship must be informed as well.'

'Shall I not go down to the bridge and cross with you?' She was uncertain, not wanting to feel that she did not at least attempt to return to her brother.

'I truly think Septimus believes it better you stay up here.' He gripped her hand. 'Perhaps you could see that the fires are lit in the gatehouse and ask Sturry for any old blankets and such. If we do have people coming up, they will need warmth and something comforting. Soup! Soup would be sustaining and can be kept until the morrow if not required.'

She smiled at his enthusiasm. 'I shall certainly ask about blankets and soup. You . . . will take care, if you are in the boat?'

'I shall, but remember I am used to boats, and in vast oceans, not just angry rivers. Have faith.'

She nodded, and he let go of her hand to go and seek out Lord Athelney. She sighed, both with worry but also with a warm, and, she admitted to herself, entirely explicable, glow of happiness deep within her, and set about the tasks that Mr Bitton had set her.

His lordship received the information from the parson without surprise. He nodded when Mr Bitton suggested the second boat be taken to the bottom of the hill, and then announced that he would supervise its transport and then its deployment if needed.

'Miss Greenham is quite capable of organising things up here. I will take some of the younger men as boat's crew, and we can work together. I have as little doubt as Greenham that the banks will be burst today. Let me change my clothes and I will be with you directly. Oh, and send Sturry in will you, please.'

'Aye aye, my lord.' The response was automatic. This was Captain Hawksmoor ordering the clearing of his decks for action.

Sturry came in a minute later. 'My lord?'

'I want Haskins, Joseph, William and the gardeners to muster outside in ten minutes. We are taking the second boat down to be of use in the village. In my absence Miss Greenham is in com—control of the preparations for receiving any villagers driven from their homes. Miss Greenham, not Lady Willoughby. You understand this?'

'Yes, my lord, but if her ladyship—'

'Her ladyship is unlikely to wish to have anything to do with "peasants", as she so charmingly terms the villagers, but just remember this is my house, not hers, and my orders are clear.'

'Yes, my lord. I understand.'

'Good. Then let us be about our duties, Sturry.'

The butler thought his lordship sounded better than he had since Christmas. Having something active to do was good for him, not a doubt of it.

Clothed for warmth and practicality, and sartorially so badly that Cottam nearly assisted him into his coat with his eyes shut, Lord Athelney met his designated boat's crew in the courtyard. Mr Bitton had had the boat hauled out and placed on a cart, and a horse put to in readiness. The men looked unsure of themselves, but his lordship's leadership soon instilled them with a sense of purpose and faith that they could do the job. They set off down the hill a little after the lieutenant. Anne Greenham, hearing the hoofs striking the cobbles under the gatehouse arch, offered up a prayer for them all, and one in particular.

* * *

The Dower House was still in a state of flux. Barwell was struggling to keep the maids from hysteria, since once one had decided that they would all be drowned they all took up the panic. He had asked permission for his favoured chair and a few personal items to be brought up from his little private parlour, which was his refuge from the predominance of women in the house, and accepted that it might be a considerable time before he might sit in peaceful isolation with a glass of her ladyship's better brandy. Cook was in tears, having been told to abandon the majority of her pots and pans that could be rescued and scoured after the water subsided, and was sending glassware and china upstairs.

Eleanor Burgess was not panic-stricken. She knew the house was certainly of a height that there was no fear of drowning unless the water arrived in such a flood as to force its way in before the occupants had abandoned below stairs. She was concerned as to whether they might have all the moveable items up on the first floor in time. She had commenced with the moving of all those things that were easy to remove, but there were those that were heavy and cumbersome. The library, a room which Lady Willoughby rarely used, was perhaps the greatest worry. Rescuing all the volumes would take too long, and Eleanor had been forced to make a decision as to the height above which she thought the books might be safe. Even if she had miscalculated, she told herself, she could not be so far out that more than one or two shelves would be lost, for the ground floor of the house was some four feet above ground level. She could only assume that the house had been built in a period when it had been very dry, or perhaps it had been intended that the rooms used by the aristocratic inhabitants should be above all but the worst inundation. It certainly seemed to have been sited with far more attention paid to the view than its position with reference to the river. The library table was too large to move, but she had got the footmen to raise it on as much lumber as they could find, and get it some two feet from the floor. The bookcases would simply suffer if the water got in. The gardener's lads had filled some sacks with soil to place before the door, but she thought it no more than a token. She had been up until nearly midnight, and risen in the darkness at half past six. Besides clearing as much as possible, she had to make provision for some basic cooking, and a supply of wood. The large fireplace in the drawing room was now adorned by a spit from which pots might be hung, and the hearth filled with an assortment of kitchen utensils Lady Willoughby would have never even seen.

One of the youngest maids had been detailed to watch from an attic window, and give warning when the riverbanks were breached. A little before midday a high-pitched cry was heard, and a minute later Sukie was bobbing a curtsey whilst gabbling that there was water now turning the puddles into a lake. Eleanor took a deep breath, rang the bell to below stairs, which was the signal for everyone to leave, and said quietly, 'Now we shall see.'

* * *

By the time the marquis's boat reached the Sittford bridge, it was raining heavily, and the river was beginning to spew over the top and swirl about either end, since no more could gush beneath the arches. It was already a foot in depth, and expanding and deepening by the minute. Lord Athelney had the boat removed from the cart, and sent horse and wagon back up the hill. The boat was inverted and carried across the bridge to the churchyard, where he met Lieutenant Bitton, who saluted.

'Boat's crew mustered and ready, sir. Septimus has got some people into his house already, but many wish to defend their homes as long as they may. Persuading them to leave might prove hard until there is no alternative. Those with an upper storey have moved upstairs with whatever they can move, but they are few in number.'

'Good. The water is now eddying about both ends of the bridge. Since the hill rises quite sharply on the Kingscastle side I think we will shortly be getting far more than our feet wet here. Until it reaches knee depth we might as well push the boats, unless there is a very strong current.' Lord Athelney smiled as a rivulet of water ran down his neck. 'Almost like old times, Mr Bitton, but we have no sails to reef.'

'Indeed, my lord. Shall I take the west or east side of the thoroughfare?'

'It matters not. The west, go on. I fear my idea of the boarding has proved pathetically inadequate. This is going to be deep, very deep. Tell the reluctant ones that, Mr Bitton.'

'Aye aye, my lord.'

They set about their business. The villagers seemed to have divided between those who had accepted their fate and departed for the vicarage early, those who held on to the faint hope that it would not be as bad as they feared, and the few who remained adamant that they would not abandon their homes, until, that was, the waters rushed within. The boats were greeted with relief from most and as admissions of surrender by others.

The first crash of splintering glass heralded the victory of the floodwaters over the Dower House. Several maids screamed, but Eleanor told herself that to expect anything less would have been foolish in the extreme. One of the gardeners began quoting scripture, but, despite being a clergyman's daughter, Eleanor did not think it very helpful to hear of the ark bobbing about with no sight of land.

'Thank you, Samuel. The Dower House neither floats nor will it sink, and dry land is visible less than a hundred yards away.'

'It is a judgement upon the ungodly, ma'am.'

'Well, none of us are perfect, but the floodwaters will affect those who are more godly as greatly as those who are less so.'

'And the Reverend Greenham expects the church and parsonage to flood, and where could be more godly in the parish?' added the under-footman.

Old Samuel shook his head, and remained unconvinced.

CHAPTER NINETEEN

ELEANOR BURGESS CHASTISED HERSELF for foolishness. She felt an irrational glow of pleasure simply because she thought that she understood what Captain Hawksmoor had felt in command of a ship, the ultimate authority and with the ultimate responsibility for those within it. Her command would not float away, certainly, though it was now surrounded by swirling waters that came up to the fourth stair on the main staircase, but everyone so obviously looked to her for advice, though she had no experience upon which to draw.

The afternoon had eventually settled into calm, once the youngest maids accepted that the water was not going to go over the roof and drown them all, there had been an end to the cracking of window glass, and Barwell had in his turn agreed, reluctantly, that the servants might sit upon the chairs in the public rooms. Since their beds were in the attics, his sensibilities would not be overwhelmed by the thought of those from below stairs curling up on the fine upholstered sofas, though he was pained to see them eating at her ladyship's highly polished mahogany dining table. There was also the problem of where to put foodstuffs. Cook, having taken possession of the drawing room fireplace, was quite content to have boxes of vegetables to hand, but the butler was resolute that they must remain upon the landing until required. Eleanor had to intervene in what was fast becoming a heated dispute.

Once darkness fell, the Dower House felt different, and, though she denied it publicly, she could see why the maids disliked leaving the drawing room unless accompanied. Looking down the stairs into a blackness that was silent and yet threatening, was eerie. The house had been invaded, possessed by a malevolent water spirit that sought mindless destruction. Before she sought her bed, Eleanor stood with her candle at the top of the stairs and looked down to the inky darkness, and felt very alone. The water below was that same river that had tried to drown her. He had saved her before, but now? She did not really need saving, did not want him to save her, fickle-hearted man that he was, and yet . . . Her dreams were full of cold currents and swirling water, and being held safe in arms that would not release her.

In the parsonage, Septimus Greenham was guiltily aware that he wanted peace. It was not the fault of the infants that cried, the nervous mothers, fraught by worries about their few possessions at the mercy of the waters in their homes, who scolded sharply, or the older children who could not resist, especially when prohibited from doing so, exploring the grandeur of the parson's private quarters. He had already shooed three girls from his sister's bedchamber, where they were prancing about like 'ladies', draped in a shawl she had left on the bed in her rush to pack, and dabbing her lavender water behind ears that would better see soap and water.

'Oh Lord, grant me patience and charity,' he murmured fervently, hoping that he might rise with the winter dawn and see the waters at least receding.

That part of the prayer was not heeded. If anything, the water level had risen overnight, and he thought the ground floor must be a good five feet deep in water, and mud. He dared not think about how long it would be before the place was properly habitable again, nor the cost. It did not occur to him that the living being in the gift of the Marquis of Athelney, the costs of restoration would fall to him.

His sister's concerns about so many persons living in what were essentially the parsonage bedchambers proved valid. There were nineteen villagers in addition to himself and the three house servants: twenty-two souls in need of meals, a place to sleep and make their ablutions. Water was the greatest problem. He had every container that could hold more than a cupful of water filled and placed in the smallest bedchamber, but this would not last more than another day. Boiling bucketfuls collected from the swirling murk was not appealing. Tomorrow, he decided, he would get the boat and its still inexperienced crew, and begin ferrying people to the Kingscastle side.

'I do not see why these . . . persons . . . are given the right to enter the house. Surely it would be sufficient to send out food and water to them. Think of the risk, Athelney.'

'The risk, ma'am?' Lord Athelney was dangerously calm. His aunt had appeared at breakfast and not stopped in her monologue about how her rest had been disturbed by fears of what was happening in her beloved home, and that the peasantry occupying the gatehouse might not, overnight, develop republican tendencies and murder her in her bed. He had reached the stage at which he might give three hearty cheers to whoever did the deed. 'Of contagion?'

'Well, that too, yes, for they carry all sorts of ghastly diseases and vermin, of course, but I meant to your property. I should lock away the family silver and keep the key about your person, but do not let even the servants know you have it, lest it become a motive for your being attacked.'

Charlotte walked in, in time to hear the last part of this doom-laden scenario. She frowned. 'The villagers would not steal from Kingscastle, Mama.'

'Of course they would.'

'No. They are good, honest people, and grateful for

278

being given shelter in their time of trouble.'

'You are starting to sound like a Methodist preacher,' remarked her mother waspishly. 'You can have no knowledge of them.'

'On the contrary, Mama, since I spent yesterday afternoon reading stories to the children and have this morning already been with Anne to see that they all passed a comfortable night.'

Lady Willoughby dropped the spoon she was stirring in her coffee cup with a clatter. 'You did what?'

'I need not repeat myself, Mama, surely? I could not do much, but as Anne says—'

'Anne. The Greenham . . . woman, you mean. I forbid you to consort with such an ill-bred female.'

'Her breeding, I have every reason to believe, is impeccable,' interjected Lord Athelney, quietly.

'She is impertinent, opinionated, and she has no concept of the niceties of society.'

'Put a shot across your bows, did she?' The marquis managed a smile.

'I do not pretend to understand what I assume is vulgar seaman's parlance, Athelney, but she spoke to me yesterday in such a way as to make it impossible for me to suffer her presence.'

'She did, then. If she refused to let you have the running of what happened when those seeking refuge reached Kingscastle, she had my sanction to do so. I did not think,' he lied smoothly, 'that you ought to be concerned with such, er, menial matters.'

'Nor should I, but she ought to have referred to me upon all points.'

'Why?'

'Why? Because . . . Because I am the . . . This is . . .' Lady Willoughby faltered, and looked daggers at her nephew.

'No, it is not. It is my house, and I gave instructions that Miss Greenham was to be in charge in my absence.'

'Would you have a mere vicarage virgin running Kingscastle?' Lady Willoughby had lost her temper. 'Do you have no idea what is due to your name? Are you so easily beguiled?'

He looked suddenly very angry. Charlotte paled. He rose from the table, made his aunt the slightest of bows, then a deeper one to Charlotte, and stalked towards the door.

'Be careful, Athelney, before you commit yourself to a nobody who will drag the name of Hawksmoor in the dust.'

He turned.

'I think you will find, ma'am, that your son did that most efficiently, some time past,' he snapped, and very nearly slammed the door behind him.

He was fuming, in part at himself for having riposted as he did. The woman was insufferable. She was all the things she claimed to find in Miss Greenham, and she had ruined his breakfast. For one brief moment the image he had once had, of Eleanor Burgess sitting in a green gown, brightening his breakfast, not gabbling but making plans for the day, flitted through his mind, and his heart ached. That Lady Willoughby had taken the idea that he was now trying to fix his interest with Anne Greenham was ridiculous. She was an excellent woman, but she was not the object of his affections. She was, however, Harry Bitton's. Anyone with eyes could see how things lay between them, and if the next few days of enforced proximity did not bring things to a head, he might be giving fatherly advice to his erstwhile first lieutenant.

At that moment, Miss Greenham herself came down the stairs to the hallway. Her hair had been a little disordered, since she had crossed the courtyard in the wind and rain, and she had been to tidy it before breakfast. She smiled at him as she made a curtsey.

'Good morning, my lord. I say "good" in the broadest sense, for it is foul weather out there.'

'Good morning, Miss Greenham. Have you been making your rounds?'

'I have checked that all is well with your enforced visitors, yes, and seen to it that breakfast is being provided. I suggested to Cook that a large pot of porridge would be best, and could be carried over to the gatehouse, if covered, and distributed there.'

'Is Mr Bitton in the gatehouse at present?'

'Indeed, my lord, he was removing the estate books to his bedchamber in the, perhaps vain, hope that he might work upon them there in some degree of peace.'

'I shall go and suggest he beats a retreat here, temporarily, while he is "invaded". Is there anything you require, Miss Greenham?'

'Oh no, thank you, my lord. I was about to take my own breakfast if I may, and then I thought Miss Charlotte and I could gather all the children who attend Sunday school and keep them busy with a little learning. How silly! I do require some paper and a pen and ink with which I might draw the letters of the alphabet. If they could be left here in the vestibule.'

'Of course. Enjoy your breakfast, Miss Greenham, and thank you.'

It was not very fair, casting the poor girl into the lioness's den, but Lord Athelney thought Anne Greenham would not be put off by his aunt. He headed to the gatehouse to find Harry Bitton.

The gatehouse was not full, but seemed so at first glance, since he had only previously seen it with at most two other people in it. A respectful hush descended when he walked into the constable's chamber, forelocks were tugged, curtseys bobbed. It was not that dissimilar to being between decks, and he acknowledged everyone with a cheery 'Good morning' and a slight smile. He received the same reception in the 'parlour' and went up to the bedchambers above. Mr Bitton looked a little beleaguered. His books were cast about his bed, and he blinked at his visitor.

'My lord, you find me at sixes and sevens.'

'So I heard from the estimable Miss Greenham. I believe she is going to take school below. I suggest I help you with these tomes and you come back to the house for some sanity . . . Unless you bump into my aunt, in which case sanity will leap out of the window.'

'I can manage th—'

'I have not lost the use of my arms through elevation to the peerage, Mr Bitton. Now, hand me that ledger.'

There were times, thought the incumbent of the parish, that one knew one was being tested. In his calling it was most often a testing of faith, but this was a simple test of strength of will and body. Well, he was no Samson, but nor was he a weakling. He could pull an oar as well as most men, and it seemed wrong to act as if he was a master of the tiller. Better he leave that to Jem Rickling, who had at least been watching Harry Bitton at the helm the day before yesterday. The boat had been attached by two good ropes to one of the two stout pillars of the parsonage's neat little portico. Getting to it, and moreover getting women and children into it, would be more problematic. The water was so deep that only by swimming might one reach the front door. The only reasonable way would be to climb out of the sash window above the portico, hoping it would take the weight of more than one adult, and assist the passengers down the two and a half feet into the boat, without it tipping up. It was a good day to pray.

Bravado, or genuine excitement, enabled many of the children to get into the boat without delay, but each trip was hampered by the elderly, the women with infants in arms, and the simply nervous. It was ten of the clock, according to the long-case clock that had been lovingly manhandled up onto the landing, before the first party was ready to go. With a full complement of rowers, there was only room for another six people in the boat. Rowing was not especially hard until they neared the full flow where the river ran its normal course, and then it took all their strength to get across and not be swept further downstream. Once in the quieter eddies where the hill rose out of the water, they took great lungfuls of air, and let aching muscles relax. He would not say so out loud, but what they faced in ferrying was not without risk. They disgorged their first party, and saw them begin their trek up the hill. Then they set off back towards the village.

By the time they had brought a second group to shore, a cart was waiting to carry the villagers up to the castle, and the second boat had been removed from it and was about to set off. Septimus Greenham, already with blistered hands, expected to see Harry Bitton in charge, but it was the Marquis of Athelney himself at the helm, and looking in remarkably good spirits for a man already thoroughly wet.

'Good morning, Greenham, or rather,' he consulted his pocket watch, which declared it just after twelve, 'good afternoon. Forced to abandon ship, so I hear.'

'Alas yes, my lord. Not only too cramped but not enough fresh water for so many beyond today.'

'Water, of course.' His voice dropped to a murmur the parson could only just discern. 'I did not think of that, and I'll wager nor has she.' He smiled at the parson. 'We shall endeavour to ease your burden to and fro. I take it the flow of the river is . . . invigorating.'

'I think you can safely say, my lord, that we rowers are exceedingly invigorated.'

'Well, do not become too exhausted. Take a few minutes before you head back, for we are on our way. How many more cargoes have you to ship?'

'I would say we need another two trips, my lord.'

'Very good. We will be about the first of them. I shall see you later, no doubt. Good luck.'

With which Lord Athelney had his boat's crew unship their oars and set off across the floodwaters.

It was nearly three o'clock when the last of the parsonage refugees was ferried to the hill. Septimus Greenham packed a small box with consecrated wine and the silver chalice and paten so that if required he might hold Sunday service in the castle, using the shawl he had rescued from being played with to pad it. Another shawl would not come amiss to his sister. For his own needs he had two shirts and some linens, his razor and comb and the Bible his father had given him upon ordination.

Lord Athelney sent him and his men up to the castle, and ordered the cart to return for the boat, but then to make its way down the track towards the Dower House. He would be bringing the staff from there up to the castle before dark. He asked the parson to request Miss Greenham to arrange for a guest chamber to be prepared for Miss Burgess and to have a fire lit in it.

The boat had to go against the current to round the bend to the east side of the promontory, but they kept to where the flow was less turbulent for as long as possible, and then cut across to where the Dower House loomed out of a lake of water. The ground was lower than the riverbank and the water had cascaded into the depression with such force that windows in the lower ground floor had been broken. They were dimly visible below the level of the water, so that the house appeared like a sinking ship. The water was now nearly three feet deep at the front door itself, and Lord Athelney's first thought was how he might hail the shipwrecked inhabitants, and then get them from the building. Fortunately, on the south side of the house there was a small balcony attached to the library, and the boat could be grappled to it, even though it was fractionally below the water level. His lordship climbed onto the balcony and simply broke a pane of glass to enable him to break into his own property and slowly push the window open. Disregarding the cold water, which reached midway up his thighs, he made his way across the room, and forced open the door into the hall. He then promptly tripped over the bags of soil that had been left there in a fruitless attempt to keep out the water. Spluttering, and muttering seamanlike obscenities under his breath, he sloshed to the stairway and called up to the floor above. Upon his third shout Miss Burgess appeared, already with a candle, for it was very gloomy within the house.

'My lord? You gave us somewhat of a fright. Er, you are all wet.' *He could not possibly have swum into the house, could he?* she wondered illogically.

'I am, ma'am, and would therefore be obliged if we kept social niceties to a minimum. I am come to remove you all to the castle.'

'We shall not drown here, my lord.'

'No, but tell me how many days' supply of fresh water you have, Miss Burgess.' His tone was not amicable.

'I . . . oh.' She had not asked Cook about the water situation, and that lady had thought poor Miss Burgess had enough to worrit herself about without the news that water would have to be collected from the flood and boiled by the morrow. 'But we are surrounded by water, my lord.'

'Water that is full of the detritus washed from upstream, and which will require boiling, ma'am, when we at the castle have our well, plenty of food, every facility.' He softened his tone. 'The Reverend Greenham has brought his "waifs and strays" to the castle today for that very reason. Show sense, ma'am, and do the same.'

He was climbing the stairs now, his breeches clinging to his legs, his coat dripping.

'I . . . shall inform the staff, my lord, but do you expect us all to struggle through the water to the library window, which I take it was your place of entry?'

'The men can do so. Some of the women may be too short to do so safely. I shall carry any that require it.'

That, she thought, was more than enough to give Cook hysterics.

Entering the drawing room, he was favourably impressed by the organisation he found there. Cook had soup bubbling away, and a kettle whistled, reminiscent of a bosun's call piping the side for him.

'Listen to me, everyone. We have a boat downstairs to convey you to the cart at the water's edge, which will take you to the castle. There is no room for possessions, excepting perhaps a change of footwear that will be dry. It will take two journeys, and I wish to mix male and female members of staff in each trip, for weight. Miss Burgess will nominate the first group.'

'What about my soup?' asked Cook practically.

'Leave it and douse the fire. It is more important to try and get the evacuation completed before it is totally dark. I shall be at the bottom of the stairs to assist you all. Now, Miss Burgess, if you please.'

Eleanor reeled off the names of the first half dozen servants, who went apprehensively down the stairs, the men with their boots, laces tied together, about their necks. Barwell had also provided himself with a soft muffler, being, as he said, prone to take chill. Upon seeing the depth of the water he jibbed like a frightened horse, but Silas, the journeyman gardener, a large young man, offered to carry him piggy back to the boat. Twenty minutes later the other staff members were assembled on the stairs in readiness. Eleanor stood at the back. Eventually his lordship returned for her and held out his hand.

'Your turn, Miss Burgess. You at least know for

certain that I can carry your weight.'

'I am not going, my lord.'

'What?'

'There is plenty of water if only I remain, and I shall be perfectly safe. I was ordered to—'

'You were ordered by a woman of no sense and are acting like a woman of no sense.'

Part of her knew this, and yet the thought of being at the castle and seeing him with Miss Greenham, bestowing upon her the looks and words she had but so recently enjoyed, was more than she could bear.

'I am sorry to give you so low an opinion of me, my lord, but so it must be. I do not abandon my post.'

'You will do as you are told, ma'am,' he barked. 'I said I would come for you, and come for you I have. I do not intend to leave my men, who are cold and wet and have laboured at risk all afternoon, to pander to your foolishness. Come, give me your hand, or, by God, I shall come and put you over my shoulder, and if you struggle you will still end up at the castle, only as wet as I am.'

He was cold, tired, and certainly in no mood to let her dither and potentially put the lives of those waiting in the boat at risk. She paused for a moment, wondering if she might retreat to the garret and elude him, but logic told her he would not leave without her. She trod purposefully down the stairs, her face a mask of calm that she did not feel, though the gloom made it almost impossible for him to discern her features.

'You need not threaten me, my lord.' She tried to

sound in control, though patently she was not.

'It was not a threat, ma'am, merely a declaration of intent, because you cannot safely remain here. It is madness to suggest it.'

'No doubt you could explain the difference at some point,' Eleanor could not help retaliating.

Her antagonism was like a slap in the face, but was followed, in sharp contrast, by her slipping her arm about his neck. She was not going to let him think her afraid, of the situation, or his embrace. In other circumstances it was an act that would have sent a frisson through him. She felt his hair, damp still from his earlier immersion, cold against his neck, and blushed in the darkness. He swung her up into his arms, and ploughed his way through the water to the library. She lay passive in his hold, acutely aware of the last time he had carried her. He crossed the room to the balcony, where he set her gently into the boat, and then took the tiller. His only words thereafter were to the oarsmen.

The cart was waiting to carry them up to the castle. He detailed two men to remain and assist in the loading of the boat onto the cart as soon as the Dower House servants had reached shelter, and promised the men hot punch and an extra day's pay for their efforts.

When the cart stood in the castle courtyard, he reached to offer Eleanor his hand. To refuse it would seem petty, and so she let him assist her from the cart with a murmured thanks. He ushered everyone into the house to get warm and dry by the hall fire, where

Miss Greenham stood, directing the provision of warm blankets and hot toddy. Miss Greenham saw Eleanor's cold, pinched face, and came forward solicitously.

'Oh, Miss Burgess, you must be frozen to the marrow, without even a cloak to keep you warm. Let me take you to your bedchamber immediately.'

She spoke in all kindness, but Eleanor could only think how much at home she sounded, as if greeting guests as lady of the house. Her throat constricted, and she simply nodded. Anne Greenham took her by the arm, promising a warm foot-bath and a tray of supper in her room, and his lordship watched the pair as they went up the broad stairs. At the half landing Miss Burgess turned, and thanked him very soberly for his aid. He only wished he felt that she really meant it.

CHAPTER TWENTY

ELEANOR'S SPIRITS WERE LOW, EVEN AS her body warmed. Anne Greenham did not fuss over her, but left her to recover and set about the practical things that would aid her. Eleanor felt crushed. Supper, taken hiding in her room, seemed all she could face. Lady Willoughby would probably interrogate her about which items had been abandoned to the water and then harangue her for not achieving the impossible. Worse was the thought of seeing Lord Athelney with Anne Greenham. She had looked so at ease, so much at home, and with that indefinable glow about her that betokened a woman in love, and confident of its reciprocation. However circumspect, there would be those moments when eye met eye and unspoken thoughts passed between them in the telepathy of mutual adoration. If seeing her look lovingly at him would be hard, seeing that affection returned would be like a knife in Eleanor's heart. She tried to persuade herself that she had been wise to refuse a man whose affections could be transferred so swiftly. Whatever he had hinted to her of being ready to love her had simply been a readiness to love anyone. No, that was unfair. Anne Greenham was not anyone; she was a sensible, attractive and thoroughly decent young woman, and hating her for those qualities was as indefensible as it was ungovernable. Eleanor Burgess slept badly.

She went down to breakfast the next morning with a feeling of dread, and entered the breakfast parlour with a face as sombre as if attending a wake. The atmosphere was heavy with animosity, which took her aback. She made her curtsey to the assembly and took a seat midway down the table. Lord Athelney appeared to be in a state of simmering wrath, the Reverend Greenham both surprised and offended and, more surprisingly, Mr Bitton was in a brown study and paying no attention whatsoever to what was being said.

This was all coming from Lady Willoughby, and although Miss Greenham's manner was one of tolerating a child with a tantrum, Charlotte looked visibly distressed. Whatever the diatribe, it ceased upon her entry into the room, and Lady Willoughby turned her anger upon her paid companion. She looked Eleanor up and down, sniffed, and demanded to know how she had the effrontery to come before her employer having failed so miserably to fulfil her duties.

'I can assure you, ma'am, that there was no more that could be done to secure the contents of the house. We were merely stranded there. Besides, I did not leave from choice.'

'You can scarcely expect me to believe that you were abducted.' Lady Willoughby snorted.

'Yet in effect that was what occurred.'

'My nephew carried you off by force?' Her eyebrows were raised in disbelief.

'I did, actually.' Athelney did not look at his aunt, but kept his eyes upon Eleanor. His voice was very calm.

'Impossible.'

'On the contrary. Any attempt at struggling would have resulted in her being dropped into the water. Miss Burgess was not that foolish.'

Eleanor threw up her chin at that, thinking there was the faintest of stress upon the word 'that'. He thought her foolish, did he? Presumably not like the perfect Miss Greenham, calmly nibbling a piece of buttered toast and with the hint of a smile in her eyes.

'Oh, indeed, my lord, I am not *that* foolish, though I admit to it in the recent past.' Her words were barbed, and she knew they stung, for a look of hurt surprise came into his eyes, and his mouth set in a hard line.

Lady Willoughby did not look in any way appeased. 'Then she should have come to me immediately upon arrival here and made her explanation and apology then, not waited until today.'

'She has no reason to apologise to you at all, ma'am. You should rather be apologising to her for putting her in such a position,' Lord Athelney growled at his aunt.

Miss Greenham, in an attempt to pour oil upon the waters, interjected gently, 'Miss Burgess was so wet and chilled that presenting herself before you, ma'am, would have been most unwise.'

If oil was poured, it was then ignited.

'If I required your view upon the matter, indeed upon any matter, Miss Greenham, I should have asked for it. I did not.'

Anne Greenham merely acknowledged the snub with an inclination of the head. Her brother frowned. He knew Lady Willoughby to be an unpleasant woman, but her behaviour this morning was the outside of enough. No wonder their host looked so irate.

Charlotte gave Miss Greenham a look of acute embarrassment and entreating apology, which received a smile.

'I think,' declared Miss Greenham sweetly, 'that I should make my preparations for school. If you would excuse me, my lord?' She looked at Lord Athelney, who managed a small smile. Eleanor felt as if her toast had turned to ashes in her mouth. 'Would you care to join me, Miss Burgess, when you have breakfasted? I feel that I have usurped your place.'

'Usurped my place?' murmured Eleanor weakly. Did she know of Lord Athelney's declarations to her? Had he confessed them?

'As teacher of the Sunday school.'

'Oh.'

'Eleanor is not paid to teach. She is paid as my companion.' Lady Willoughby sounded like a child unwilling to share a toy. 'She will be unavailable to you.'

'I, however, will therefore be at liberty to assist you, Miss Greenham, if you think me equal to the task,' piped up Miss Hawksmoor.

Charlotte did not look at her mother, but at the parson's sister. Having felt triumphant, Lady Willoughby found herself trapped in a corner. To claim that she required her daughter's presence also sounded precious in the extreme. She was reduced to making a huffing noise, and announcing to the world in general that 'things had come to a pretty pass'. Which things, and to what pass, were not specified.

Miss Greenham rose from the table, and the gentlemen did also, her brother smiling encouragingly at her, and Mr Bitton, suddenly roused from whatever he was contemplating so deeply, went to open the door for her, announcing that there were a few papers that he had neglected to bring over from the gatehouse the previous afternoon.

Eleanor drained her teacup. Her appetite had disappeared. She also got up, since the breakfast party was dispersing, and promised to adjourn to Lady Willoughby's private sitting room within a very few minutes.

'Might I speak to you before you do so, Miss Burgess?'

Lord Athelney sounded very serious. She nearly jumped.

'No. I mean, it would not be convenient this morning, my lord.' She blushed, and did not meet his eye.

Rebuffed, he bowed, and did not repeat the request. It was a morose marquis who withdrew to his library, where Septimus Greenham found him some half hour later.

'My lord, I . . .' He stopped, seeing the marquis's expression, which was troubled. Technically, of course, his lordship was a parishioner as well as his patron, but he hardly felt that he could enquire as to what troubled him.

Lord Athelney gave a wry smile. 'Carry on, Mr Greenham.'

'I was wondering how we return to normal. Even if the waters recede within a few days, the damage is done. I am not at all sure the houses in the village will be habitable for some time, being begrimed with mud and exceedingly damp. I would be very surprised if the parsonage doors were not so swollen as to prevent any of them shutting, and as for the papered walls . . .' He sighed. 'I imagine there will be artisans in Shepton Mallet I could employ.'

'I shall be presenting a considerable list to the Trustees, for the repair of the village houses, and the parsonage. I cannot see how they could refuse. If the money were in my hands . . .' He paused. 'There would be no doubt about it. I do not shirk my duties.'

'I was not mentioning this in order for you to cover

the repairs, my lord. I was simply wondering how everyone might live if their homes were uninhabitable until at least partially dried out.' Septimus Greenham was caught between affront that Lord Athelney might think him angling for aid, and respect for the man who had no intention of avoiding the expense that this natural disaster had brought about. Not all landowners would have reacted as he had.

'I imagine that they will return to clear up as best they can, but remain here to eat and sleep for some time after the waters drop. If you also require accommodation, you know that it is at your disposal. This house is large and rambling and can easily cope. Whether I can cope with the presence of my aunt is not the same thing.'

'She is . . .' Words failed the parson.

'Oh, she most definitely is. She would drive a saint to sinning, and I am no saint to start with. Could you add a prayer for deliverance to your orisons, Greenham?'

'I shall, my lord.'

Lord Athelney's wry smile had become a grimace.

Anne Greenham rather liked teaching, even if the level was very basic, and at times it was more an exercise in the containment of youthful spirits. Charlotte Hawksmoor was seated in the corner of the room, reading a story to the youngest children. Both felt a twinge of guilt that Eleanor was trapped with Lady Willoughby. When the parson entered the chamber, the children stood respectfully, and he gestured for them to sit down again.

Miss Hawksmoor coloured, and smiled shyly at him. She rarely smiled in her mama's presence, and he was struck by how singularly sweet she looked. It was as if she had previously been invisible to him.

'Ladies, I am come to remind you that it lacks but a quarter hour until luncheon. Lessons may end for the morning.'

'Is the hour so advanced? Goodness me,' declared Charlotte, quite surprised. 'How quickly the morning has passed by.'

Brother smiled at sister. Miss Hawksmoor had, in all innocence, just indicated how much the morning felt an entertainment.

'May I escort you both to the house?' he asked, with tongue-in-cheek gallantry.

'Why yes, brother dear, for it is so very perilous and far across the courtyard. I do hope we are not attacked by bandits.'

'Or lions,' offered Miss Hawksmoor.

'Now, Miss Hawksmoor, that is most unlikely for lions were eradicated from Somerset some years ago.' His eyes danced but his voice was as serious as when he delivered the sermon.

Miss Hawksmoor giggled. A child looked up, puzzled, understanding the words 'lions' and 'Somerset' and connecting the two. He also assumed that whatever the parson said was serious and 'gospel truth'.

'Lionses? Here?'

Miss Hawksmoor raised her eyebrows as if to say,

See if you can explain.

'Er, no, Thomas.'

'But you said, sir.'

'I said they were not here, Thomas.'

'But do lionses not hide and leap out and eat you?'

'Well . . .'

'So how can you know they aren't here, hiding?'

Miss Hawksmoor and Miss Greenham were struggling to control their features. The clergyman was floundering.

'There are no lions in Somerset, Thomas. We are very fortunate in England that we do not have animals that eat people. You should say thank you to God that you live in England when you say your prayers tonight.'

He glanced at the ladies with a hint of triumph.

'What about monsters?' another child piped up. 'Mama says if you don't go to sleep the monsters get you.'

This left Septimus Greenham in a quandary. He could not undermine the parent, but nor could he say monsters existed to grab naughty awake children. Miss Hawksmoor came to his relief.

'Monsters do not eat people, dear. They growl at them and make them frightened.'

The child accepted this explanation at face value, and nodded sagely. 'Growling would frighten me.'

'School will start again when I ring the bell, children,' announced Miss Greenham decisively.

The three adults made their escape.

'I have committed the sin of telling a falsehood, Mr

Greenham. Will I be forgiven?' Miss Hawksmoor looked up a little shyly as he took the arm of each lady.

'Since it saved me from an impossible position, Miss Hawksmoor, I think you will be. Besides, children are often afraid of monsters, and what better reason than them growling. Perhaps you spoke the truth, as a child sees it.'

'That is rather more hopeful than accurate, Septimus.'

'I am an optimist by nature, sister.'

Eleanor arrived at the luncheon table with a frown that was only partially the consequence of her headache. Lady Willoughby had sent her on various errands of an entirely spurious nature simply to penalise her for something over which she had had no control. Remaining in the Dower House had not been possible when Lord Athelney was fully prepared to remove her by force, but her ladyship refused to acknowledge this. It required little more to persuade Eleanor that he was thus responsible for the situation in which she now found herself, and only one further step to see it as intentional. Her sound common sense decried this as rank stupidity, but she was stressed, tired and at the lowest possible ebb.

She had resolved not to rise to the frequent cutting remarks her employer might make, and simply plan her letter of resignation, which she would place before Lady Willoughby as soon as the weather would not preclude long-distance travel. It was the obvious answer to her problems. Remaining in Lady Willoughby's service would be unthinkable, and in the neighbourhood of Lord Athelney and his bride impossible. She would even be home for her sister's wedding, though the contemplation of any nuptials could not be said to thrill her at the moment. She would tell Mama, tell her everything, and Mama would understand, at least everything except the second refusal, and since he could not have been sincere, she would see that it was, with hindsight, the right decision.

The trio from the gatehouse, spared any attack by lions hiding in the courtyard, arrived in good spirits, which incensed Lady Willoughby. She saw the parsonage pair as dangerous, and Charlotte's pleasure in their company as tantamount to mutiny. Eleanor assumed that Lord Athelney's unapproachable demeanour sprang from his antagonism to his aunt, but a fleeting thought did wonder why Miss Greenham's smiling face did not give him respite from the natural irritation of a man whose hospitality is not only abused but who has one guest who ruins the stay of the others.

'Charlotte, you have neglected your Berlin work. You should remain with me this afternoon and complete that corner of the cushion.' Lady Willoughby smiled, but it was a patronising smile. 'You may then tell me all about your morning with the others, but do change your gown first. I do not want anything to spread from it in my rooms. The maid can brush it down and hang it apart from your other gowns.'

Charlotte opened her mouth to speak, and then closed it. She simply did not know how to respond. She was not even totally convinced that her mama was referring to the village infants and not the Greenhams. The same thought occurred to the parson, but he contented himself with remarking that the tidiness of the villagers, and their progeny, was remarkable, especially given the nature of their evacuation.

'They do not know wealth, but there is no squalor in Sittford. While it is more common in cities, it is not unheard of in rural communities. The parishioners of St Dunstan's are clean of habit and secure in their own simple worth.'

'Worth? You mean they aspire to mimic their betters?' Lady Willoughby's lip curled.

'I take issue with the word "better", ma'am. They are respectful of those whose social position is higher than their own, but wealth and privilege do not equate with moral superiority.'

'Are you daring to lecture me, sir?'

'Not at all, Lady Willoughby. I am simply stating that lack of wealth does not equate with moral turpitude.'

'You will be saying next that that old servant woman who now resides with the wheelwright is my equal.'

'Only in the sight of God, ma'am.'

'Bringing the Almighty into this is blasphemous. I shall not attend to you.'

With which Lady Willoughby pointedly turned to the unfortunate Mr Bitton, and began to lecture him on the likelihood of being hoodwinked into spending his employer's funds.

Charlotte threw the Greenhams a look of profound apology, and whispered that she was terribly sorry that she might not continue in the gatehouse after luncheon.

Eleanor had said nothing during the interchange, but watched. She did not realise that she herself was being observed by Lord Athelney. He took in the dark rings beneath her eyes, the pale and slightly hollowed cheeks, the slight sag to her shoulders. She looked worn to death, he thought, and wished he might alleviate her burdens. Being hampered from doing so frustrated him, but worse was the idea that he might in some part be their cause.

'Miss Burgess.'

She turned, startled, though he spoke softly enough that it did not halt Lady Willoughby, now in full flow. 'My lord?'

'Since my cousin will be with her mama this afternoon, you should be free to at least let me speak with you for a short while in the morning room.'

'Miss Hawksmoor's presence is not usually a signal that my services are to be dispensed with, sir.'

'Yet an absence of perhaps as little as ten minutes could not be seen as a dereliction of duty.'

'By a normal person, perhaps not. But we are talking of one who holds me accountable because I could not hold the river back from flooding the basement of a house set below the level of the riverbank, nor forgive me for being removed from my post by force.'

'Would you really have preferred to remain in the Dower House alone?'

'I . . . It was my duty.'

'While a captain faces court martial for losing his ship, he is not expected to sink with it.'

'The Dower House is not, unless you have knowledge of the foundations that I do not possess, sinking, my lord.'

'Ten minutes, Miss Burgess. Shall we say in the morning room, at three o'clock?' He disliked pressuring her, but saw no alternative.

'I cannot guarantee it, my lord, but I will endeavour to be there at that hour.'

'Thank you.'

CHAPTER TWENTY-ONE

LORD ATHELNEY ADJOURNED TO THE MORNING room some considerable time before three o'clock, and paced up and down, which familiar activity was remarkably calming to his spirits. The clock struck the hour without the appearance of Miss Burgess, and he wondered whether she had been delayed by the caprice of Lady Willoughby, or had simply chosen to hide behind her. However, before the quarter hour she stepped quietly into the room, with an apology for her dilatoriness.

'I would have been punctual, my lord, but for her ladyship requiring me to check that the pastilles she had ordered to be burned in her bedchamber had been lit.'

'A servant might have done that.'

'I am a servant, my lord.'

'I do not understand you.' Something in the deadness

of her tone annoyed him. 'You rail against it, at the unfairness of being treated in this manner, or at the least you did. I thought you unbowed.'

'You seem to have thought many things, my lord, and found yourself mistaken.' She resented his anger.

'What do you mean?'

She ignored the question. 'It is as the Reverend Greenham said at luncheon. I know I am Lady Willoughby's equal in the sight of God. In the sight of man . . . What does it really matter?'

'You are defeatist, and I cannot fathom, for the life of me, why that is so. What has changed, Miss Burgess?'

She looked away. It occurred to him that perhaps Lady Willoughby had revealed to her what she had told him. Having her terrible secret laid bare to another might have made her as she was now. His tone softened.

'You are not Lady Willoughby's equal, you know. You are her superior, in intellect, in character, in every womanly virtue.'

'Thank you for the compliment, my lord. What a pity that I know you hold Lady Willoughby in the lowest possible regard.'

'Why must you cut up at everything I say? Why misconstrue it?' He had wanted to be gentle with her, get her to confide in him at least why she now seemed so repelled by him, but at every turn she blocked his advance, and his frustration found voice in anger.

'Because I have learned that men do not mean what they say. Or rather that they say a thing and then change their minds as they change their coats. How ironic, when it is women whose reputation it is to be fickle.' She sounded very bitter.

So William Hawksmoor had seduced her, promised her what? Love? Was it not only the kiss but the indication of real feeling that had made her recoil from him? Yet that made no sense, for it had been she who spoke of love when he had first proposed, had indicated that if her feelings were engaged she would not refuse him. She had been so superior in understanding, he had thought they would always have that ability to comprehend the other without a full explanation in words, and now he did not understand her one tiny bit. Not that it altered his feelings for her, although logic said that it should. He believed she was still the strong, intelligent, lithe-witted Eleanor Burgess with whom he had fallen in love, but that she lay as if under some malign spell, a spell he could not break. He ran his hand through his hair. He was backed into a corner. He could not ask her about what had happened, and if she did not tell him then he could not, in turn, let her know his feelings. She would not want his pity, but he wished that he could tell her that he respected her, loved her whatever had happened a year ago.

'Miss Burgess, I . . .'

There was a knock on the door. He turned, frowning at the unwanted interruption, but it was repeated with some urgency and he bade it be opened. Sturry appeared, apologetic, since his lordship had sounded so gruff, but with a very worried expression.

'I am sorry to disturb you, my lord, but there has been a calamity.'

'A calamity, Sturry?'

'Yes, my lord. A child has fallen down the well.'

'What?' It was more an exclamation than a question, and all personal matters were forgotten in an instant.

Miss Burgess's hand went to her cheek as Lord Athelney ran from the room, and she followed as fast as her skirts permitted. The well was normally covered, but from the garbled explanations that could be heard through the cries of the child's mother, it appeared curious youngsters had pulled it off so that they might drop stones into the well and listen to the plop far below. One child had leaned too far and toppled in. The well was no more than four feet across, and deep.

'Have we a rope?' Lord Athelney was already stripping off his coat.

'Yes, my lord.' Mr Bitton came forward, with a rope at one end of which he had fashioned a small loop. 'I'll go down.'

'No. My castle, my well, my responsibility, Mr Bitton. You can lower me away, Mr Bitton, with a couple of good men to aid you and none too slowly if we are to have success.' He did not actually say that the chances of a child surviving the fall conscious and not drowning were small and that the absence of any splashing did not bode well. 'Look lively now, Mr Bitton.'

He set his foot in the loop and climbed over the

stonework, as Mr Bitton and the men lowered him into the gloom. Miss Burgess arrived just in time to see the top of his head disappear below the parapet. The wailing was reduced to a sobbing as everyone unconsciously held their breath. There was a very slight splash as Lord Athelney was lowered into the water, and after only a few moments an echoing cry for him to be hauled up. Hand over hand, the men heaved on the rope. Lord Athelney's head reappeared and almost immediately afterwards the child's body slung over his shoulder. The mother screamed.

'Take him.'

Hands reached to grab the limp form, and a very wet and rather grimed marquis climbed out of the well. The child, a blonde-haired lad of about seven, was laid on the ground on his back, with his mother wringing her hands over him. There was blood oozing from a wound on the scalp. Without compunction, Lord Athelney pushed the woman out of the way.

'Give me room there.'

He turned the child over and thumped him, very hard with the heel of his hand, in the back. He repeated the action but nothing happened. Then, to the astonishment of the villagers, he turned the boy onto his back and, holding the little nose closed, appeared to kiss him. There were exclamations of horror, until it was realised that he was in fact blowing air into the body. Between breaths he looked up.

'Check for a pulse.'

He was looking at Miss Burgess, who was standing close. She knelt, and took up a wrist as he resumed. The onlookers watched, mesmerised, and after a minute or so Miss Burgess cried out that she could feel a pulse, thready but definite. She called for a blanket. Lord Athelney continued breathing into the child's lungs until she announced a strengthening of the pulse. A blanket was passed forward, and the child wrapped in it. Then his lordship carried his small burden into the gatehouse, up the stairs to the constable's chamber and laid the little boy in front of the fire.

Miss Burgess followed immediately behind. 'Will he live, my lord?'

'I do not know. If the injury to the head is severe, he may not wake.'

'Head wounds can bleed prolifically and yet not be too serious,' she offered, more to console herself.

'That I know, ma'am.'

'Why did you think to blow air into the lungs?'

'I have seen it done, and successfully on one occasion. I also recall a ship's surgeon say that if cold, and that water was very cold, a child may be revived after an adult would be lost.'

'You should have a care to yourself and get warmed.'

'I will dry soon enough here, but once others have him in care I shall do so. I must send Fittleton to Wells or Shepton for a doctor. Which one attends Lady Willoughby?'

'Dr Newton of Wells.'

'Then we send for him.'

Mr Bitton brought in the discarded coat and boots. 'Will he . . .'

'I do not know, but if Greenham knows some strong prayers, they may be useful.'

Fittleton having been sent on the fastest horse in the stables to Wells with a note for the doctor, Lord Athelney left the injured child in the care of Miss Burgess and Miss Greenham, and returned to the house, where Cottam sighed over the state of his buckskins, but said nothing. He did not reappear in public until the dinner hour, and when everyone sat down to eat, Miss Burgess was not present.

Lady Willoughby had been shocked to hear of the calamity from Sturry, but her horror was not at the fate of the child but that the well had been violated by the immersion of an unclean child into it. She sought assurance that any water brought to her for her ablutions must first be boiled.

'Does my immersion also count, ma'am?' Lord Athelney enquired.

'I do not care for it, Athelney, but you are a relative.'

Miss Greenham choked.

'Has there been any improvement in the boy's condition?' He ignored his aunt but turned to Miss Greenham.

Lady Willoughby's bizarre concern had distracted everyone for a minute.

'Not as yet. Miss Burgess is sitting with him and his

family. Dr Newton said that the skull was not broken, nor was there any damage he could see to the spine from the fall, but whether there is damage to the brain he could not say, either from the immersion or hitting the walls or surface of the water with force.'

'It should be a lesson to them to keep their progeny under the strictest of supervision,' declared Lady Willoughby, as though it was a judgement.

This was greeted with a general silence, which she chose to take as approval.

The events of the afternoon cast a damper over the evening, and before the tea tray was brought in rather earlier than normal, Lord Athelney went across to the gatehouse. Miss Burgess appeared to be giving support to the boy's mother, but there was presumably little she could do by way of nursing. She looked up as he entered. The other villagers had drawn back to give the family a little space, but there was a scraping of chairs as they rose in deference. He waved such a show aside. The boy's father took his hand and shook it, whispering that whatever happened, his lordship had done a fine thing and that he and his poor wife were eternally grateful. Lord Athelney denied doing anything of note, and addressed himself to Miss Burgess.

'If there is nothing practical to be done, ma'am, might I suggest you return to the house and get to your bed. Watch will be kept here, and you will be better for a night's sleep if there is need of you tomorrow.'

His tone was measured.

She nodded, took the woman's hand and assured her that she would return in the morning, and preceded Lord Athelney from the chamber. The stairs were dark and she hesitated, as her eyes grew accustomed.

'Shall I go first, if you are concerned? I did not think to bring a lantern.'

'My concern is only that I do not trip over my skirts and break my neck, sir. I am not afraid of the dark.'

His brow furrowed. In the emergency all antipathy had been forgotten, and he had entertained, for a brief moment, the hope that it would be set aside. It was not to be. Miss Burgess was as stiff as a poker once more. A piqued voice in his head queried why he should let himself maunder over a woman who disliked him so much, but he knew the answer. He had not expected to love, had not really understood how it felt to fall in love, but having done so he could not throw it off like a garment. It suffused him.

Crossing the courtyard, he took her arm, and she did not resist. Having claimed she did not wish to fall down the stairs, it would have been ridiculous not to take care when crossing the uneven cobbles. Once within the house she drew apart from him.

'I think I would prefer to retire without taking tea, my lord.'

'I understand your wish for privacy, Miss Burgess, but I shall send tea and some supper up to you, for you have not eaten.'

'I am not hungry.'

'But yet you should eat, and certainly drink.'

'I think I may judge that for myself, sir.'

'I am not ordering you, ma'am, simply . . . Oh, I shall send them up, and if you choose to go to bed hungry and wake with a headache through not drinking, it is no fault but your own.'

He was tired, too tired to argue.

The dawn found him feeling remarkably unrested, though he had slept longer than he usually did at sea. Once shaved and dressed, he went to see if there had been any change in the condition of the boy, whose name, he had discovered, was Billy. He was unsure what he might find, but was relieved to see everything calm within the constable's chamber. He was also surprised to see Miss Burgess already in attendance.

'There has been no conclusive change, but he did stir a little, his mother says, in the small hours, not enough to know anyone, but he tossed his head about.'

'You must promise to return to the house to eat breakfast, Miss Burgess.'

'I must, my lord? Will you drag me by force otherwise?' Just for a moment there was a ghost of a smile.

'No, ma'am, that I shall not. But I shall send over Miss Greenham if you wish your absence to be covered. She is most competent.'

The smile died, and the shutters came down once more. 'And most obedient, it seems, if she is content to be sent by you. However, it will not be necessary.'

'Not obedient, but she does not take everything I say and turn it into something it is not. Please take breakfast, Miss Burgess. That is all I have to say.'

He turned to give words of encouragement to Billy's mother, and left.

Eleanor fought back tears. She despised herself for her jealousy, and marvelled at her ability to take umbrage. In a few short weeks she had become a crabby old maid. No wonder he preferred Miss Greenham. She was angry with him, and had tried to make that anger prise her from her feelings for him. It had not worked. When she had seen him disappearing into the well, although she knew he did not stand in great danger, yet her heart had pounded. He had had no thought for himself, of his position. How could one not love such a man?

It was a little after nine when she entered the breakfast parlour, having washed her hands and tidied her hair once more. Miss Greenham was alone at the table, gazing thoughtfully across the top of her cup of coffee. She looked up as Eleanor entered.

'Is there news?' Eleanor wondered at Miss Greenham being back in the house.

'Yes. He stirred a few minutes ago, and took some sips of water. His mother is convinced he recognised her, although I could not swear to it. I think he will live.'

Eleanor sat down a little heavily, and when she picked up the coffee pot her hand shook slightly. Anne

Greenham rose and came to take it from her and pour.

'Thank you.'

'It is nothing. Lord Athelney asked that you be cared for most particularly today, because of the strain.'

'I am not enfeebled.'

'Not at all, but yesterday was very difficult, especially for you, becoming so involved. Please rest when you can. I know Lord Athelney is most concerned.'

'Are you privy to all his thoughts?' Eleanor winced at her own shrewishness. 'I am sorry. I am indeed a little overwrought. Forgive me.'

'Of course.'

Why was it, thought Eleanor, despairingly, that even Miss Greenham's calm dignity now filled her with ire? The answer came instantly in her head. The answer was William Hawksmoor, Marquis of Athelney.

CHAPTER TWENTY-TWO

F OR THE BETTER PART OF A week following the accident with the well, the castle remained in a state of tension that had little to do with the sheer numbers of persons within its walls, but everything to do with the personalities and situations among those who slept in the main house. Mr Bitton was torn between the delight of having Miss Greenham in such proximity and within view at every meal, since he carefully judged when to break his fast, and the conflict between his desire to ask for her hand and his growing perception that he was too lowly in society to aspire to the granddaughter of an earl. At best he was the younger son of a country squire, and a naval lieutenant. Looked at another way, he was an estate steward, and by no stretch of the imagination would Mitchum, in his youth, have been considered worthy of a young lady of

Miss Greenham's lineage. He therefore oscillated between bliss and misery, which left the object of his affections confused. At times he was in joyous mood and engaged in light-hearted, even slightly flirtatious, conversation, and then within the hour he might be so absorbed in some deep thought that he scarcely noticed her. Added to this, the children took badly to confinement, and by the week's end were trying her patience with their rebellious spirits.

Eleanor crept about the castle like a wraith, assiduous in her attendance upon Lady Willoughby not just because of that lady's increasingly petty and wayward demands, but because Lord Athelney did his level best to absent himself from wherever his aunt might be. Although she had a parlour to call her own, Lady Willoughby still used her time to go about the castle, finding fault, raising the hackles of the senior staff, attempting to use her own staff as if they now lived in Kingscastle, much to their embarrassment, and generally upsetting everyone. If he was unfortunate enough to enter a room where she was prowling, as he described it, his lordship withdrew in short order. That Eleanor treated him as if he were a cross between the serpent in the garden of Eden and Bluebeard, simultaneously despising and fearing him, helped not at all. For her part she felt ill, ate little and was thoroughly miserable, whilst he was, for a man renowned by his subordinates as fair and unflappable, tetchy, inconsistent and much like a bear with a sore head, as Harry Bitton described him to his friend.

Septimus Greenham was busy with his parishioners,

who were living in stressful circumstances, cheek by jowl, and concerned for hearth and home beneath the river's torrent. He was also aware of the unhappiness around him and somewhat at a loss as to how to alleviate it, though there were times when even he, a man of the cloth and with a realistic tolerance of the weakness of his fellows, wished that Lady Willoughby Hawksmoor might turn into a pillar of salt. She thoroughly upset everyone, not least her poor daughter, whom he was coming to watch more closely. He had assumed at the outset that mother and daughter would be of the same mould, then decided that Miss Hawksmoor was a spiritless, if beautiful, dab of a thing who did not even think about what her mama said and believed. He acknowledged that this was an error. Charlotte did think for herself; she had just grown up in an atmosphere where to show it meant ill treatment and mockery. The sight of his sister Anne standing up to the petty despot had clearly given her courage, and the innate sweetness of her disposition was no longer totally overwhelmed. He had noticed her wince on several occasions, blush for her parent's ill-manners, and evince every sign of distress at Lady Willoughby's complete lack of feeling for anyone but herself. That made his attitude to her ladyship harden.

He watched Miss Burgess and Lord Athelney and came to the same conclusions as Harry Bitton, but could see neither why a chasm existed between them, nor how he might aid them to close it. His sister and friend were a different matter, and he believed that Harry only needed a push to do what both of them desired, and make a declaration. It would not be fair, however, to encourage his friend without being absolutely certain of Anne's feelings. He had little time alone with her, but on the Friday afternoon, when he had persuaded her that any further attempt at educating the 'Sittford rebels' would only result in her suffering an attack of nerves, and that a cup of tea was just what she needed, he found his moment. Mrs Ablett, who thought Miss Greenham a lovely young lady, sent up freshly made biscuits to accompany the tea. Anne sat, one hand to her brow, and sighed.

'You are working yourself too hard, my dear.'

'Oh no, Septimus, I am sure it is just that I am not used to the intensity and . . .' She sighed again.

'Are you unhappy, Anne?'

'Unhappy? Not unhappy, no, but I confess in agitated spirits. I am sorry.'

'Do you reciprocate his feelings?'

She blushed, but did not pretend that she did not understand him. 'I . . . Would you disapprove if I did, brother?'

'Not at all. Harry Bitton is a good, kind and honourable man, and he is head over heels in love with you.'

'He is? Part of me knows that for certain, and yet the other wonders if I am just seeing things as I want them to be.'

'I am at a loss to discover why he has not already made you an offer.'

'I wonder that too. Is that vain of me?'

'Vain? Oh Anne, my dear sister, you were never

vain. The only strange thing is that you never noticed how smitten Father's chaplain was with you, nor the archdeacon's nephew, that chap in the dragoons, who came home on furlough wounded.'

'They admired me?'

'Oh yes.'

'Goodness me.'

'But you have noticed Harry Bitton's admiration.'

'Yes. Septimus, he is . . . I feel . . . he is wonderful.'

'Not the word I would choose, but I agree with the general sentiment, my dear. Now, I recommend that you do not fall into a melancholy but be patient a little longer. I am sure Harry will offer for you, you know.'

What he did not add was that he would make every effort to ensure that he did so. It was not, of course, the most straightforward of matters. He could not simply go up to him and ask why he had not asked for Anne's hand. He considered the problem and then went first to Lord Athelney. After all, as his commanding officer he had known Harry Bitton, the man, for some years, whereas he had known him as a schoolboy and only recently re-established the friendship.

His lordship was run to ground in the small parlour where once he had defeated the 'ladies' from London. He was sitting with a book, but was not reading, merely turning the pages.

'My lord, might I ask your advice upon a delicate matter?'

'Why yes, of course, though I hardly think myself more qualified than a man of the cloth with such

322

things. What is it?'

'Harry Bitton.'

'Ah.'

'I knew him very well, long ago, and we are on excellent terms now, but you, my lord, have the greater experience of him in recent years. I would swear that he is besotted with my sister, and yet he seems in some quandary, and has made no declaration to her.'

'And your sister would welcome it.' Lord Athelney did not pose it as a question.

'Yes, my lord. She is as enamoured of him as he is of her, I believe.'

'I have known him for several years and cannot commend him too highly as a naval officer or as a man. That he is in love with your sister seems beyond doubt to me. The only reason I can imagine he is in a quandary is about whether he is worthy of her.'

'Worthy of her? But of course he is.'

'I fear it is his slightly awkward position here which may be the problem. Mitchum was a local man, a simple man. I would be happy to elevate the position of Estate Steward. There is much that he could do here, and I value him as a friend as well as employee. He is a self-effacing fellow, and I think I ought to let him know just where he stands, don't you?'

'Yes, my lord. I think that would help, and I will give him the hint that he need not be afraid to ask her.'

Lord Athelney thought a hint might not be enough.

* * *

Harry Bitton was engaged in the logistics of catering for upward of forty extra mouths at the castle. The housekeeper had thrown up her hands in horror and was of limited use and so he, taking it as just another aspect of managing the estate, was balancing supplies with requirements, and had already sent to a tenant farmer on the higher ground for the provision of a pig, and more eggs. The supply of dry goods would last well enough, but the castle stocks would need replenishing when the crisis was over.

Lord Athelney found him in the library, rather than the little room that had become Mr Bitton's hideaway, and contrived to look as though he merely happened to be passing.

'Ah, Mr Bitton. Did Waddington Farm have a pig to slaughter?'

'Yes, my lord, and it is being carted over today. It has not hung, of course, but he had a side of bacon also, and that I purchased in addition.'

'What would I do without you?'

Mr Bitton grinned. 'If nobody else was competent you would be doing this yourself, my lord.'

'Ah, but think what that would do to my reputation. I am supposed to be above actually doing anything.'

'Well, that hare won't run, not after you were out in the boat ferrying to and fro.'

'But please note I did not actually row.'

'I should think not!' Mr Bitton sounded outraged.

'Beneath my dignity, or you think I would be

uncoordinated at it?' Lord Athelney enquired, one eyebrow raised.

'A marquis cannot row, nor for that matter a post captain.'

'That did not answer the question.' The other eyebrow was raised.

'You are roasting me, my lord.'

'Yes, but if that pig does not arrive, perhaps we will have to resort to cannibalism and have roasted Bitton.' His smile broadened, and Mr Bitton realised it was something he had not seen in days.

'I may be rather tough and salted after all those years at sea, my lord.'

'True, but far less tough and unpalatable than Lady Willoughby. In the past they burned women like her at the stake, I am sure of it.' He was no longer joking.

'Goodness, yes.'

'I am pleased to see your Miss Greenham does not bend to her whims.'

'She's not "my" Miss Greenham, sir.' He blushed, and dropped his gaze.

'Of course she is. The only thing you have not yet done is make it public.'

'I . . . She is . . .' Harry Bitton floundered.

'She is an excellent young woman who is probably highly perplexed as to why a man whose every glance speaks devotion has not proposed marriage to her.' His lordship sounded brisk.

'But . . .'

'But, Mr Bitton?' The crispness of tone was all Captain Hawksmoor.

'I . . . I am not a suitable husband for her, sir.'

'On what grounds?' He folded his arms and looked Mr Bitton straight in the eye.

'She is a bishop's daughter, granddaughter of an earl, used to the elegances of life and I am . . . What am I, my lord, but a half pay lieutenant with little chance of more sea time, acting as a steward.'

'Circumstance, not ability, has dictated the former, Mr Bitton, and since Mitchum need only provide advice from this juncture, you are the steward of Kingscastle, which is the equivalent of a sea command in my eyes. I will not run this estate, watch the squalls and order the reefing of sails, the turn of the rudder so to speak. I will make strategic decisions. I value you, and whereas Mitchum could do less and less, you can do more and more. The steward of Kingscastle is perfectly worthy of asking for the hand of the local parson's sister. Do you think Miss Greenham regards you as unworthy?'

'No.'

'Then for goodness' sake, man, make her happy, make yourself happy, and ask her to marry you.'

'Is that an order, sir?' Mr Bitton gave a wavering smile.

'Yes, Mr Bitton, it is.'

If his mind had not been upon other things, Mr Bitton might have suspected collusion between his lordship and Septimus Greenham, although when the reverend gentleman came into the library he was not contemplating giving his friend a hint but rather attempting to regain a Christian perspective and control his anger. It took Harry Bitton back to when he was twelve.

'That woman!' Septimus Greenham exploded.

There could only be one candidate for 'that woman'. Mr Bitton looked sympathetic.

'Lady Willoughby gone beyond all bounds, has she?'

He watched his friend clench and unclench his fists, and take deep breaths.

'Since I felt the call to the ministry, Harry, I have not found anyone who truly tested my capacity for charity of spirit, until her. I have tried to see her as a test, but can only see the havoc she wreaks.'

'Most of the time she is down at the Dower House so I can avoid her, thank the Lord,' declared Mr Bitton devoutly.

'But that only means we do not see how she goes on there. Miss Hawksmoor . . . That poor young woman. When you think she has spent her entire life living with . . .' The parson shook his head. 'I was with her but a few minutes ago, and she was telling me how her mama thinks that the villagers are all disease-ridden and keen to take advantage. She never truly believed such a thing, but is now outraged that anyone could hold such beliefs. She said there is a boy she heard singing, and he sings with natural pitch. She thinks that though unlettered, he is not at all lacking in promise. She is bringing him to me after she has taken coffee with Lady Willoughby. I wonder if I might tutor him so that he could apply for a choral scholarship at Wells.'

'That sounds a capital idea.'

'Yes, and Miss Hawksmoor said that she fully expects to be rung a peal over if involved, because it would count as "raising peasants above their station".'

'Very feudal, Lady Willoughby.'

'Very.' Septimus Greenham paused. 'I happen to think men should be judged upon their merits, not who their ancestors were.'

There was a silence, then he spoke again. 'I count you a good friend, Harry, and a man I would trust with my life, and that of my sister too.' It was about as pointed a comment as he could make.

'You mean that?'

'I would not say it otherwise. Anne is the best of sisters, and I would not trust her to just any man.' He looked his friend in the eye.

'Septimus, it seems presumptuous.'

'Rot. If you want the fraternal blessing, you have it, but you are a chump if you did not realise that already.'

'I am a chump.' Harry grinned ruefully.

'Then, my dear chump, ask her.' Septimus glanced at the clock upon the mantelshelf. 'I am promised to Miss Hawksmoor. Don't tack too much, or whatever you sailor types call it.'

'No, I'll try not to.'

* * *

Lord Athelney's brighter mood faded when he left Mr Bitton. He had been giving such sound advice and yet in his own case he had made such a mull of it as defied explanation. Perhaps he should corner Miss Burgess, make her listen to him, make her tell him his failings. It would at the least clear the air between them. It was a pensive marquis who found Miss Greenham in the hallway, her hand to her cheek, and her brow furrowed as if trying to recall something important.

'You appear very serious. Are you looking for something, Miss Greenham?'

'It is nothing really, my lord, just that I wanted a pencil, so that I might draw some objects with the word beneath in order to help my class. I did not want to ask Sturry, for he is quite, er, occupied, with Lady Willoughby's frequent requests.'

Lord Athelney saw his opportunity to play Cupid.

'I believe there should be several in the drawer of the library table. I recall using one when Mr Bitton and I were studying a map of the estate there last week.'

'Thank you, my lord.' She smiled, and his lordship went about his business feeling marginally better.

Lieutenant Bitton had never felt this nervous even before going into action. He told himself it was foolishness, for both his friends, one of whom was also the brother of the lady to whose hand he aspired, had told him he really ought to put it to the touch. Added to which he knew deep in his heart that Anne Greenham favoured him.

Her smile told him; the warm blush of her soft cheek told him; the look in her eyes shouted it at him. He had admitted to Lord Athelney that he dreamt of her, but he had most certainly not revealed that he had dreamed of her in his arms, with nothing but one of the constable's chamber curtains wrapped about them and a ledger as a pillow, lying in a field of summer grass, and she was soft and sensuous and everything he imagined a woman would be. Anne. He savoured the name, yearned to be able to use it, see her turn as he spoke it and smile at him.

She would say yes. Septimus said so. Lord Athelney said so. It was just . . . getting it right. His neckcloth felt too tight, and the room up and down which he was pacing was far too warm. It was the coming alongside manoeuvre that was so problematic. Once he was into his proposal, telling of his love, it would just happen naturally, but the opening phrases eluded him. He could not just blurt out, 'I have something to say to you. Please marry me.' Nor could he do it in front of the villagers, his employer, her brother, or the ghastly Lady Willoughby Hawksmoor. He had to get her alone, and not make his declaration as if pouncing on her. It was so very difficult when one had no experience, and what young lady would want a proposal from a man who was used to proposing?

He sat down, feeling rather dizzy, and rested his head in his hands. He did not hear the door open. Miss Greenham walked in to go to the drawer of the library table. She caught her breath when she saw Mr Bitton sitting before the fire in an attitude that indicated deep perturbation or distress. Her heart constricted, and she rushed forward, the rustle of her skirts alerting him so that he raised his head just as she, all concern, dropped to her knees before him.

'Mr Bitton. Oh, you poor man, is it some bad news from your family? Can I help? Oh, what a foolish thing to say, if . . . But if there is anything I might do, truly . . .'

Without thinking, she took one of his hands between her own, and her eyes, full of tenderness, met his. For a long moment his mind was a total blank, and he could not have said what day it was, nor even be certain of his own name. There was just the feeling of his hand in hers and those eyes, limpid pools that one could drown in, that he wanted nothing more than to drown in.

'Not . . . bad news,' he eventually managed, in a husky whisper, and it suddenly occurred to him that it was very awkward going on one's knee to propose to a lady who was already on her knees.

Her lips parted, and had he not been transfixed by her eyes, he might have seen that the freshly laundered tucker at her bosom rose and fell rapidly.

'Not bad news,' she echoed.

He swallowed rather hard. 'You should . . . I mean . . . chair . . . seated.' He had now lost the ability to speak in a coherent sentence.

Feminine intuition could sometimes be most astute. He was not miserable, but he was nervous. She had a very good idea why that might be, and wanted to help him.

'You want me to let go of your hand, sir?' she asked, half teasing.

'No.' He gulped. 'Like that.' The blush rose in his cheeks, and she, mirroring it, lifted the hand she held to her cheek, her expression encouraging.

'I am very comfortable here,' she whispered, and smiled slowly, 'and I am listening.'

'Miss Greenham . . . Anne . . .' He slid forward so that he too was on his knees, and they looked remarkably like the effigies of Tudor Hawksmoors in the castle chapel, facing each other in alabaster. He made one last attempt to order the words in his head into pretty sentences and gave up. 'Will you marry me?'

It was at least unequivocal.

'Yes, I will.' Her smile trembled then.

'You will.' It was an exultant whisper, which was then repeated as a triumphant cry. 'You will!'

His free hand went to her other cheek and her face was cupped in his hands. He bent his head and kissed her, and suddenly the floodgates opened and he was hugging her, telling her how much he loved her, how beautiful she was, how undeserving he thought himself, disjointedly explaining his circumstances while listing the myriad virtues he perceived in her, and she was laughing and crying and caught in the whirlwind.

'Oh, but you see me as some angel that I am not.'

'My angel of the cushions.'

She giggled, and began to get up. 'I do not recollect that in any scriptural book, sir.'

'I cannot offer you all I would wish.'

'I have not asked for anything. Besides, you have offered me yourself. What more could I need?' She saw him frown. 'You are valued by Lord Athelney, very highly. I have no doubt you will make the position of steward not only respected but important, and besides, I do so like the way you have arranged your quarters.'

He laughed out loud then, and almost immediately afterwards the door was opened to admit Lord Athelney and Septimus Greenham, who had been wondering at what point they might interrupt without interrupting. His lordship had sought out the parson to tell him what was in the wind at last.

'She said yes,' announced Harry Bitton, as if this was the greatest surprise ever.

'Well, we did suspect that might be the case, since if she had turned you down you would be unlikely to be laughing,' remarked Septimus, advancing to shake his friend by the hand, and then kiss his sister's cheek.

'Are you saying he asked you before asking me, brother?'

'Of course, my dear. He did the honourable thing.' It was nearly the truth.

'And you, my lord, did you really send me here to find those pencils?' Miss Greenham raised an eyebrow, and advanced towards him, for he had held back so that her brother might give the first congratulations.

'Oh, they are there, I promise, but . . . I confess to putting you on a converging course, so to speak.'

'I take it then, my lord, that our marriage has your blessing?'

'My blessing is hardly required, but you can be assured that I think it an excellent match. My only concern is that now I shall definitely have to get the courtyard window of the gatehouse parlour enlarged and the wall panelled, so that the new Mrs Bitton can do her embroidery without straining her eyes. Such an expense!' He grinned, and Miss Greenham, quite overcome, laughed and held out her hands. He took them in his own and, casting a roguish look at Harry Bitton, brushed one and then the other with his lips. 'And that, I promise, is the limit of *droit de seigneur* in this castle.'

Eleanor heard voices in the library and opened the door to see Miss Greenham, her hands held in those of Lord Athelney, who looked delighted. She did not step into the room to see Mr Bitton and the parson at the other end but froze on the spot. Anne Greenham turned a face wreathed in smiles towards her.

'Oh, Miss Burgess, I am the happiest of women.'

Eleanor felt suddenly faint.

'Congratulations,' she managed, in a strangled voice, and shut the door. She caught her breath on a sob and hurried, blinded by tears, along the passageway.

CHAPTER TWENTY-THREE

LORD ATHELNEY LET GO OF MISS GREENHAM'S hands suddenly, the smile wiped from his face.

'You must excuse me.'

His brain was reeling. Eleanor had thought that he and Anne Greenham . . . And that thought had hurt her. There had been one moment of patent devastation on her face. If she hated him, if she despised him, that would not have been her reaction. He must find her, explain to her, and perhaps, just perhaps, she might listen, despite the past.

He strode from the room and when he reached the staircase took the stairs two at a time. He knocked at the door of her bedchamber. There was no reply. He knocked again, and entered to find it empty. He had assumed she would retreat here, but . . . He ran a hand through his unruly hair. The house was a warren of rooms and passages. Finding her could take ages, but find her he must. He went out into the passageway and almost collided with a maid bearing linens. She dropped her armful of folded sheets with a hurried apology.

'Miss Burgess. Have you seen Miss Burgess?'

'My lord?' She looked at him in surprise. 'She was downstairs but a minute ago, my lord, I'd swear. I thought I saw her go into the breakfast parlour.'

'Thank you.'

He almost ran. At the door of the breakfast parlour, he halted, tried to compose himself, and then opened the door. Eleanor was standing with her back to him, apparently gazing at the rivulets of water coursing down the diamond panes.

'Miss Burgess . . . Eleanor . . . Please, may I explain?'

She did not turn around, but her hands clenched into fists and he heard a distinct 'Go away,' which he ignored. He approached her, and took her hand, which she immediately tried to snatch away. She would not look at him.

'You do not understand . . . What you saw was . . .'

'You have my congratulations, my lord. Let that suffice. I do not deserve that you should be cruel.'

'Cruel?'

'You have made your feelings perfectly clear, my lord, or rather your change of feelings. Did you really ever have any for me?'

The accusation baffled him.

'But it was you who avoided me. I do not blame you; how could I do so . . . after . . .' He took her by the shoulders and spun her round to face him. Her cheeks were wet. 'Listen to me. I am not my cousin. And I know that whatever happened, it was not your fault.'

'"Whatever happened"?' She looked perplexed.

'Lady Willoughby told me no details, but enough. Whatever he did, whatever the . . . consequences . . . there is no blame upon you.'

She stared at him then, realisation of what he was trying to say hitting her. 'Blame? Oh! You think he . . . You think me so weak or foolish that I let a rake seduce me?'

'You mean he forced his attentions on you?' The disgust was clear in his voice, and she took it as disgust of her.

'Would I be that sullied in your eyes? Of course. So you shunned me, like some leper.'

She flung away from him, and did not see the pain etched into his features.

'You would be just as you are now to me,' he whispered, 'just as precious. But I can see that it might be hard to feel for any man, let alone one bearing my name. I would not force my presence upon you, Eleanor . . .' His voice tailed away. What could he say?

'Precious?' She picked up upon the word. 'But not more precious than Miss Greenham, clearly?'

'Miss Greenham . . .'

'Miss Greenham, who toils, smiling, up the hill so often; the Miss Greenham who chooses new furnishings for the castle, who acts as if she were already the chatelaine; the Miss Greenham aglow at being made an offer by the Marquis of Athelney.'

'Anne Greenham is a fine young woman, but she is not precious to me, nor have I made her an offer. She is very precious, however, to Harry Bitton. She will make him a good wife.' He spoke very softly, and hardly heard his own words for the pounding of his heart.

Eleanor turned, her eyes wide, staring at him. There were no words; she simply stared at him. The stirring embers of hope glowed strongly.

'You cannot think that I love any other woman but you, surely. I knew I loved you, that day I held you half drowned in my arms. I did not say it properly for I did not understand it until the moment had passed. I should have said then, that in the water I could not find you. For one awful moment, Eleanor, I could not find you,' there was a tremor in his voice, 'and in that moment my life seemed to have no purpose. And then you threw my name in my face, refused me when I had thought we had something meaningful connecting us. I did not understand, until I put together the pieces. One of Cousin William's friends talked of his wicked behaviour "closer to home". I had thought he meant chasing the poor serving maids, which Sturry had told me all about, but then you avoided me, would not come to the castle, and my aunt . . . She said her boy had "unfortunate habits" and that you . . .' He stopped, and looked at her, his heart in his eyes. 'I cannot undo it, but it does not make me love you the less, want you the less, Eleanor.'

It took an effort of will just to take a breath. He loved her, he wanted her, and she could see how truthfully he meant it.

'You should never trust what your aunt tells you, my lord. She saw . . . She saw how I felt, would not let me accompany her and Charlotte up to the castle, implied I was not invited, and then I saw Miss Greenham and I . . .' Eleanor's voice dropped to a whisper. 'I hurt so much.' She bit her lip. 'As for William Hawksmoor, your aunt assumed, but did not listen to me. I did find him in my bedchamber one night. He was drunk. He thought because his mama paid me, I was available to him. He grabbed me, kissed me, but no more, for I thrust the candle from my nightstand in his face, and then chased him out with the poker. Perhaps he did not tell her the full tale, or rather she did not tell it all to you.

'That day, that day you saved me, I was shaken. When you kissed me it half reminded me . . . And yet it was so different. I did know it was so different. I never really thought you were like . . .' She took a great trembling breath, but before the emotion could entirely overwhelm her she was in his arms, enfolded, the strong beat of his heart in her ear, and he was pressing kisses into her hair, which was all that was available to him, and murmuring disjointedly.

'Eleanor, my love . . . My darling girl . . . Never anyone

but you . . . I won't let you go . . . I love you.'

She looked up then, and laid her hand against his cheek. Even as she parted her lips to speak, any response was prevented by his seizing the opportunity to cover her mouth with his own. Once, a William Hawksmoor had attempted such an act, and she had taken steps to repel him, but this William was so very different. Her hand moved quite naturally to the nape of his neck, and she responded, as eager, as passionate, as he was himself.

'Say it . . . again,' she managed, between kisses, and though she trembled, it was not with distress.

'That I love you, or you want me to ask you to marry me, for a third time?' He laughed, though there was a catch in it. 'Eleanor, my foolish love, it is banns that have to be repeated three times, not the proposal.' His voice dropped. 'Yet I am not so proud I would not ask a third time, beg if I must, but . . .'

'You know you do not have to beg, sir.' She blushed, but met his eyes boldly. 'I am in your arms, have accepted . . . and returned, your kisses. I am yours, if you want me.'

'If I want . . . Oh, Eleanor, I . . .' His kiss was far more expressive than any phrase.

The door was almost flung open. Lady Willoughby, in high dudgeon, advanced into the room as if she owned it, all ready to demand that the vicar be deprived of his parish, and then stopped dead at the sight of her paid companion in the arms of her nephew, in an embrace so intimate and impassioned that she gasped. Eleanor would have disengaged, but Lord Athelney held her firm, and his lips lingered on hers.

'How dare you!' Lady Willoughby shrieked.

Neither his lordship nor Miss Burgess knew whether she was addressing them as a couple or one of them in particular. Lord Athelney disengaged slowly, turned his head and raised an eyebrow. One arm remained about Eleanor's waist.

'It is scarcely your business, ma'am.'

'Of course it is my business, when my employee betrays my trust, flaunts herself in the most disgusting manner and degrades me by her licentious behaviour.' She glared at Eleanor with undisguised loathing. 'You are dismissed, here and now. Pack your bags and leave forthwith, and do not expect a reference, hoyden.'

Eleanor did not move, but she did permit herself a smile, of which Lord Athelney approved. It was he who answered.

'You forget yourself. Firstly, this is my house, not yours. In fact, the house in which you reside is also mine, though that is perhaps beside the point at this moment. You cannot send Miss Burgess from it. Nor can you dismiss her, since she has, er, of this moment resigned her position.'

'I have?' whispered Eleanor, looking up, but still smiling.

'Yes, my love, you have.' He resumed his list to Lady Willoughby. 'Thirdly, she will not need a reference, from you or anyone else, since she has done me the immense honour of agreeing to become my wife in the near, the very near,' his hold tightened to a squeeze, 'future.'

Lady Willoughby's glare grew venomous. 'Hussy! What a viper have I held to my bosom. You have plotted and schemed this, ingrate. When I think how I have treated you . . .'

'And when I think of how you have treated me, ma'am, I am doubly certain that I have nothing to say to you.' Eleanor stood a little taller, with no pretence of inferiority.

'You little fool,' spat Lady Willoughby. 'How will it look when half the county hears how you wove your web and caught Athelney in it? You think I shall not make it known?'

'You may of course say what you wish, ma'am, but the first time such wilful lies leave your lips, it is you who may pack your bags, and depart the Dower House immediately.'

'You would turn me out of my house?'

'Out of mine, yes. The Dower House is a grace and favour residence, and you are without grace and not in favour. For Charlotte's sake, and hers alone, I do not make the demand that you seek a roof elsewhere immediately.'

'Ah, so you are plotting with that . . . that . . . monster?'

Lord Athelney was so taken aback he forgot his anger. 'Monster?'

'That wolf in a surplice!'

Eleanor giggled. The idea of the parson as a wolf was so outrageous.

342

Lord Athelney blinked. 'You mean Septimus Greenham?'

'Septimus! Hah! "Septic" would be a better name for one so poisonous.'

Lord Athelney began to wonder if his aunt had taken complete leave of her senses. 'The Reverend Mr Greenham is a very moral and—'

'He has seduced my daughter.'

'He has done what?' Lord Athelney's voice was raised, more in surprise than anger. He could not imagine the vicar 'seducing' the shy Charlotte.

'It is easy to feign shock, Athelney, but do not pretend you did not know how he has lured her into disobedience, into breaking the commandment. Beneath that religious exterior lies an evil revolutionary wretch who has turned my daughter's head,' Lady Willoughby now drew out a lace-edged handkerchief and dabbed at her eyes, 'so that she will not heed her mama.'

'Ah, so you mean Charlotte has actually said "No" to you, has she? Good for her.' Lord Athelney sounded buoyant.

'She will be ruined, ruined. I will forbid any further contact, of course, but in eighteen months she may marry as she wishes and if he should . . . it is unthinkable. You must send him from the parish.'

'I shall do no such thing.'

Eleanor had been so envious of Anne Greenham that she had almost ignored the changes in Charlotte over the last few weeks. She had thought the influence of Miss

Greenham had been at work, but now, thinking about it, here was the greater reason for her unfurling her petals into a personality of her own. She had formed a quiet *tendre* for the incumbent of the parish. This last week had perhaps shown him the previously hidden Charlotte, and if he as much as showed a fondness for her, she would defy her mama in an instant.

'I shall write to the bishop,' announced Lady Willoughby stridently.

'And much good it will do you, ma'am. From what Mr Greenham has said to me, I gather the bishop is an old family friend.' Eleanor could not keep the delight from her voice.

Lady Willoughby made a strange huffing sound, and looked as if she might burst with ire, then turned on her heel and slammed out.

'I am not sure that I can bear the thought of my aunt remaining here to greet us on our return from honeymoon, my love.'

'Honeymoon?' Eleanor sounded surprised.

'Yes. Where would you care to go?' He sounded as if he would not mind if she said the far-flung Orient. 'We shall, I take it, be going into Cheshire so that your father can marry us, but the Holyhead post road is very good. We could be in London, or the Continent, within a few days. You have but to say.'

Her eyes misted at the thought of Papa pronouncing her the wife of William Hawksmoor, Marquis of Athelney.

'Eleanor? Have I upset you?'

'No.' She shook her head. 'It is just . . . This is not a dream, is it?'

'If it is, then I am having the same dream.' He wiped a solitary tear from her cheek with his thumb, and rested his cheek against hers. 'But it is not a dream, my love; it is real. We cannot desert Kingscastle while the villagers are forced to remain, but I want to marry you as soon as we can head north. I shall write to your father, immediately.'

'And I shall write to Mama. She will be so shocked.'

'Shocked?' He laughed. 'Will she think it so bad a match? Has she a duke in mind for you?'

She pulled back in his embrace and looked up into his face, suddenly serious. 'I do not think she has had any expectation that I would receive an offer.'

'Let alone three, from the same man.'

'It shows . . . persistence.' She gave a small giggle.

'I was going to ask you . . . for the third time, when I visited a few days after the bridge broke. I was so certain of my heart then, but . . . I have been a fool, my dearest.'

'And I have not? I have been jealous, and miserable and . . . Kiss me again.'

He obeyed her command with alacrity, and a thoroughness that left her pleasurably breathless.

'Where . . . shall we go, then?'

She had almost forgotten the question. 'Go? Oh, I do not desire to travel, my lord. I think it would be wasteful.'

'Wasteful?'

'Yes, for you give me reason to believe, sir, that I should

see very little of the locality.' She blushed, but placed her hand on the thin cambric of his shirt, and looked into his eyes boldly. 'To which plan I do not anticipate having any objection.' The look she received in response made her pulses race the more. She attempted to distract him. 'You will obviously be trying to fulfil the stipulations of your uncle's will, which is a serious matter.'

'The only thing I will be trying to fulfil is my desire for you. I want you because you are you, not because I must find a wife. You know this.'

'I know this. I . . . I refused you because the first time I felt unworthy, thought I was protecting you, that to accept would be taking advantage, and then because I wanted more than affection. I was so greedy, for I wanted . . . your love.'

'Which you have, Eleanor. Every ounce or drop or whatever love is measured in.' He was euphoric.

'Which I have.' She clung to him, unashamed, and laughed. 'But now you know all my bad points, sir. That I am jealous, greedy, foolish . . .'

'Then I may spend a lifetime learning your good ones, and as for the "bad", I shall prove that you have no need of jealousy, feed your "greed" for love, and adore what you term your foolishness.' He grew more serious. 'A few short months ago I thought Kingscastle, the title, all of it, a burden to be borne, a duty and no more. The exciting part of my life seemed at an end, and I was leaving the only "family" that remained to me. That is all changed, because of you. Perhaps Kingscastle was filled with my uncle, faded and aged. We will change that, and if Harry Bitton and his Anne are in the gatehouse we will certainly replace age with youth, and I do not refer to the rather raucous village children.'

'Ah, I said you were thinking of that stipulation.' She blushed. 'Perhaps you ought in fairness to warn me now how many you think a suitable number.'

'The number is more the consequence of what I am thinking about.' The laughter in his eyes was augmented by something rather warmer.

'I ought to be shocked, my lord.'

'But you are not.'

'No. I just think I ought to write to Mama this afternoon, for the moment the floods recede I can see we will be heading north to Cheshire, at the gallop.'

'Unfortunately not that fast, my love. I am never sick at sea, but I confess carriage travel disturbs my, er, digestion somewhat.'

'At the canter then, and I will hold your hand all the way.'

'A post chaise is suddenly quite appealing. But best you practise the hand-holding.'

This important activity was interrupted only by Mr Bitton, who informed his lordship, with every sign of delight, that Lady Willoughby had withdrawn to her room in what looked like strong hysterics, and that since Septimus would be conducting the wedding ceremony, would his lordship be prepared to walk Miss Greenham up the aisle.

'With the greatest of pleasure, Mr Bitton. But make sure your nuptials do not coincide with ours, in Cheshire. We,' he glanced down at Eleanor's smiling countenance, 'are getting married.'

'Of course, my lord. I mean, you hoisted that signal ages ago.'

'I did?'

'You will have to teach me about signal flags then, Mr Bitton, for I did not see it at all.' Eleanor dimpled.

'That I will, ma'am.'

With which Harry Bitton withdrew to inform his own beloved of the news they were hoping to hear.

'Is there a signal for "I love you"?' Eleanor murmured.

'I have never seen it hoisted in flags, but this is the best I know.'

Lord Athelney pulled his betrothed into his arms, lifted her chin, and kissed her.

It was a very long signal for three short words.

SOPHIA HOLLOWAY describes herself as a 'wordsmith' who is only really happy when writing. She read Modern History at Oxford, and also writes the Bradecote and Catchpoll medieval mysteries as Sarah Hawkswood.

@RegencySophia

sophiaholloway.co.uk

Captain William Hawksmoor of the Royal Navy never expected to inherit Kingscastle, his family's estate, and finds himself all at sea when he does so. Especially when he learns that he must marry within a year or be forever dealing with trustees.

As the new Marquis of Athelney, the captain takes command of Kingscastle and discovers much to be done to set it in order. He must also contend with his aunt, Lady Willoughby Hawksmoor, who is determined that her daughter will be his wife. When she discovers he is far more interested in Eleanor Burgess, her underpaid and much put-upon companion, Lady Willoughby shows she will stop at nothing to keep them apart.

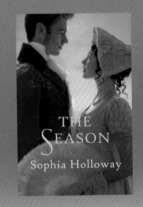

THE
SEASON
Sophia Holloway

ISBN 978-0-7490-2783-4

a&b
Fiction
£8.99
US $12.95

9 780749 027834 >

allisonandbusby.com